SHADOW LAND

GORDON POPE THRILLERS, BOOK 3

B. B. GRIFFITH

Griffith Publishing

Publication Information

Shadow Land: Gordon Pope Thrillers, #3

Copyright © 2020 by Griffith Publishing LLC

Print ISBN: 978-1-7353058-3-7

Ebook ISBN: 978-1-7353058-2-0

Written by B. B. Griffith

Cover design by James T. Egan of Bookfly Design

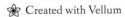 Created with Vellum

For Lee Z., who doesn't have an ounce of quit in him.

"It's Baltimore, gentlemen. The gods will not save you."
—Commissioner Ervin Burrell, *The Wire*

CHAPTER ONE

In the Maryland hill country at the foot of the Patapsco mountain range, night came early—especially in the bone-cold month of February. When the sun dipped below the jagged mountains to the north of Ditchfield Juvenile Correctional Facility, the five buildings making up the property were plunged quickly into darkness. The repurposed manor house-turned-administration center looked like a part of the craggy valley itself, a grand building crafted from soot-colored stone with brickwork the same dried-blood black of the surrounding rock.

Veteran correctional officer Andy Bagshot liked Ditchfield best at night. He requested night shift whenever he could. Darkness suited the old estate. Fewer eyes were watching his every move. Plus, it paid better.

Andy started his nightly rounds for bed check at 8:00 p.m. If the inmates cooperated and signaled during roll call the way they were supposed to, he could usually do it in thirty minutes. Sometimes, the inmates didn't cooperate with the other guards, which dragged things out. They always cooperated with Andy, though, because they didn't want what would come to them if they made his job difficult.

He started on the south side of the property at Pod A, a housing block for the "low-risk" kids. He walked around the outside of the squat brick building and gave every window and door a perfunctory check. He scanned the exercise yard and picked up a basketball blowing slowly across the empty court in the freezing night air. He tossed the ball into the nearby rec basket and slammed the cage shut. A lot of kids on the south side—in Pod A or Pod B—were still allowed to play basketball. They were the warden's favorites.

Andy didn't think any of the little shits should get to play anything, no matter what pod they were locked up in, but that wasn't his call.

Kids on the north side were different. Pod C and especially Pod D housed the crazies, kids that went through life getting *stuck and stowed*—a lot of solitary confinement and a lot of prescription drugs. Many of the guards hated working Pod D in particular. The general consensus was it creeped out the staff—but not Andy. He liked Pod D the most.

Unfortunately, the warden had taken Andy off north-side rounds after a little incident in the fall in which his nightstick happened to pop the orbital bone of one of the Pod D kids. He probably should have lost his job, but the warden and Andy understood one another. Sometimes nightsticks slipped.

He pressed his key card to the reader beside the front door to Pod A, and the lock snapped back like the sound of muffled gunfire. He swung open the door and was greeted with the musty, dirty-penny smell of teenage boys—forty of them—criminals, every one bad enough to get the Ditchfield treatment, which usually required committing a violent crime or repeat offense. Assault and theft ended up in Pods A and B, mostly. But Pods C and D housed juvies sent up for aggravated crimes, including attempted murder and in a few cases straight-up murder, things that would get them sent away for twenty plus at the Chesapeake supermax prison in Baltimore but, because they had the dumb luck to be under eighteen when they committed them, had landed them here instead.

As far as Andy was concerned, a criminal was a criminal. Age didn't matter. They were all lost causes. Almost all of them would end up in Chesapeake anyway, one way or another, whether for the crime that got them here or for the crimes they would commit in the future.

"Up against the wall," he said, his voice carrying.

All the routine nighttime shuffling about and side conversations ceased. The boys were already in their cells because they retired straightaway after dinner, but now they backed up against the far walls of their cells. At Ditchfield, each kid got his own cell. The pods were always at capacity.

Andy would just as soon double them up in the cells. Free up more real estate for new arrivals and transfers both. *Pack 'em in and let 'em break each other down.* But again, that wasn't his call.

"Roll call," Andy said and started walking. When Andy walked, his arms stuck out a bit, like a bodybuilder's, although Andy came by his bulk naturally. He had a big frame and a gut that filled it almost to overflowing. He wasn't much predisposed to exercise of any sort. He liked being big. In his line of work, having some weight to throw around helped.

First, he did the cells on the right side. Each boy said his last name as Andy walked past. When one muttered, Andy stopped and told him to repeat himself clearly. The new kids still required some teaching. The day before, the boy in Cell Ten had been up against the bars, so Andy had to punch his nightstick into the kid's throat. Tonight, Andy was pleased to see him lined up nicely against the back like everyone else.

He made an about-face and scanned the cells on the left side, noting each last name with a slight bob of his head as he passed. But Cell Twenty-six was silent.

Andy stopped and turned around, ready with his nightstick. He didn't know who this kid was, maybe Jones or Jackson—just another black kid—but whoever he was, if he didn't shape up, he was sure as shit gonna come to know Andy real well.

He took in the whole of the cell in an instant. A thin green mattress lay on a thick cinder slab. A brown blanket was rumpled but flat near the steel toilet and bolted stool—nothing else.

Cell Twenty-six was empty.

Fat drops of sweat sprang up on Andy's brow. He smeared them up into his buzzed hair. *Remain calm. Show no emotion.*

He kept walking. Cell twenty-seven called out roll and twenty-eight, too, after a moment's hesitation. Under normal circumstances, Andy would have barked at him, but his mind was racing. All other inmates were accounted for, none doubled up.

He had a missing kid.

At the door once more, he turned around and took a breath to steady himself. "Where is twenty-six?" he asked.

No answer.

"The first person to tell me where twenty-six is might have a shot at getting out of their cell in the next forty-eight hours. The rest of you get weekend lockdown."

No answer.

Andy squeezed the rubber grip on his nightstick until his knuckles went white. He turned, slapped his key card on the reader to unlock the door, then pushed it open and walked out into the night air. His sweat froze to his brow, but he hardly felt it.

The inmates were already jawing behind the closed door. He flexed his fingers and pulled his comm from his belt. "This is Bagshot. We got a problem. South side, Pod A, Cell Twenty-six is empty."

The line was silent. A twinge shook Andy's gut as he waited. He couldn't quite remember the protocol for when an inmate missed bed count. It was in a book somewhere in his locker, gathering dust. He was supposed to be handing off a full pod to the morning shift in a little over an hour. He was supposed to go home and start his weekend off with a long and happy night of drinking malt liquor and diddling himself to his favorite cam girls.

So much for "supposed to."

His comm crackled. "Say again, Bagshot?" Ken Abernethy's tone was icy.

"I think I got a kid missing bed count here in Pod A, boss."

"You *think?*"

"Cell Twenty-six."

The shuffling of papers sounded over the comm, with a few taps on a computer. "That's Jarvis Brown."

Brown, Andy thought offhand. *I wasn't even close.*

"You better be damn sure, Bagshot," Abernethy said. "Because I got my finger on the button here. I press this button, and the valley lights up like a Christmas tree. We'll be neck deep in Baltimore Police."

Andy could hear the boys whispering frantically inside.

They sounded scared. Nobody was calling for Jarvis Brown to get his ass in his bed or to knock it off.

Andy had worked for eight years to cultivate the fear in inmates' eyes when he so much as touched his baton. If a boy under his watch didn't make bed check, he wasn't pranking around. He was gone.

"I wish I had better news, boss."

"Hold up, Warden," someone else chimed in—Jack Mitchell, by the sound of it. He would be making the same rounds on the north side right then. "Can I get a description on Brown?"

Andy held his breath. That was an odd request and maybe a blessed stroke of luck. Visions of malt liquor and cam girls crept back into the periphery of his brain.

Abernethy tapped on his computer. "Jarvis Brown. Black male. Six foot one. One hundred and eighty pounds at intake. Raised scarring on the right shoulder. Unidentifiable tattoo on the left."

"Yeah, this is him," Mitchell said. "He's here in Pod D."

Andy let out a breath and pumped a fist in the air. He still might catch shit for this, but at least it wasn't light-up-the-valley shit. Why this dumbass Brown would run from Pod A to Pod D was beyond Andy. No kid in their right mind wanted to be anywhere near D. Then again, most of these kids were even dumber than they looked.

Mitchell chimed in again. "I knew this wasn't Cunningham. He's too fat."

Andy froze with his fist in the air.

"Say again, Mitchell?" Abernethy said.

"Well, we got Jarvis Brown here. He's all doped up in Cunningham's cell. I'd probably have passed him right by if the kid hadn't just fallen out of bed."

Andy closed his eyes. Everything about what Mitchell just said was wrong.

"And where the hell is Charlie Cunningham?" asked Abernethy.

"Don't know, Warden. But I know he ain't here."

Andy didn't even jump when the emergency lights kicked on all down the line, turning night at Ditchfield into day. The sirens overhead worked themselves into a blare as all Andy's weekend plans turned tail and ran.

CHAPTER TWO

SIX YEARS EARLIER

Gordon Pope sat on the edge of his bed and stared at an envelope in his hands. The letter was from Baltimore Urology Associates and was addressed To Be Opened Only by Dr. Gordon Pope. He thumbed the red lettering underneath the address window that read Test Results Inside.

Gordon had been waiting for that letter for a week. Every day, he'd scampered down to the letterbox the moment he heard the mailman, in order to catch it before Karen had the chance to come across it, but now that it was in his hands, he couldn't bring himself to open it.

"What are you *doing* up there?" Karen called from downstairs. "We're going to be late. You know Waterstones doesn't hold reservations."

Gordon snapped back to reality and cleared his throat. "I'm coming, I'm coming," he called back.

He put the letter in his nightstand drawer and stood then wiped his hands on his slacks as if washing them clean of the entire ordeal. He would open it the next day, maybe. Birthdays were bad times to look at medical results, fortieth birthdays in particular. He felt fragile enough already, confronted baldly with the fact that half his life was behind him. *If I'm lucky*, he thought grimly. He smoothed his sparse hair, tucking his tufts behind his ears. *Speaking of "baldly."* The first present he seemed to be opening at the end of his fourth decade was a healthy dose of male-pattern baldness. *Happy birthday to me!*

Karen was already at the door, settling an elegant camel-hair overcoat around her shoulders. She pulled her newly blond hair from inside the collar and checked her reflection in the window. "I don't know why your mother insists upon going to this place all the time," she said. "They haven't changed the menu in ten years."

"I like Waterstones," Gordon said. "It was my idea. And it's my birthday."

"I mean, I get it. The Cobb salad is good," she went on, uninterrupted. "It's been the same Cobb salad for a decade. Your shoes are mismatched."

Gordon squinted at his shoes. "You sure?"

"Yes, darling. That one's black. That one's dark brown."

"Huh," Gordon said. "I think you're right." He turned and took the stairs up again, two at a time.

"I swear, Gordon. What would you do without me? Our reservation is in five minutes. We're going to be late."

"They'll hold it for Mom," Gordon called back, scuffing off the black shoe and dragging on the correct brown one with his foot. He paused by the bed again and glanced at the nightstand.

"Sometimes I wonder what's going on in that head of yours," Karen called from below.

If only you knew.

. . .

DEBORAH POPE WAS SEATED in the back of Waterstones, by the window, with a clear view of the Patapsco River feeding Baltimore's inner harbor. It was a prime table. Gordon expected nothing less for a woman who ate there weekly, at least.

"My son!" she said, standing as Gordon and Karen approached. "You don't look a day over forty." She hugged him fiercely around the waist.

Gordon wasn't a tall man, but Deborah was an even smaller woman. She'd settled naturally into her seventies and never looked back after the death of her husband, a man she described as so self-absorbed that she had no choice but to become a successful couples' therapist just to stay sane living with him.

She turned to Karen and smiled primly. "Karen," she said, with a good deal more reserve.

"Hello, Deborah," Karen replied.

The two women gave each other a delicate embrace.

Karen eyed the half-drunk martini in front of Deborah. "Sorry we kept you. I hope you weren't waiting too long."

"Oh, barely five minutes. The martini was ready for me when I sat down," Deborah said. "They know me here. There's this wonderful waiter, fairly new."

As if on cue, a young Latino with slicked-back black hair appeared and settled another chilled martini glass in front of Deborah, substituting old for new with a touch of flair. Deborah smiled and clapped, her silver bracelets tinkling softly. Karen rolled her eyes.

"Young man, what is your name?" Deborah asked.

"Caesar, ma'am," he said, standing tall, hands behind his back.

"I like you, Caesar. We're celebrating my son's fortieth birthday tonight. Let's start with champagne."

Caesar bowed slightly and backed away. An awkward silence followed, in which Karen arranged her coat carefully behind herself and Gordon stared into the polished cherrywood of the table, thoughts of the envelope lingering in his head. Deborah finished off her martini and reapplied her lipstick. Moments later, three glasses and a chilled bottle were produced.

"This ought to liven things up," Deborah said as Caesar poured.

Gordon was momentarily lost in the whirling tornado of bubbles rapidly chilling his champagne glass.

"Just a little for me," Karen said, and Caesar obliged.

"I'll take the rest of hers," Deborah said, smiling.

"I'm off alcohol at the moment. Caffeine too. And dairy. I've heard it helps with..." Karen rolled her hand as if she didn't want to speak the word.

"Fertility," Gordon said. He grasped his glass and held it aloft. "Karen is doing everything she can."

"I've no doubt," Deborah replied, keeping her eyes on Gordon. "I hope you two aren't beating yourself up too much about all of this."

Gordon took a long sip of ice-cold champagne. By "you two," his mother clearly meant *"you, Gordon."* Karen approached all problems clinically. She never beat herself up about anything. Gordon was the self-loather. Karen lived her life knowing a solution would eventually present itself if she methodically and efficiently narrowed down variables.

He wondered if she knew that one of those variables was Gordon himself.

Before he knew it, he'd taken down the whole glass of champagne. He coughed as the bubbles tickled his nose.

"Gordon, I haven't even proposed a toast yet," Deborah said.

"That's all right," Gordon said. "We'll have another chance." Gordon looked around until he caught Caesar's eye. "Hello, Caesar. I'll take a scotch on the rocks, please. Heavy on the scotch. Thanks."

Both women looked squarely at him. "Oh please, Mother. That was your second martini, and you know it."

"Tough day at work?" Deborah asked.

"Gordon's just feeling fragile at forty. This happens to him on birthdays," Karen said. "As a matter of fact, it was a great day at work. The APF likes the work we did with the Hazel School last summer. They're pushing it for a Rosenblatt Foundation grant."

"*Your* work with the Hazel School. *You* developed the plan to care for the deaf kids," Gordon said.

"Not true. You helped," Karen said, although even she seemed to hear how lame that sounded.

Gordon had "helped" if you called sitting with troubled deaf kids while they angrily signed the answers to a series of questions about their daily routines helping.

"Anyway, it's fifty thousand a year for four years," Karen added offhand, although Gordon knew she was particularly proud of the grant size.

"That's your grant, Karen. You were brilliant in that study." Gordon reached for her hand under the table and gave it a squeeze, to which she responded faintly in kind.

Deborah cleared her throat. "Sounds to me like it could be a wonderful opportunity for Jefferson and Pope, LP."

Caesar came around with the scotch, and Gordon almost picked it right from his hands.

"And you, Gordon? How is work going for you?" asked Deborah. Gordon's mother was very good at redirecting conversations back to focus on her son even if he didn't want the spotlight.

"Well, it's no government grant or anything, but last week, I submitted an appeal on behalf of a kid I worked with briefly when Karen and I did that consulting gig for the Baltimore City Public School System. It's a..." He rolled his hand, not sure he wanted to say the word. "It's a pro bono thing."

"Gordon likes to do the work that takes the most time and makes the least amount of money for the practice," Karen said.

Gordon was pretty sure she meant that as a joke, but she was never very good at jokes.

"I remember that consulting gig," Deborah said. "As if any two psychiatrists on the planet could straighten out the Baltimore public schools."

"Yeah, well, our patient zero in the study was a kid named Charlie Cunningham. I spent a fair amount of time with him before the city cut funding. Very troubled kid—tough upbringing, but bright."

"Textbook antisocial personality disorder," Karen chimed in drolly, ticking symptoms off as she spoke. "Multiple violent run-ins at school and at home. Callous and hostile in general. Almost no empathy."

Gordon swallowed a hefty swig of scotch. "Yes, well, I respectfully disagree. Those markers are extremely difficult to diagnose in a twelve-year-old. I think it's more like standard anger issues, maybe intermittent explosive disorder. I sat with this kid for hours, trying to document the structure of the school day, when he felt like he was spiraling, what his triggers were. He's no sociopath."

Karen pursed her lips. "I wanted to believe you. I almost did. Then Charlie put a pencil into a classmate's eye," she said. "Didn't break a sweat. He partially blinded the kid at lunch and walked away. Cops found him spattered in blood, flipping through magazines in the library. Textbook sociopath."

"He still doesn't belong in Ditchfield," Gordon said, setting his tumbler down with a smack.

Nearby tables perked up and looked over as their pocket of the restaurant grew suddenly quiet.

Gordon looked at the shining red wooden table again. "No child belongs in Ditchfield," he finished quietly. "He got the sentence yesterday. He ships up at the end of the week. So I petitioned the city, crafted a plan of care. I'll take him as a full-time patient if they'll let me."

As Karen shook her head softly, Deborah nodded. "A little life from my son," she said quietly, a hint of pride in the small smile on her lips. "That said, try not to get us kicked out of here. This is one of very few half-decent martinis in Baltimore."

"Long shot," Karen said. "Especially once the courts have ruled."

"I'll take it anyway," Gordon said.

He thought that might have been a great time for Karen to reach out and pat his knee... maybe give his hand a little squeeze under the table. Instead, the three of them sipped in silence until, mercifully, the Cobb salads arrived.

GORDON FOUND he had to sit on the bed to get his shoes off later that evening. He was a good deal more buzzed than he'd planned, even for a birthday dinner. In fact, he'd been drinking a little bit more than usual across the board recently—nothing irresponsible, just a little bit of a heavier hand during cocktail hour. That was hardly a red flag. Maybe it was a bit of a yellow one, though.

That said, he still wasn't buzzed enough to open the

envelope in his nightstand drawer, especially not with Karen just in the bathroom, getting ready for bed.

Instead, Gordon perfunctorily checked his phone before plugging it in for the night. He'd missed a call, one of those generic numbers that was either a spam call or a government office. They'd left a message.

"Dr. Pope, this is Jackie with the Juvenile Board of Appeals…"

Gordon listened to the message, and when it was done, he simply closed his eyes. Not only had the board denied Gordon's appeal, Jackie felt Gordon should know that another incident had occurred.

Charlie Cunningham had broken parole and stolen a car. Then he'd run that car through the wall of a church in east Baltimore during a funeral. Three people were taken to the hospital.

Not only was Charlie Cunningham going to Ditchfield, he was now going to Ditchfield's Pod D under full psychiatric protocols.

In the bathroom, Karen was humming "Happy Birthday" while she washed her face. Gordon took off his clothes and flopped back on the bed then stared at the ceiling fan, slowly rotating above. When Karen came in, he pretended to be asleep.

CHAPTER THREE

PRESENT DAY

Detective Dana Frisco parked her minivan in one of two visitor's spots outside Ditchfield's main manor house. The sun was still hours from rising. The walls of the valley loomed pitch black all around her, but Ditchfield itself was blazing with light, like an angry bare bulb hanging in a cold basement.

She took in the sight of the central manor house in much the same way she took in the old climbing wall at the police academy in Dundalk back in the day, before endurance training and years of dealing with chauvinist cops and petty police politics had turned her from petite to powerfully jaded.

All right, you cruel hunk of rock. Let's get this shit over with and never see each other again, shall we?

The first time she came to Ditchfield, she'd been a regular rank-and-file officer following up on an assignment, volunteering for work nobody else wanted in the hopes of getting her name on the map. Now she was a sergeant, directing the assignments. And that wasn't because she'd taken on more work or volunteered for the tough cases back in the day. She'd found out the world wasn't that simple—the Baltimore city cops that took on shit work only found themselves rewarded with more until they were buried by it.

The reason she'd made sergeant was that she surrounded herself with people who cared about her and gave her the leverage she needed to keep clawing forward. One of them was Gordon Pope. The other was Detective Marty Cicero, who was sitting in his souped-up Dodge Charger just to her right.

He looked over and gave her a two-fingered salute as he stepped out of his car. "Morning, Sarge!"

"I keep telling you not to call me that," Dana said. "You're the only detective in my unit."

"You got the chevrons?" Marty asked, referring to the three little wonky strips of fabric that designated her current rank.

"They're somewhere in my closet."

"You still got 'em though," Marty said, pointing at her. "And you got the pay bump?"

Dana snorted. "If you could call it that. You're the one who should be wearing the chevrons, Marty."

"Nah," Marty said, waving her off. "I keep tellin' you they took care of me fine. Plus, I'm not a chevron guy."

The case that got both of them commended had also nearly killed Dana. She couldn't run quickly enough from an explosion that put her in a coma for three days. Marty's commendation came because he ran *into* a fire to save Gordon and two others, including a twelve-year-old girl. Marty's writeup cited his "heroic decision to place himself in mortal danger in the hopes of saving others," but Dana knew that the real "heroic decision" Marty made that night was to set aside his dislike of Gordon Pope and save him anyway. Marty didn't like Gordon and never would, for one simple reason: Marty loved Dana. And Dana loved Gordon.

Dana also knew Warren Duke had offered Marty a promotion before he offered Dana a promotion despite the fact that Dana was the veteran. And she knew Marty had declined because it would have meant moving him into another department... away from Dana. Duke reluctantly gave it to Dana because Gordon Pope had leverage over him. If it was up to Duke, Dana would be pushing papers in some forgotten office and Gordon Pope would be in jail, but the firebug case had involved Duke personally, in ways he wanted to keep quiet, so for once, Duke didn't get what he wanted.

Instead, Duke made her a sergeant over the Child Protective Investigations Unit, a unit of one. That had been a nice little backhanded compliment.

Marty affixed his badge and chain between his sizeable pecs and unzipped his leather jacket. His gun peeked out from its shoulder holster. As far as Dana could tell, the worst part of the whole fire-rescue business for Marty was that the second-degree burns he'd suffered on his hands and arms had kept him out of the gym that first month afterward. He'd made up for it since. Both Dana and Marty were plainclothes officers now. They could wear what they wanted, which in Marty's case was mostly dark jeans and expensive T-shirts that looked about ready to blow off him.

"My first Ditchfield run," Marty said. "Looks about how I pictured it. Is it haunted? Sure as shit looks haunted."

Dana clipped her badge to one hip and her gun to the other. "Haunted? Doubt it. Everybody gets out of here the second they can. Even the ghosts."

· · ·

EVERYTHING ABOUT DITCHFIELD WAS DAMP—THE air, the ground, the bricks of the walls. The windows looked old and ill fitted. The wet-earth smell of the night had leaked into the hallways of the main manor. Dana and Marty followed a spooked-looking receptionist to the office of the warden, escorted them in, and closed the door behind them.

Ken Abernethy was bent over a drafting table, looking at an overhead topo map of the valley through a brass magnifying glass on a stand. He wore a matching two-piece tracksuit that looked cleaned and pressed, and he held a walkie-talkie in both hands. He reminded Dana of a gym teacher, the kind that kept even the rowdiest kids in line: clean shaven, gray hair neatly parted, fit but aging.

"BPD?" he asked, looking up as they walked in. "Hate to bother you folks, but we had to call. Protocol's protocol. Take a seat."

"I think we'd like to get right to the boy's cell," Dana said. "Set up a perimeter. We can talk on the way."

"Suit yourself," Abernethy said. "But the young man is long gone."

"You sure about that? This ain't exactly an easy place to get in and out of," Marty said.

"It is if you steal a truck," Abernethy replied. "One of my officers just noticed it missing. Matter of fact, I'd say Cunningham's got a decent shot at being in Baltimore proper by now if that's where he's going. You two could have saved yourself the drive." His tone was even and calm and had a touch of Southern gentility, but his eyes were bright and calculating.

"Your problems don't just disappear with the kid," Dana said. "That's not how this works. You'll probably get a full review from the state. Which, quite frankly, is long overdue."

Abernethy nodded and looked down apologetically, but in the aw-shucks way that meant he wasn't, in fact, worried about any type of retribution. Old white men in places of power often had that look when they messed up. They weren't so different from some of the foolhardy young criminals she came across. Both types thought they were invincible.

"What's the description on the truck?" Marty asked coldly. "I'll call it in."

"It's the groundskeeper truck. An F-150 that's probably twenty years old. Silver with a lot of rust on it." He picked up a scrap of paper on the drafting table and handed it to Marty. "Here's the plates."

"We'd still like to see the cell," Dana said.

"Of course, of course," Abernethy said. "This way."

Dana followed the warden down the hallways of the main house, with Marty close behind, speaking quickly to the city dispatch. The swollen wood of the old main stair creaked and popped under their feet. Outside, the night was still. Mist hung heavy in the air, barely moving in the bright emergency lights. A pair of flashlights swept slowly across the road in the distance, but otherwise, the three of them were all that moved.

They approached a squat brick building with a single metal door front and center. The words Pod C were stenciled above the door in black lettering. Dana thought they might go inside, but Abernethy instead took them around and along a thin concrete walkway that spanned the length of the bunker, about half a football field.

"Don't want to rile up the youths if we don't have to," he said.

Dana looked up at the small slits for windows, evenly spaced above their heads as they walked by. She tried to picture a boy or a girl looking out and almost convinced herself that she saw dark shapes moving inside, watching them.

"Don't worry, Officer... Frisco, was it? The windows are too high for them to see you."

"It's Sergeant Frisco," Dana said.

Abernethy nodded sagely.

"And I'm not worried. Does every cell have a window?"

"No," he replied. "Here we are."

The three of them rounded the corner to the back side of another brick bunker. It had the same flat brick face, the same type of metal door. The black lettering above read Pod D.

Abernethy stepped up and removed a sizeable keychain from his pocket. He plucked up a key card and pressed it against the reader, which showed a red light then a green light. Dana flinched as a lock within the door snapped back like a whip crack. Abernethy pulled open the door and revealed what at first glance looked like a darkened dentist's office. Thin, sharp medical instruments glinted in the light that crept past them. A freestanding chair, inclined slightly, sat in the dead center of the room.

"This is our treatment facility. The cells are just beyond that door," Abernethy said, stepping up and in. His fingers lightly touched the headrest of the chair as he passed. Dana followed, noting the four-point restraints bolted to the chair's arm and leg rests. A machine that looked a bit like a wine fridge whirred softly in the corner. Plastic bottles and metal clamps glowed underneath a magenta light within. Row upon row of cabinets lined the wall to her right, each with a strip of tape scribbled with a name. She scanned them until she found "C. Cunningham."

Marty stepped in last. He'd finished calling in the truck,

and the hand holding his cell dropped slowly to his side as he took in the room, muttering under his breath.

"Treatment facility?" Dana asked.

"Yes. Pod D houses criminal youths with severe mental disorders. They often require assistance with their medical regimens."

Marty walked over to a closet-sized door beside the cabinets and looked inside the darkened inset window.

"That's our padded room," Abernethy said evenly, "a place where the youths can fight through episodes without hurting themselves."

Marty muttered under his breath again. "Stop saying *youths*," he said aloud.

"What would you have me call them, Detective?"

"I dunno. Kids? Boys and girls? Little shits? Anything else."

"I run a facility for troubled youths. There are no boys or girls here. They forfeited their childhoods when they made the decisions that led them to my front door," Abernethy said, with a flat finality.

Dana thought of Chloe, almost nine. The Cunningham boy had been shipped here at twelve. That any twelve-year-old could forfeit their childhood based on a single mistake, no matter how bad, made her stomach turn.

Abernethy reached the second door, leading into the bunker. "We also consider them patients, in the case of Pod D," he added.

He pressed his keycard to the reader, and the lock snapped back. The door opened with the scraping sound of a rough broom.

The smell hit Dana first—soiled sheets and greasy hair, not overpowering but ingrained, a bit like opening an old, empty gym bag. She was surprised at the level of light, given the hour. It was more than she'd be able to get to sleep with. And the fixtures all buzzed.

Abernethy led Dana and Marty down the hall. The center aisle was little more than two shoulder widths. The straight shot led to another closed door at the far end, where a big security guard was standing at uncomfortable attention.

They passed cell after cell, each with a single occupant dressed in a single-piece gown, thin and papery. The kids were all behind thick, clear plexiglass. Each was on a bed—a small slab of concrete that most of them hung over at the arms or legs. Their toilets looked more like freestanding bowls than seats. They had no other furniture or adornment of any kind, aside from a series of small steel hoops embedded in the concrete high up on the walls.

Few of the kids moved. One rocked quietly on his side on his concrete bed, arms clasped around his knees. Two were restrained in their beds at the wrists and ankles. Not one of them took any notice of their passing.

Dana was struck by how young they looked.

"How long have those two been in four-point restraints?" Dana asked, her voice a low growl.

"Inmate Fourteen bit a medical assistant today during meds. When patients bite, we restrain them to deliver their doses and keep them restrained until they are copacetic," Abernethy said.

"He looks pretty damn copacetic to me," Marty replied.

"You'd be surprised. The other, Inmate Twelve, is chronically bulimic. It's all we can do to keep him from jamming his hands down his throat. Here we are. Cell Seventeen. Charlie Cunningham." Abernethy ushered them inside with a sweep of one hand.

Dana took a small flashlight from her jacket pocket and clicked it on. "Has this cell been disturbed by anybody?"

"Possibly by the youth they found here, Jarvis Brown. He was supposed to be in Pod A."

Both police paused in their inspection and turned to Abernethy.

"Wait a minute. You found *another kid* in here?" Marty asked.

Abernethy took a deep breath. "We did," he said, disappointment heavy in his voice. "And for more on that, I'll direct you to Andy Bagshot here." Abernethy gestured toward the security guard Dana had seen upon entering. "He'll be more than happy to answer your questions. Won't you, Andy?"

Andy Bagshot stepped forward slightly and nodded. His drawn face and narrowed eyes looked anything but happy.

"If you'll excuse me, I have a good deal of paperwork to attend to," Abernethy said, withdrawing. "Take good care of them, Andy."

"We'll have additional questions for you, Warden," Dana called out, low, after him.

"I'm sure you will," Abernethy said without looking back.

They watched him go until, a few moments later, Marty said, "What a prick, right?"

Dana nodded slowly.

"You can tell him I said that too," Marty said, turning to Bagshot. "Now, mind tellin' us how some other kid ended up in Charlie Cunningham's cell?"

Bagshot was big, taller than Marty—not nearly as cut, but with enough meat on him to make up for it. For a moment, the guard just stared at the detective long enough for Dana to know she didn't like Andy Bagshot at all.

Dana was about to speak up when Andy answered. "Not sure. But the boy we found in here, Jarvis Brown, was pretty messed up."

The way Bagshot said *boy* actually made her prefer the way Abernethy had said *youths*.

"Messed up like injured?" she asked.

"No, he looked drugged. Barely responsive," Bagshot said, only eventually turning to look at her. "Had to shuttle him to Johns Hopkins Hospital. Didn't want him dying on us."

"Did your medical people drug Brown?" Dana asked.

"The same people give the same meds to the same kids every day. They'd notice Brown ain't Cunningham."

Bagshot tongued a bulge in his lower lip and swallowed what Dana assumed was a hefty glob of tobacco juice. She didn't bother to hide her disgust as she turned back to the cell.

"So who did, then?" she asked.

"Ain't that why you're here?" Bagshot asked.

Marty stepped toward him, but Dana laid a hand softly on his back, and he paused. The two men stared at each other in silence.

"Let's check the cell," she said softly.

Marty shook his head at Bagshot but eventually took out his own flashlight and clicked it on, turning away. Dana followed him into the cell. Together, they ran their lights over every inch of concrete, starting in opposite corners.

"Were you on duty when Charlie escaped?" Dana asked.

"I was, but not here," Andy said, adding noticeable derision to the word *here*. "I was doing bed check in Pod A."

"That where Jarvis Brown's cell is?" Dana asked.

"Yes, it is," Andy said after a moment.

"Thought so," Dana said.

"What's that supposed to mean?" Andy asked, peering down at her as she scanned the crevices in the concrete where the slab of bed met the floor.

"You're acting like a man who just got busted down by his superior and needs to take it out on someone else. I had a feeling you screwed up somewhere tonight."

"Listen to me, you—"

"You better think real hard about the next words that come out of your mouth, Officer Bagshot," Dana said, using the hard, sharp tone that always got through to the drunks and addicts back when she booked them by the dozens. She shined her flashlight right in his face. "Or Marty here will arrest you for obstruction of justice, and I don't think I need to tell you they don't take too kindly to prison guards in the holding cells in the city."

"Cameras in there are really shitty too," Marty added, smiling wanly. "And the cops on watch are pretty hard of hearing."

Andy grimaced and clenched his teeth, working his jaw as though the words were hard to swallow, but he was quiet. Dana turned back around and looked at Charlie's bed. She pulled a black rubber glove from her back pocket and popped it on one hand then picked up the thin blanket from where it lay crumpled on the floor. She held it out in front of her, pinched between two fingers, and gave it one good shake. A fine dusting of white powder puffed in and out of the cone of her flashlight. She glanced at Marty, who popped one eyebrow.

"Did Charlie and Jarvis Brown ever interact?" Dana asked.

"No," Andy said flatly. "Pod D is kept separate from all the other kids."

"Could have been anything. Something small, even, like passing by each other for meals," Dana said as she carefully set the blanket down again.

Andy shook his head then appeared to think as his head stilled. "Could be maybe they get close enough to interact when we clear the rec yard for the Pod D boys. Those that can take the rec hour, anyway. One group shuffles out, and the next shuffles in."

"Close enough to touch?"

"Maybe."

Dana focused her light on the bed and found the pillow lumpy and stained. She tried to picture a boy sleeping there, imagining how he might lie after being fed a bucketful of pills or shot up with whatever psychoactive treatment they gave these poor souls. If she was stuck in this place, she would face the wall, curled up in the corner.

She took a closer look at where Charlie's bed slab met the wall. The concrete was whitewashed and pocked. She knelt on the bed and got within a few inches, scanning the wall with her light. The white coating of paint was streaked here and there with stains—blood, maybe, or bloody snot. But the whitewash reflected back for the most part, except in one area near the head of the slab. There, the paint seemed missing in a rough circle about the size of a quarter. The surface looked more like unfinished drywall.

Using one gloved finger, Dana scraped at the spot. A flake of white fell away. She dug some more, and a little chip of white fell out.

"What the hell is that?" Marty asked.

"Not sure," Dana said, but she had an idea.

Dana dug out the entire depression. "Looks like maybe

an eye bolt was attached here once. Bad patch job left a little indentation in the wall." She picked up the little chunks of white and put them in an evidence bag she pulled from her jacket.

"You know what kind of meds Charlie was on?" Dana asked, turning to Bagshot.

He eyed the evidence bag warily. "No idea. But probably some pretty heavy stuff. All these Pod D boys are."

She turned around and gave the rest of the cell a sweep, but she'd seen what she came for. Nothing else was there but bare walls and cold concrete.

"We're good here for now," she said. "Just one more thing, and we leave you alone. His effects."

"His what?"

"His personal effects. Whatever he had on him at intake. We're gonna need to see those."

"That was five years ago," Andy said.

"We're gonna need to see them," Dana said again.

"Fine," Andy said. "If it means I'm done standing here, I'll get you whatever you want, *Sergeant*," he said acidly.

ANDY BROUGHT them to the secretary up front and left them there without another word. Marty watched him go and shook his head.

"Man, they got a special class of people working up here," he said before turning back to find the secretary looking right at him. "No offense, ma'am," he added.

The assistant, a slightly haggard woman with a lot of hairspray in her bob, wore a name tag reading Jolene. She shrugged. "None taken. I'd say, on the whole, you're right. Andy Bagshot might be the most special of all."

"How's that?" Dana asked.

"He has a reputation for being a bit rough with the kids," Jolene said. "And a bit of an asshole to the staff too," she added dryly. "Now what can I get you, hon?"

"We'd like to take a look at the intake paperwork and effects for an inmate named Charlie Cunningham."

Jolene tapped on an old yellowed keyboard attached to a boxy computer that whirred loudly. "Cunningham... let's see. Here he is. One of our long-term kids." She wrote down a number on a pad and tore off the sheet. "Be right back."

Marty leaned on the counter with one elbow, pulled a packet of almonds from his jacket, and ripped the plastic with his teeth. He popped a few in his mouth and chewed thoughtfully. "You're right," he said.

"Thank you. About what?" Dana asked.

"This place is a nightmare."

"You've seen a fourth of it. Probably the worst fourth, though."

"What do you think is in the bag?" Marty asked, gesturing at where she'd stowed the Ziploc and glove.

"Well, we've got one kid, Jarvis Brown, who was doped up to near unconscious. We've got another kid, Charlie, who was probably getting a lot of drugs to dope him up, only I don't think he was taking them."

"You think those are crushed-up pills?"

"Maybe. I used to give Chloe a multivitamin every night before she brushed her teeth, one of those chewy things I thought she liked. I was cleaning her room out a few months ago and moved her bed frame. Fifty multivitamins fell out."

Marty snuffed with laughter. "Little pack rat," he said, smiling.

Marty and Chloe got along effortlessly. Gordon was catching up quickly, but Chloe still considered Marty her best friend, and he had a soft spot for her in return. He'd even started to teach her a few self-defense moves recently. The past four nights in a row, Dana had come downstairs to find her daughter dressed in a pink tracksuit, trying to practice an arm bar on her grandmother.

Jolene returned with a gallon Ziploc bag inside a banker's box. "Here you go. This is what he had on him. When you're done, just leave it there. I'll file it away."

The phone rang, and she looked at it warily. "We're starting to get some calls. Press sniffing around. Not sure how they figure these things out, but they do. If you'll excuse me."

Dana unzipped the bag and emptied it onto the countertop. Charlie hadn't had much on him when he was brought in, although not many thirteen-year-olds did. A keychain had a ticket-sized photograph inside a scuffed plastic covering: a picture of a skinny young black boy trying hard not to smile down at an equally skinny girl, who beamed out at the camera from behind the crook of his arm. They looked like siblings—similar flat noses and big, almond-shaped eyes, although his were slightly more sunken than hers. He also had a chunk missing from his right ear.

"Twins?" asked Marty.

"Looks like it."

The wallet looked like a hand-me-down, with thin and frayed leather and bits of plastic poking through at the edges. In it was another photograph of the girl, school-picture style. She was smirking, dressed in a frilly but worn green dress. On the reverse was written, "Tasha Cunningham—8th Grade."

Dana found a food stamp card where a driver's license might be, but the wallet was otherwise empty. She frowned.

Could that really be all the boy had to his name? She checked the itemized list.

Three items were missing, listed as "business cards."

1. Business card for "Reverend Josiah Hill—Elder and Senior Pastor. New Hope Community Church."

"That's the place he ran the stolen Buick through," Marty said. "Maybe he picked up a business card along the way?"

Dana looked at him sidelong for a moment then turned back to the list.

1. Business card for "Brighton and Associates. Thomas Brighton, Esq.—Founding Partner."

Dana knew Thomas Brighton from her days doing grunt work processing cases at the Baltimore City Circuit Courthouse. He was the guy sliding from courtroom to courtroom on tasseled loafers, defending anybody whose check didn't bounce. He was a bit of a weasel but not a bad lawyer, all said and done. He'd fight like a dog if he thought that might get his name in the papers, like he did for Ethan Barrett in the sleepwalker case. She also had to credit Brighton for introducing her to Gordon. They'd first met because Gordon used to moonlight as an expert witness for Brighton in order to fund a borderline drinking problem. That wasn't exactly a storybook start to a relationship, but it seemed to be working so far.

1. Business card for ""Jefferson and Pope, LP— Karen Jefferson, MD | Gordon Pope, MD"

Dana momentarily forgot how to breathe. Marty sucked in through his teeth. She held the itemized list up to the light as if it might somehow change. She flipped it over and back again, hoping she'd misread, but no.

"Excuse me," Dana said, gathering Jolene's attention by degrees. "Where are these business cards? They're listed on the intake sheet."

Jolene looked nonplussed. "They let the kids keep pictures and cards sometimes. They put 'em up in their cells."

If that was the case, Charlie had these cards, and he'd taken them when he ran.

That meant her boyfriend's old business card was somehow one of the very few personal possessions of a dangerous young escapee from the psychiatric ward of Maryland's most notorious juvenile detention center—along with the business card of a church the kid had attacked with a two-ton automobile and that of a shady lawyer.

"What do you make of that?" Marty asked quietly.

"I think we need to find Charlie Cunningham," Dana replied, her voice shaky, "and we need to find him quick."

CHAPTER FOUR

Gordon Pope was lying on his stomach in Dana Frisco's basement, his left cheek smushed against the carpet. His right arm was pinned like a chicken's wing behind his back. If it were pressed any farther, he would be scratching his shoulder blade in a way that might compromise healthy rotator cuff functionality down the line.

Chloe Frisco leaned over his head, her long black hair spilling onto the floor. "Do you see how I can just sort of freeze you like that? Just by pushing up a bit more? Can you feel that pinch?"

Gordon winced. "Sure can," he said, trying not to squirm. "I do definitely feel that pinch. That's for sure."

"Marty taught me that," she said proudly.

"How nice of Marty." *Next, he'll have her at the shooting range. Maybe teach her to field strip a nine millimeter.*

Maria, Dana's mother, poked her head around the corner, "Chloe, sweetheart, take it easy on Dr. Pope. That shoulder is forty-five years old. Besides, he came here to talk to you."

Maria smiled down at Gordon. She'd warmed up to him considerably over the past half year. When he first started coming around, Maria had made herself extremely conspicuous when it came to him and Dana. She seemed to find any excuse to walk through whatever room they were in, sometimes between the two of them. Gordon remembered one time, early on, when Maria squeezed herself between Dana and him on the couch while they watched a movie. She would take Chloe under her wing as soon as Gordon set foot in the door, as if he was just generally contagious.

When Gordon didn't go away, Maria settled into a state of begrudging respect, as if he was a stray dog that wouldn't leave the porch. When Gordon sat watch over Dana in the hospital during her coma, things started changing, but what really won Maria over was when Chloe decided she wanted Gordon around. Chloe had the full-to-the-brim heart of an eight-year-old girl but the observant eyes of an old soul. She was the cornerstone of the family. What she said was law— in matters of the heart, at least.

That was why Gordon was there that day, letting her practice Marty's self-defense tips on him.

"Sorry, Gord," she said, letting up. "I didn't know your shoulder was so old."

Gordon sat up and rubbed some feeling back into his arm. "Well, it's not *that* old. I mean, it's not even seven years old in dog years. Younger than you. It's the knee that's pretty much shot."

Chloe laughed. She'd been fascinated by the concept of dog years recently. Someone at school had told her that most dogs don't live past ten. Beets, their Boston terrier, was eight. She'd been distraught, afraid to let the dog out of her sight lest he poof up to doggie heaven at the drop of a hat.

Beets wasn't thrilled with the new helicopter-parenting arrangement.

Finally, Gordon had been the one that talked her off the ledge by explaining the concentrated nature of dog years. That was her first real conversation about death—not an easy topic, but one he'd tackled many times before with kids her age. His approach was to gently remind her that every minute we had here was special precisely because it didn't last forever, and he also emphasized that everyone around her wasn't going anywhere, least of all Beets, who had the constitution and general demeanor of a fire hydrant. It was a good talk.

Still, it was no arm-bar lesson.

Of course, being face-to-face with her, he was having stage fright for some reason. His two-and-a-half decades of experience with kids seemed to have gone right out the window.

"Um. Yeah. So," he began. "I was hoping I could sit and talk with you for a second. About me and your mom."

"Okaaay," Chloe replied warily.

"No, nothing bad. Nothing like that. We're fine. Totally. I just..." He paused, considering his words, then cleared his throat. "May I have a glass of water, Maria?"

Under normal circumstances, Maria would most likely have pointed out the tap. But Gordon had recently had a version of this conversation with her that went mercifully well, and she seemed inclined to help. The glass appeared in his hand, and he drank half of it in one go.

"You're being weird," Chloe said.

"I'm aware of that. Sorry. I'm just nervous. And when I get nervous, I sort of lose my filter, so here we go." Gordon rubbed a dry contact and set his water on the table. "You know I love your mom, right?"

"Yeah," Chloe said.

"Well, over this past year, I've also come to love you too. I hope you don't think that's weird," Gordon said.

Chloe thought for a minute. "No, I don't think that's weird," she said.

"I know how important you are to your mom. And also to me. And I wouldn't want it any other way. So I wanted to ask you something first, before I ask your mom—"

"Are you gonna ask her to marry you?" Chloe asked, and the tiny note of hope in her voice was like a balm to Gordon's racing heart.

He laughed with relief. "If you think it's a good idea, yeah, I was going to ask your mom to marry me. But first I wanted to ask you. You'll always be her number one, but if it's okay, I'd like to be number two."

"Three," said Maria, peering around the corner, wiping tears from her eyes. "You're her three. I'm her two."

Gordon took a patient breath. "I'll take three. I'll take anything as long as I'm in the count with your mom."

Chloe looked at him. He waited, thinking about reaching for the rest of that water, but before he could grab it, Chloe jumped into his arms instead.

"Can you get married tomorrow?" she asked. "Wait, that's too soon. Maybe next week?"

Gordon laughed again, sagging a bit as the force of her hug squeezed out a bit of the anxiety over this pre-proposal.

"Well, it's not quite that easy," he said. "I actually have to ask her first."

"Oh, she'll say yes." Chloe waved him off. "I wonder if mom wants a dress," she said, lost in thought. "I wonder if she'll get a pink one. I'll draw what it should look like." She scampered toward her art station.

Upstairs, the garage door rumbled as it opened. All three of them froze.

"She's home!" Chloe said. "Are you gonna ask her?"

Gordon's stomach flipped again at the thought, but he nodded. "I don't do well with things hanging over my head. So I prepped up a bit of brunch and brought it over."

Maria poked her head out again, her brow furrowed. "You cooked?"

"It's good, I promise," Gordon said, hands up. "Blueberry pancakes from scratch. The only thing I can do, but I do it pretty well. Not like the pork-chop fiasco."

Maria had sole dominion over the kitchen in the household and disliked anyone mucking about in the little slice of linoleum between the stove, sink, and refrigerator. She pondered the idea for a moment before allowing it with a nod.

"Anyway, I was thinking we could all sit down and eat brunch together, have a few mimosas—not you, Chloe, of course, but me—and then when I have the courage, I'd get down on one knee, and you all could be there as backup."

Chloe snorted with laughter. "Backup?"

"Yeah, in case she says no. Maybe you could talk to her. Say you're on board. Sort of like a peer review."

"You've got the ring? Can I see? Can I see?" Chloe asked.

Gordon reached into his breast pocket and pulled out a little velvet box. He found himself smiling, almost giddy. Chloe's enthusiasm was catching. For the first time since he hatched this plan, it was starting to seem real. Even after Maria had nodded soberly and kissed him on the cheeks in blessing, it hadn't seemed real. But with Chloe looking at the center stone his mother had practically thrown at him the moment he'd broached the subject of a ring for Dana,

Gordon started to allow that he might actually have a wife again... and one that loved him for who he was.

Dana called from upstairs, "Gordon? Are you here?"

Gordon took the ring box back and tucked it into his breast pocket. "I'll go up and get started. You two come up whenever. Just act natural."

Maria gave a single, solid nod. Chloe bobbed up and down on the balls of her feet.

Gordon nearly ran into Dana on his way up as she was on her way down.

"Oh, thank God," she said. "You're here." She looked disheveled, a few strands of dark hair having escaped her ponytail and gotten plastered to her damp brow. Her eyes were saddled with dark-purple bags. She grabbed Gordon by the shoulders and looked at him like he might disappear on her. Then she looked beyond him and saw Chloe. "But also, you can't be here."

"What? Dana, are you all right?"

"Not really. I've been up for a while. We'll talk about it on your way out."

"Way out? But I was going to make us a nice brunch, my special pancakes. I even brought fresh fruit—"

"That's great," she said. "Perfect. We can take it on the go. I feel like I haven't eaten in forever." She was already up the stairs and opening the refrigerator.

"Can you just slow down for a second here?" Gordon asked.

Dana stopped at the sink and took a deep breath while Chloe peeked around the corner from the basement stairs. "Yeah, sorry. I've had, like, five cups of coffee. I got called in to work at two in the morning. Been at work since 2:00 a.m."

"At the station?"

She shook her head, opened Gordon's Tupperware container of fresh blueberries, and popped one in her mouth. "Out on a call. At Ditchfield. These are delicious."

"You went to *Ditchfield*? At two in the morning?" Gordon asked.

"Yeah. Not by choice. You know how I feel about that place," Dana said then shivered. The cold light of the window picked up the gooseflesh on her slender neck, haloed in wisps of black hair.

"Dare I ask why?" asked Gordon.

Dana looked down at Chloe by his side and seemed to settle herself for the first time. She sagged back against the sink a bit, as if exhaustion had finally caught up to her and jumped into her arms like a fat cat, like it or not.

"Hi, sweetheart," Dana said, sounding tired but much more herself. "How are things?"

Chloe answered her mother much the way she'd answered Gordon earlier: "Okaaay."

"I'm just gonna walk Gord out," Dana said.

"But he was gonna cook pancakes," Chloe said, looking desperately at Gordon to intervene. "And mimosas!"

Dana looked askance at Gordon. "You were?"

Gordon looked back and forth between Dana and Chloe, trying to square the excitement he'd felt limping up the stairs with the confusion hitting him there at the top. "Chloe, let me talk to your mom outside for a sec. We'll straighten all this out."

Chloe looked like she'd been given a birthday present only to have it swiped from her hands again. She flopped her arms to her sides. "Fine," she said. "But just talk. Nothing *else*. Okay?"

"What's that supposed to mean?" Dana asked.

But Gordon was already ushering her out of the

kitchen, an arm around her waist, before Chloe could slip up and his whole plan landed butter-side down.

Gordon navigated the thin confines of Dana's cluttered garage, gingerly sidestepping lawn toys and a pile of snow tires. His knee was better, so he could walk short distances without thinking about it, which was a whole lot more than his physical therapist had told him to expect during the early days of Gordon's recovery. Still, he was one bad tumble away from starting all over again. He still had night-mares of the hellacious exercises that man had put him through.

"How about we start with telling me why you're kicking me out of your house?" Gordon asked once free of the clutter and on the driveway.

"I'm sorry. I didn't want to worry Chloe," Dana began.

"Well what about worrying *me*?" Gordon asked.

"Ditchfield had an escape last night," Dana said, pulling her coat around herself against the pervasive cold. Her breath puffed white, carried away by the light wind. "A boy from Pod D," she added.

Gordon blinked, shaking his head lightly. He wasn't sure what he'd expected her to say, but it wasn't that. *"Let's take a vacation,"* maybe. Or *"Chloe arm-barred another kid at school."* Even *"I'm not sure this is working out between us"* fell higher on his list than a Ditchfield escape from Pod D.

Gordon's mind raced. He'd known a fair number of kids in the Ditchfield system back in the day, but not many of them would still be there. Except...

But that's not possible, not after all these years.

"His name is Charlie Cunningham," Dana said, plucking the name right from the forefront of Gordon's mind.

Eventually, Gordon was able to form and float one word between them: "How?"

"Not completely sure," Dana replied. "Although I have a working theory. Marty and I are going to pay a few visits and try to flesh it out. But that's not why I need you to stay away."

Gordon wasn't fully listening. In his mind, he was walking the cold, shadowed halls of Ditchfield, pacing back and forth on the concrete between the manor house and the bunkers, waiting for the go-ahead to perform a wellness check on one of the handful of patients he'd treated that ended up there. He did so of his own volition—no prompting or state requirements. He did it because he hated Ditchfield. Every patient he'd lost to that institution was a personal failure for him. While he paced those cold walkways, he always wondered what they were cleaning up, what they might have been hiding before allowing him in.

The kids never talked much, not even the ones who were talkative before. And he noticed things: little nicks that shouldn't be there, hints of bruises peeking out from collars and sleeves, slight limps, winces when they sat.

Charlie Cunningham was the last of his patients to get sent to Ditchfield. Gordon had only checked on him once. Then came the divorce and his life falling down around him. He gave up child psychiatry for five years. Gave up on himself. Gave up on his practice.

Maybe he'd given up on Charlie Cunningham too.

"Gordon, did you hear me? We found your old business card was in his personal effects," Dana said.

Gordon looked up at her as if lost. After another moment, he registered her words. "That would make sense," he said softly. "I worked with him for a while. Even wrote an appeal to keep him out of that godforsaken place, but it never got to a judge before..."

"Before he tried to massacre a church congregation with a car?" Dana said.

Gordon remembered that phone call on the night of his fortieth birthday. He still couldn't quite believe it even though the cops had had Charlie dead to rights. He fessed up to everything and didn't even try to flee the scene.

Gordon had seen a lot of sides of Charlie Cunningham. He could be contemplative, angry, silent, even charming, sometimes all four in one sitting. But he'd never seen the side that might commit mass murder. Then he ran a car into a church and put three people in the hospital. As far as Gordon could remember, all had recovered. *Was he seeking to kill everyone?* The courts evidently thought so. Gordon had his doubts, but that hardly mattered.

"Yeah," Gordon said. "Before that."

Dana put a hand on his shoulder, pulling his attention back. Her face showed her exhaustion, but beyond that, deeper, her eyes looked worried.

"He had five things in his wallet: a picture of his sister, a food stamp card, and three business cards. And one of those business cards was for the church he hit. The last was for Thomas Brighton. I've already given his office a heads-up."

Gordon nodded, understanding what she was getting at. "You think maybe he was on some sort of revenge mission before he got locked up and now he's out again and set to pick up where he left off."

"I think that's a real possibility," Dana said. "One we need to prepare for."

"I get that. I sure as hell don't want to put your family in danger, so I think it's a good idea to take precautions. But from another angle, if you didn't know the kid's history, that wallet looks like it has the contact info for his church—which he relied on to help care for his sister—plus the numbers for his psychiatrist and his lawyer. The car wreck notwithstanding, I don't see anything super strange about that."

"Yeah, well, the car wreck is withstanding. Very withstanding."

"I'll stay away until we find him," Gordon said.

"*We?* No, no. Marty and I will find Charlie Cunningham. You will do no such thing. You'll attend to your patients and live your life with both eyes wide open."

"I know Charlie better than you do," Gordon said, shifting on his feet and easing his knee into motion with a slight wince. "I can help you."

Dana crossed her arms. Gordon knew she was too good of a cop to say no. But he also knew she didn't like it.

"You promise me you'll be careful? Watch your back and not go anywhere stupid or do anything stupid?"

Gordon nodded. That was fair. He would be the first to admit that his habit of waltzing into crime scenes like he owned the place had gotten both of them in a lot of trouble in the past—Marty too.

Dana sighed heavily. "Then I could use any info you have about Charlie's relationship with his sister, Tasha. She's his only living relative as far as we can tell."

"Tasha. He mentioned her. I think they were close. Maybe he broke out to see her? I'll check my files, see what I have," Gordon said.

A car peeled off somewhere in the distance. Dana turned her head quickly at the squealing of the tires and the revving engine even as it faded away.

"Dana, I'm not worth breaking out of Ditchfield for," said Gordon. "There's something bigger going on here."

"You're worth a lot more than you think," said Dana. "To me. To Chloe."

Gordon looked beyond Dana to where Chloe was pressed up against the glass bay window of the living room, her little nose smushed, her breath fogging the cold glass.

"Sorry about the brunch," Dana said, following his gaze. "What was the occasion?"

Gordon caught Chloe's eye and gave a tiny shake of his head. He mouthed *later*. Chloe backed off the glass, slumping a little. It broke his heart and cheered him at the same time, how invested she already was.

"It's nothing. It can wait," Gordon said.

Gordon carefully wedged himself into his beat-up old coupe, positioning his bum leg like an awkward lamp he had to cart around. Chloe gave him a sad little wave. Dana bent down and kissed him goodbye, a little harder than usual. As she walked away, she turned back twice to see him again as he warmed up the engine.

Even if Charlie Cunningham wasn't the mass killer everyone assumed he was, he was still a very troubled young man, loose somewhere in Baltimore, with some sort of agenda. Nobody escaped from Ditchfield just to grab a quick bite and catch a matinee.

Gordon tapped lightly at the ring box in his breast pocket. He could wait.

But something in the air told him he shouldn't wait too long.

CHAPTER FIVE

SIX YEARS AGO

Gordon paced on the cold concrete between the Ditchfield manor house and the north property that housed Pods C and D. The winter-damp brick of the bunkhouse steamed in the weak afternoon sunlight. He checked his watch. In another few hours, the sun would cut behind the canyon, and the brick would freeze all over again. The guards had kept him waiting for going on fifteen minutes. They didn't need fifteen minutes to move a kid from his cell to the visitation room. That took five minutes, maybe ten. Fifteen minutes meant they were stalling.

The door finally opened, and a burly security guard with a buzz cut and a fat baby face stepped out. He looked Gordon up and down, one hand on the butt of his baton. His name tag read Bagshot.

"All right, Dr. Pope," he said, after a few moments.

"About time," said Gordon. "Were you giving him a makeover?"

"Unannounced visitors often have to wait," Bagshot said dryly. "Routine is very important in Pod D."

Gordon stepped up and squeezed past the man, trying

his best not to touch him. The visitation room was on the near side of the bunkhouse, shared by Pods C and D. The warden and his band of merry men didn't want civilians seeing that hellacious exam room on the far side, with the restraining chair and the cabinets of sharp steel things. Gordon had only seen it through a window, and that was enough.

Charlie Cunningham was seated like a poseable doll on the opposite side of a thick slab of two-way plexiglass. His back was ramrod straight, his hands shoulder width apart and lying flat on the stubby counter in front of him. The sight of him stilled Gordon in his tracks.

Charlie had been in Ditchfield for only a little over a month by then, but he'd already lost all semblance of childhood. He'd always been a tall kid, but before, he'd been softer, rounder of cheek, his hair in the early stages of what would surely be an impressive afro. All that was gone. His face was longer now, sallower. His head was shaved. He looked like he'd lost about ten pounds from all the places on the body that make a person look full and healthy.

Worst of all, the intelligent glint in his eye was gone, scorched out, no doubt, by whatever drug regimen they had him on.

Gordon sat down slowly. The last time he'd seen Charlie, they joked about him growing out his hair. He'd laughed genuinely when Gordon asked him for advice on how to grow an afro of his own. That was a week before he blinded a kid with a pencil and went from having a few school suspensions on his record to having a jail term at Ditchfield.

A week after the pencil incident, Charlie got into a Buick and drove that jail term from "one year on good behavior" to "no chance of parole," and the powers that be at Ditchfield moved him from a cell in Pod C to a four-point-restraint fishbowl in Pod D.

"Hi, Charlie," Gordon said, speaking through a circular grate about the size of a shower drain. "How are you?"

Charlie stared right through him. Gordon decided to take a mental step back.

"Do you remember me?" Gordon asked.

Gordon watched him carefully. Dilated pupils. Delayed motor response. Eventually, Charlie looked slightly down to find Gordon, but his eyes seemed to have trouble focusing. His irises moved like a spastic camera aperture. He was trying to see clearly but couldn't quite get there.

"I remember you," Charlie said slowly, but he sounded like he didn't care.

Gordon ticked off medications in his head. By then, they could feasibly have built up a crushing base of heavy benzos that would explain the general apathy. He was clearly on some sort of fast-acting sedative as well, probably intravenous. Maybe that's what they'd been doing for those fifteen minutes.

"Pope," Charlie said after another long moment. His mouth began forming a slow smile then gave up, as if he'd forgotten a joke halfway through.

"That's right. Gordon Pope. I'm here to check on you. See if you're being treated fairly."

That was a joke in and of itself. He obviously was not. But Bagshot was standing just behind Gordon, who didn't want to make any more trouble for the kid than he already had. Gordon wished he could see Charlie's inner arms—they were likely all tracked up—but he was wearing a loose-fitting pair of orange scrubs that looked twisted and haphazardly arranged on him, as if thrown on in a hurry. A dark-purple bruise leaked from the left side of his collar, above where the collarbone jutted abnormally.

"What the hell happened to his neck?" Gordon asked, turning to Bagshot.

Bagshot, still looking forward, only shrugged. "I'm not the kid's mom," he said.

"You're going to need to step out," Gordon said. "This falls under physician-patient privilege. It's against the law for you to be here."

In truth, he wasn't sure if medical confidentiality applied to the situation, considering Charlie had already been convicted, but Gordon tried to speak forcefully enough that Bagshot wouldn't question him. The guy gave Gordon the creeps.

Bagshot narrowed his eyes, probably weighing if he cared enough to argue. He looked at Charlie even longer, as if trying to make some sort of silent point. Eventually, he caught the boy's eye, and only after Charlie looked down, defeated, did Bagshot nod.

"Fine. But the clock is ticking. You got five minutes." He turned around and left through the heavy metal door, which wheezed shut behind him, locking with a loud click.

As soon as Bagshot was gone, Gordon leaned in toward the grate. "Charlie, what are they giving you? What kind of medicine? Do you know?"

Charlie's eyes were still on the door. He shook his head a bit as if to clear it then found Gordon. "I dunno. They give me a little cup of different stuff. It's all white. They stand there until they see me swallow and I open my mouth and say, 'Aah.'"

"What about intravenous? Shots. Do they give you shots?"

"They did in the beginning, in the chair. But I stopped talking so much, and they stopped pricking me."

Gordon's mind was all over the place. He had so much he wanted to ask Charlie and so little time, both on the visitor's clock and with Charlie's fading awareness.

"Do they hit you here?"

"Yeah," Charlie said flatly, and his eyes flashed with a bit of that old light. "But that ain't new. Everybody hits everybody everywhere. Here, they make it a lot harder to hit back is all."

"What about that guy?" Gordon asked, nodding back toward the closed door. "Does he hit you?"

"Yeah. Bad. But you snitch on him, he'll make it worse for me," said Charlie. He showed no anger in his voice, only stating flat facts like an accountant.

Charlie seemed more alive. Gordon wondered if the boy had been faking his stupor before and, if so, how. Not for the first time, his wife's words crept back in: *textbook sociopath.*

But Gordon was still skeptical, mostly because that was an easy diagnosis—too easy.

"Why did you run a car through that church?" Gordon asked.

He realized that wasn't the smoothest segue, but they had no time to beat around the bush. He wasn't looking for a criminal motive, really. That ship had sailed. Gordon was concerned with what was going on inside Charlie's head.

But Charlie's eyes glassed over again. An act? He'd seemed all there moments before.

"Charlie. I know you can hear me. You're not a killer. I need to know what you were thinking. Maybe I can help you."

Charlie looked at the door then at the ceiling where a

camera perched in the corner like a red-eyed bat. He looked carefully at the grate between them, as if scanning for a microphone. "Nobody died?" he asked carefully.

"A few people had some long hospital stays, but nobody died. How does that make you feel?"

His face was a blank slate. Unblinking.

"Charlie, my wife says you're a sociopath. Help me prove her wrong."

"Tasha," Charlie said, barely above a whisper. His eyes briefly flicked up at the camera again then down. "Find Tasha."

"Your sister?"

He settled back into a dull gaze, as if he'd been wound up, performed his motions, and returned to an inert state.

"You still with me, Charlie?" Gordon asked, tapping on the glass.

The lock on the front door snapped back, and the door opened. Andy Bagshot clomped one boot inside and held it.

"Time's up, doc," Bagshot said. "Out."

Gordon stood, bent low, and tried to look into Charlie's eyes once more, but he'd shut down.

GORDON DROVE the twenty miles back to Baltimore with only the low whine of his old coupe's engine and the wind whipping past the wobbly side-view mirrors to accompany his thoughts. He thought about Ditchfield, about the menace of a place where every threat seemed just out of sight, like a mote in the eye flitting away as soon as one tries to focus on it.

"Nobody died?"

If Gordon had to pin an emotion to those words, which

was hard to do given how flat Charlie was, he'd say the kid was disappointed.

Gordon thought about Tasha. He knew Charlie had a sister, a twin. He'd spoken of her before. Once, she came to get him from one of their sessions after school. She was a tall, quiet girl, pretty but deflated, eyes on the floor. She carried herself hunched forward, while Charlie walked with his shoulders pulled back. At first blush, Charlie didn't appear to care much about her or even really acknowledge her.

Then some kid "said something about Tasha"—according to the police report, at least—and Charlie nearly gouged his eye out with the fine point of a mechanical pencil.

Gordon made a mental note to hit the boxes—to check all the recorded sessions, anything he'd written—for any mention of Tasha Cunningham. Obviously, he would search Charlie's sessions, but sessions from the other kids in the study might also prove useful. Maybe something more was going on.

Gordon had plans all itemized and laid out in his head —where to look in the filing cabinets and even a few spare notepads he'd tossed into his everything drawer.

He parked the coupe in the driveway of his home, wincing at the rattle the engine made when it shut off. He would have to get that checked sooner rather than later.

He hung his keys on the hook inside the front door and decided against taking his coat off just yet. The air was freezing outside, and the coupe's heater was a C+ at best.

"Karen?" he called.

No answer.

Her new Benz was in the driveway, though, so she was there somewhere, probably reading in the study. But first things first: he needed a drink. He headed straight to the bar and plucked up a tumbler. *The good stuff tonight. Macallan 15 oughta do the trick.* He poured a generous three fingers and rolled the amber around. He took down one finger in a single sip and felt Ditchfield melt away a bit.

He turned around and found Karen seated with a drink of her own. A glass of wine, almost gone, sat on the table next to a nearly empty bottle. She was holding an open envelope in one hand and a folded slip of paper in the other. Her eyes were a spent color of red.

As soon as Gordon saw the envelope, he closed his eyes briefly then looked away, not unlike the way Charlie had shut down at the end of their visit. His tumbler hung from limp fingertips, waist high.

Karen's lips trembled. "When were you going to tell me about this?" she asked hoarsely.

Gordon tried to put some purpose back into his body by standing up, at least. He grasped his drink like it was a drink once more and not a tissue.

"When I got the courage to open it up," he said after a moment.

"It's been sitting in your drawer for over a week," Karen said.

Gordon decided right then wasn't a great time to ask *how* she'd come across the envelope. Perhaps he deserved to be found out this way. Part of him wondered if he would ever have opened that envelope on his own. Maybe he would've just let it sit there in the back with the phone cords and ancient, unused condoms that they'd never needed to begin with. He knew what the results would say. He didn't need to see them. Opening that envelope only meant he had to act on them.

"Do you know what it says?" Karen asked.

Gordon took a sip.

"It says you're sterile, Gordon. Sperm count is too low to register."

Gordon managed a nod then took another sip.

"How long have you known this?" Karen asked, looking at him like a stranger.

"I've never known. That's why I got the test. But I've had a hunch for a while."

"You care about that Cunningham kid but not this?" Karen flopped the test results onto the table then picked up the rest of her wine and slugged it in one go. "I've been getting cupped, down there. Did you know that? Acupuncture, too, all over, twice a week. Not drinking what I want, not eating what I want. I'm juggling doses of clomiphene and metformin. I've been jamming a steroid pill up my vagina for months. And the problem was never me. The problem has always been you."

"It's not really a *problem*," Gordon said, loosened by the scotch. "It's more the way I am."

"I think I'm understanding that now." Karen pushed her wine glass away and stood.

The glass lolled around on the fine edge of its base until it tipped. Nothing spectacular—just a slow fall until it toppled onto the wood, the delicate bulb shattering.

Gordon moved to his wife, put his scotch down, and started gathering the broken wine glass carefully until she leaned into his arm and started sobbing. Gordon set the broken glass aside on the table and settled himself carefully beside Karen, and she leaned further into his arms. Her hair smelled sharp and clean.

"It's all I ever wanted," she said. "A baby."

"It's not all you ever wanted," Gordon said, steely eyed now, aware of this space in time—of living a watershed moment as it unfolded around him. Perhaps visiting Charlie had prepared him, somehow, to meet this crossroads. "But it's what you want now, as bad as you've ever wanted anything. And I get that."

As she sobbed quietly in the crook of his shoulder, he eyed his scotch, sensing that he had a lot of it in his future... and maybe not much else. He felt his wife firmly in his arms yet slipping away from him at the same time.

"I'll clean this up," he said. "You go lie down."

She pushed up and off him blindly, her lips leaving a red stain on his white shirt. She left the kitchen without another word.

Gordon wasn't sure how long he stayed in the kitchen. Eventually, the Macallan 15 sat empty next to him on the table, and he still hadn't looked at the results. Nor did he think anymore of Ditchfield or Charlie or Tasha. He thought of when he first met Karen. They were undergraduates together at Hopkins, pre-med. Her hair was light brown then but bright with summer sun. He remembered she wore a little butterfly clip that pinned it back at her ear and caught the harsh lights of the lecture hall, flashing every time she bent over her notepad that first week in Psych 101. It caught Gordon's eye one day, and he'd never looked back.

That flash had led him here, to this table in this time. *How strange*, he thought, *what a flash of light could do. How much can change in a single moment.*

When he went upstairs, he held on to the handrail. He wobbled on the edge of the bed and took off his shoes and his clothes as quietly as he could. He knew he'd had too much scotch to be quiet getting into bed, but when his head finally hit the pillow, Karen still didn't move.

She was pretending to sleep. Gordon knew that move well.

CHAPTER SIX

PRESENT DAY

Dana found Marty sitting on a concrete bench outside the entrance to the Children's Center of Johns Hopkins Hospital, eating almonds. *The more some things change, the more they stay the same.* She said a quick prayer of thanks for her staid and steady partner, who always seemed to get there just a few minutes ahead of her. *Or maybe it's just his road-eating car.*

Marty flicked a salute at her, badge glinting on his chest. He wore the same black leather jacket with a different T-shirt—this one was black with a V-neck that stopped just short of nightclub attire—as tight as ever. He fell in place beside her as they walked inside.

The Children's Center at Hopkins was bright and airy, with wide open spaces where kids could run and play while their parents waited nervously. Floor-to-ceiling windows looked out upon a peaceful center courtyard. Dana passed a big piece of functional art, a type of loop-the-loop where a few kids jumped and played. That exam chair at Ditchfield seemed a world away.

"The jewelry's new," Dana said, nodding at a flash of

gold peeking out from Marty's cuff.

He looked down at his wrist and started to put his hand in his pocket before stopping himself. "Yeah, just a little bracelet thing. Thought I'd wear it."

"Let me see it," Dana said.

Marty seemed to think twice before popping his wrist out. The bracelet was fine chain link, maybe a quarter inch wide. That type of thing would have looked ridiculous on anybody else.

"I used to wear a chain, remember, but then I started wearing my badge around my neck, and it was too much. She got me this so I could keep a little flash, you know?"

"She?"

Marty cleared his throat. "Yeah, you know, the girl I'm seeing. I thought I told you."

Dana just stared him down—no easy feat when she had to look up. "You told me no such thing, and you know it." Then she smiled, unable to help it. "You're dating someone?"

"Yeah. You could say that."

When they reached the front desk, Dana held up a finger at him. "We will continue this. I have questions."

"It's no big deal."

But both of them knew it was a big deal. Dana thought it was a huge deal. Although she tried not to show it, the fact that Marty had feelings for her that she just couldn't return had kept a sort of distance between them, which she hated. She did love Marty, but not the way he wanted, and she was terrified of showing him the former in case he mistook it for the latter. It had constantly fueled an awkward undercurrent between them. If he really was moving on, or at least trying to, Dana counted that as some of the best news she'd heard in months.

The woman at the front desk looked quizzically between them because Dana's finger was still aloft. But Dana wasn't about to let Marty change the subject.

"Can I help you?" asked the front desk attendant.

Dana let her finger linger in the air.

"Okay," Marty said, exasperated. "Later."

Dana turned to the woman and flashed her badge. "Sergeant Dana Frisco, here to see Jarvis Brown. This is my partner, Detective Marty Cicero."

The attendant looked briefly at their brass and typed something. The printer behind her whirred to life and rattled off some paperwork and two wristbands.

"Sign, please," she said. "Jarvis Brown is on our secure wing. Floor seven. Elevators to your left."

In the elevator, Marty was the first to speak, probably fending off any more questions about this new lady. "So, what's our angle here?"

"According to the ER doc that transferred him, he just slept off enough lorazepam to bring down a horse. They almost intubated him at one point."

"And you think he got it from Charlie?" Marty asked.

"Maybe. The lab got back quick with detail on the white powder. It's a pharmacological cocktail, but mostly fast-acting benzos. So yeah. Same stuff. But we're not playing bad cop here, not accusing him of anything. We want him to open up."

A security guard for the hospital stood outside Jarvis's room. He scanned their wristbands and checked their badges before moving aside without a word.

Jarvis Brown was lying on top of his covers, watching cartoons on TV and eating a cup of pudding like he'd never been fed in his life. Four more empty pudding cups sat on a half table extending over his bed. He turned to look at them when they walked in, but his spoon never stopped moving.

"Hi, Jarvis. I'm Dana. This is Marty. We're Baltimore Police. How are you feeling?"

He looked back and forth between them, blinking. Either he still had a fair amount of the drugs in his system or he just wasn't all that bright. Dana recalled the picture of Charlie Cunningham and his sister in the keychain. The resemblance wasn't dead-on, but it was strong—similar big, almond eyes and high brow. He had the height too. The boys could feasibly pass for one another.

"Jarvis?" Dana asked again.

"That depends," he said, his voice rolling with a drawl. "You takin' me back?"

"No," Dana said. "Only the docs can do that."

"Then I'm doing incredible," Jarvis said, spooning another glob of chocolate pudding into his mouth.

Marty pulled up a chair and sat down while Dana gave a whiteboard on the wall a once-over. Under the heading Medications, the board had a few scripts Dana didn't recognize, for the purpose of Reversal Agent. Time stamps showed the nurses had checked on him several times already that morning—for pudding requests, by the looks of it.

"Let's talk about how you ended up in Charlie's cell the other night," said Dana.

"Man, I already told everyone. I don't remember shit," he said. "I ate lunch like every other day, and at rec, I didn't feel so good. I sat down for a bit, and next thing I know, I woke up here."

He spoke with authority, even looking Dana in the face, but he didn't look her right in the eye. The anger he put behind his words was trying to cover a lie.

Marty leaned forward, elbows resting on his knees. "You ain't super eager to get back to Ditchfield, are you, Jarvis?"

Jarvis looked warily at Marty. "Man, what do you think?"

"You talk with us, maybe we can see about getting you transferred somewhere," Dana said.

Jarvis turned back to the cartoons, scraping the bottom of his pudding cup, but Dana could tell he was considering it.

"As a matter of fact, one of the reasons you're still here is because we told the warden we needed to speak with you," Dana said. "Maybe we tell him we need another day, say you're still too out of it to answer."

"How many pudding cups you think you could eat in a day?" Marty asked.

Jarvis looked thoughtfully at his pudding cup.

"And these doctors and nurses, they gotta be nicer than what's his face..." Marty snapped his finger to remember. "Bagshot."

Jarvis visibly tensed at the name. The little balsa-wood strip of a spoon trembled for just a moment in his fingers. Marty and Dana shared a glance.

"Andy Bagshot was on patrol that night. He messed up bad. Maybe we can get him removed from his position," Marty said carefully. "You're going back to Ditchfield either way, sooner or later. If you can help us, your time there might be a lot easier."

"What do you want?" Jarvis asked, but his tone was softer.

Dana knew they were in. "Tell us how you ended up in Charlie's cell."

Jarvis put his pudding down with the rest of the empty

cups and picked at the thin hospital blanket bunched around his legs. "I told you the truth. I got no idea. I just walked where Charlie told me to walk. That's all. It's hazy."

"You talked to Charlie? How?"

"Before they clear the rec yard, they line the next pod up on the other side of the fence for a while. Ain't no problem to talk. Even fist-bump if you want."

"If you can fist-bump, you can pass something through too," Dana said.

Jarvis looked back up at the TV, but he seemed not to see it. "The Pod D kids that come to rec don't talk much, but Charlie was different. He whispered at me whenever I passed by, like he was working a corner."

"He was dealing in Ditchfield?"

Jarvis shrugged. "He never seemed to call out to anyone else. Just me."

"Because he was targeting you," Dana said. "And it worked."

Jarvis scratched at his neck. "I got sent up to Ditchfield 'cause I worked a few corners of my own pretty hard in West Baltimore. Sometimes I liked to sample. I thought I'd maybe get clean inside, but then someone starts whispering at you, know what I'm sayin'?"

"What did Charlie say he had?" Dana asked.

"Pills. Painkillers. And he'd just hang his hand through the fence. I ignored him for weeks, but then I looked at Bagshot wrong, and he popped me with his stick, and it hurt like a bitch. So the next time I heard Charlie whispering, I took him up on it."

Dana could picture it—one group of kids milling about the exercise yard while the quiet and broken boys of Pod D waited their turn on the other side of the fence, airing out, nobody looking their way. None of those kids could do much more than shuffle about, anyway. But one of them, Charlie, had been squirreling away his tranqs in the broken concrete of his cell wall. He wasn't nearly as quiet or as broken as he looked.

"I asked him what he wanted. He said first hit's free, but I had to take it at a special time. That's how the pills worked. If I didn't, he'd cut me off."

"And you believed him?" Marty asked.

Jarvis nodded. He pulled down the neck of his hospital gown to reveal a mottled patch of black spreading out like an oil slick from a lumpy break in the bone, just recently scabbed over. Marty sucked through his teeth as he looked at it then away. Dana moved in closer, and as she did, she forced herself to contain the cold fury beginning to flicker inside of her. That cold fury came to life anytime she saw a kid taken advantage of, no matter if they lived in a mansion or the projects or a prison.

"Yeah, I believed him. It took everything I had not to sniff it all up right there in the yard, but I didn't want to be cut off. So I waited until the next day, before lunch, like he said."

"And rec is an hour after lunch?" Dana asked.

Jarvis nodded.

Dana counted back the time. The tranqs would be fully on board by then. Charlie knew what he was doing.

"I was feelin' real faded already by the time I went out with the rest of the pod to the yard. It got hazy—that's all I remember."

In Dana's mind, she saw Charlie lined up with Pod D on the other side of the fence, ready to get his hour in the yard. He scans the yard and finds Jarvis Brown sitting nearby or maybe leaning hard against the fence. As soon as the shift changes, Charlie moves. Swapping places with the boy wouldn't be that hard. All he had to do was shuffle off with the Pod A kids and leave Jarvis sitting nearly comatose in his place behind the fence. Guys like Andy Bagshot, who couldn't even keep the kids' names straight, probably wouldn't notice until it was too late.

"He gave you sedatives, not painkillers. Tranquilizers," Dana said.

"Yeah, I figured that out pretty quick when I woke up here," Jarvis said. "Don't even remember being in Charlie's cell or Pod D. None of it."

"Has Charlie reached out to you?" Marty asked.

Jarvis shook his head and winced a little, favoring his neck. "Like I said, I didn't know the kid in the first place. But even if he did give me stepped-on trash or whatever, at least he got me out of Ditchfield for a day. Worth it."

Dana stood back, signaling to Marty that they were done. She'd gotten what she wanted. Jarvis was already reaching for the call button as they left. That pudding wasn't going to eat itself.

"Hey, wait. You really think you can get Bagshot fired?"

"Maybe. You willing to testify about that collarbone?" Dana asked.

Jarvis looked down at the bedspread again.

"Thought not. But I'll see what I can do," Dana said. And she meant it.

OUTSIDE THE ROOM, Dana started to give her rundown to Marty but stopped when she noticed the guard had changed. Instead of the bored hospital security, a city policeman was standing at attention. He wasn't just any city cop, either, but Tommy Packman, the cop Marty had popped in the jaw a long time before, back when Dana was

trying to get Ethan Barrett out of a run-down theater. Marty
had laid Packman out after he grabbed her. He'd apologized
later, saying he was only doing what Lieutenant Duke
ordered.

That lieutenant was now a lieutenant colonel and offi-
cially the chief of the Detectives Division. Tommy
Packman was one of his chosen ones—an absolute
bootlicker and a terrible cop, totally in Duke's pocket. Also,
he was apparently guarding the room of Jarvis Brown.

"Morning, Sergeant," Packman said evenly. "Marty," he
added after a moment.

"What the hell are you doing here?" Marty asked
flat out.

He'd never bought Packman's "apology" either. Others
deferred to Packman because of his standing with Duke,
but Marty was never one to play politics. That was one of
the things Dana liked most about him.

"The chief wanted me to keep a special eye on the kid,"
Packman said and sniffed.

But Dana knew he would be reporting everybody that
visited and probably what they said too. She had no idea
how long he'd been there, but the door wasn't thick, especially for a weasel like Packman, who wasn't above pasting
his ear to the wood to listen.

"We want to make sure the young man gets back where
he came from as soon as possible," Packman added, which
came out with the quality of a Duke soundbite, probably
word for word.

"Come on, Marty," Dana said, pulling her partner away
before he said something stupid that would immediately get
back to Duke.

He came reluctantly. On their walk out, Dana spoke
with a white coat about maybe letting Jarvis recover for

another night. She said she might have more questions for him.

"More questions?" Marty asked when they were in the elevator.

"I lied. I kind of feel bad for the kid. Told him I'd try to buy him another day."

"If Duke wants him back at Ditchfield, he's going back sooner rather than later."

"It's why Duke gives a shit at all that bothers me," Dana said.

Marty pulled out his almonds again and ate them one at a time, lost in thought. "He wouldn't be able to help us find Charlie anyway," Marty said. "He was just a tool. A stooge."

The two of them walked back out into the parking lot, zipping up their jackets. The winter cold seemed to totally ignore the high-noon sun.

"I wasn't holding out much hope of a lead on where Charlie is, in the first place," said Dana. "But Jarvis helped paint a picture. Charlie is very bright. He manipulated everyone and slipped away. He planned this escape for weeks. Maybe months."

"You think this kid is really dangerous?" Marty asked.

Dana sighed. "He's out for a reason. I don't think it's just to go on a crime spree. But there are a lot of different types of dangerous, and he's definitely one of them."

Dana's mind kept returning to that keychain. She wished she'd taken a picture of it. Somehow, she felt that was a better representation of the real Charlie Cunningham than the photo stills and recent mugshots on file with the city. She was less and less concerned with the *how* of Charlie's escape. She wanted the *why*. And the longer she thought about that keychain, the more convinced she was that the *why* had something to do with Tasha Cunningham.

CHAPTER SEVEN

The office of Brighton and Associates was located on Bail Bond Row, a short and gaudy city block just south of the Baltimore City Circuit Courthouse. A strip of old-style Baltimore row homes had been repainted in every color of the rainbow and renovated into the offices of bondsmen, lenders, pawn brokers, and various catch-all attorneys —sometimes all four under one roof.

Brighton had opted for a Gilded-Age look. Gordon thought the gold lettering on the sign out front was a nice touch, but the dual-lion setup on the outdoor stairway was a bit much—the same with the hanging chandelier on the porch and the faded golden shutters. Around the city circuit, Brighton had a reputation as a bit of a fop and occasional hustler, but even his colleagues had to admit he was at least a halfway decent attorney. He also didn't discriminate in his clientele, which was why Gordon had decided to reach out to him.

Gordon banged twice with the oversized brass knocker on the front door and stepped back from under the chandelier, waiting. The door comm clicked on.

"Can I help you, hon?"

"Yeah, I'm Gordon Pope, here to see Thomas Brighton. I have an appointment."

During a pause on the line, Gordon could hear the woman chewing gum and flipping through something.

"Here ya are," she said. "He put you down as Gordon Plop. I swear. Come on in."

Buzz, click. The snap of the lock instantly brought Gordon's mind back to Ditchfield. He opened the door and stepped inside.

The interior of the office was narrow and smelled like dusty wood. All around him remained the faded evidence of the home long gone. The receptionist sat behind a desk that took up most of what had likely been the old dining room. She was a young woman, buxom, with a low-cut dress and platinum-blond hair pulled up in a curated mess on the top of her head. She was in the process of spitting her gum out.

"Take a seat, hon. He'll be out in a second. Can I get you a water?"

"No, thank you." Gordon sat in a faded red wingback.

Behind her, a pair of frosted-glass sliding doors led into the back of the house. A figure was walking back and forth inside, loudly wrapping up a phone conversation with, "Thanks, buddy. I owe you one."

Moments later, Thomas Brighton slid apart his office doors with gusto and stepped through into the waiting room. He was shorter than Gordon expected, wider, too, or perhaps that was just the effect of the double-breasted pinstripe suit. He found Gordon and smiled. His face was tan, his dark hair slicked back into a little duck tail.

"Thomas, this is Gordon *Pope*," the secretary said. "Your eleven o'clock."

Brighton clapped once loudly then pulled Gordon to standing, shaking his hand at the same time. "Gordon *Pope!* Of course. Here I was thinking, *Dr. Plop? That's an unfortunate name.* Come on in. I'm yours for the next—" he popped a gold wristwatch from under his cuff and glanced at it "—twelve minutes."

He ushered Gordon into his office and walked around to the other side of a large desk of worn mahogany. He sat grandly in a large executive chair of slightly cracked leather and steepled his fingers at his lips, waiting.

Gordon took a seat in the companion of the faded wingback out front and tried to shrug off the exhaustion that had been creeping into his day-to-day ever since Karen confronted him about the letter. Karen had suggested they undergo what she called a "period of processing" during which they simply mulled the information over.

They were going on two weeks without really having discussed it. However, Karen had withdrawn in a million small ways—going to bed without him, working away at the office on the weekends, making long calls to her family in California behind closed doors—that told Gordon a lot without her having to say anything. Feeling a sense of unraveling, he knew his window to act on Charlie's behalf was closing, like a child doing chalk art with black storm clouds on the horizon.

"I want to shut down Ditchfield," Gordon said, point blank.

Brighton's laughter dissolved when Gordon didn't join in but only leaned forward and stared at Brighton more intently.

"Wait, you're serious?" Brighton asked.

Gordon nodded. "I hear you're looking for splashy cases. That you're not afraid of a challenge."

"A *challenge*? Running a five-K is a challenge, Dr. Pope. Learning origami is a challenge. Going after Ditchfield is career suicide."

"The evidence is right in front of you. All you've got to do is go see it. Gross negligence at best, straight-up abuse in many cases. I've seen it time and time again," Gordon said. "And it's not going to stop. It's like they don't care who sees."

"I know," Brighton replied.

Gordon looked blankly at him.

"I've only been in this line of law for a few years, but I've already seen what Ditchfield does to kids. You're right. It's like they don't care who sees. Now, why do you think that might be?" Brighton asked.

Gordon supposed he did know. Perhaps the reason he'd been afraid to go right at the beast was because he'd known all along.

"Because it's connected," Gordon said.

Brighton nodded slowly. "Did you know that Ditchfield is a nonprofit?" he asked cheerily. "It's classified as a charity. Funded by a whole mess of special interests. You oughta take a look at their 501c3 filing sometime."

"It doesn't get much splashier than that," Gordon said, grasping at straws. "I could help you. I'm the psychiatrist of record for some kids up there. I can get evidence."

"We would lose," Brighton said, point blank. "Definitely the case. Maybe a lot more."

Gordon sat back in the dusty wingback, rested his head, and closed his eyes.

"You've still got eight minutes," Brighton said. "You can sleep if you want. Wouldn't blame you. You look a little run down. Nothing personal."

Gordon felt trapped between a rock and a hard place.

Ditchfield was quite literally a monolithic brick wall that refused to be moved. And on his other side was Karen. He'd never be able to give her a child, at least not the way she wanted. His wife was another immoveable stone. And there he was, trying to wring blood from both like a fool.

"Say," Brighton chimed in, "you ever do expert testimony? I've been looking for someone to moonlight. I'd prep you for the stand. And pay you, of course."

Gordon opened his eyes, stared at the ceiling a moment more, then heaved himself upright. "Thanks for your time. But I'm not that desperate."

At home, Gordon placed his key on the hook and tossed Brighton's card in the trash. He took off his coat and turned to the bar, only to find Karen already there. In her hands was a dusty bottle of Bordeaux that Gordon recognized at once. It was a rare vintage his mother had given them on their wedding day to drink on their fifth anniversary. Karen cradled it in front of her in two hands, not unlike a swaddled child.

"I keep waiting for my mind to settle," she said, talking to him while looking down at the wine. "For everything to click back in place so I can be fine with not having the child you and I would have had. But it's not clicking."

"You know there are other options," Gordon said carefully, as if talking her off a ledge. But he knew she'd already jumped. "We can adopt. We could look for a sperm donor together. Start researching IVF."

"I don't want someone else's child, not even if it was half mine. Does that make me a bad person?"

"A little," Gordon said before he could stop himself.

Gordon was only recently admitting to himself that he'd never be a father any other way.

"I've studied children all my adult life alongside you. I wanted to have a child that was ours. To watch them grow and explore and all the while wonder whether they got more of your heart or more of my head. We would debate it over wine whenever they did something wonderful or stupid."

Gordon didn't know whether to be flattered or offended. *Heart versus head?* He was coming to realize just how good Karen was at disparaging him with a kiss. "Heart isn't all genetics, you know," he said. "Neither is brains."

If Karen heard him, she gave no indication. "I'm going to stay with my parents in California for a few weeks," she said. "My flight leaves in the morning. But before I go, I thought maybe we could share a bottle of wine together."

Gordon's voice caught in his throat. He felt a slow weight pulling him down and reached out to the kitchen island—one finger to steady himself. He thought of the stretch of time in the months after they were newly married, when a new and fresh wind blew at the sails of their relationship. They would work in their shared office, he at his desk and she at hers, while soft classical music played just under the sound of the last rains of fall hitting the skylight above, sometimes sipping a glass from a bottle of red that would glow in the light of the Tiffany lamp between them.

They didn't even need to speak then to communicate. Now, nothing Gordon could say seemed to get through to her. Or, worse, it did get through to her, but she didn't care.

"Yeah, honey," Gordon said, defeated, and he failed to keep his voice from breaking. "Let's have a glass of wine."

So Karen went to the glassware cabinet and pulled out two big tulip-bulb wine glasses and looked at them through the light, wiping away a few stray hard-water stains as Gordon got the corkscrew. The Bordeaux opened with a soft pop, the sound of a peck on the cheek.

They drank the bottle of wine and talked about the past. With each sip, the room took on more of a sepia feel, as if the living colors were slowly draining from the story they shared—the day they graduated as newly minted Hopkins psychiatrists and kissed under the statue of the Christus Consolator in the rotunda of the hospital's old great dome; when Gordon plucked up the guts to ask if they might go into business together—as husband and wife; the room with the skylight, where he proposed.

That night, they made love for the first time in months, holding each other as tightly as Gordon could remember in all their years together. Very early the next morning, Karen woke him with a soft peck on the cheek and said goodbye. Gordon started to get out of bed, but she put a finger on his chest and held him in place.

"Just let me go. The cab is already here," she said.

"Call me when you get there," he said, wanting to say so much more but not finding the words.

Karen took a small roller suitcase and left their bedroom. He heard the luggage skate along the wood then out the front door, which closed behind her with a whisper. Gordon heard the cab pull away and felt the sudden and crushing silence of the bedroom.

He flopped back down and stared wide-eyed at the ceiling like a man who'd just been robbed. He could hear his blood whistling in his ears and thought distantly that he might be having a panic attack. Karen had said a few weeks, but he knew he would be naïve to think she really meant that. He stood up and wandered through their condo, moving from room to room, picking things up and putting them down again in a daze while the coffee brewed.

Half of his brain insisted Karen would be back in three weeks. The other half was in triage mode, working to keep him alive. The triage half wondered about immediate things: how he would work without her, if he even could afford to. His patient pool was deep but not wide. She brought in all the money. In a fit of inspiration, he went to the trash can and pulled out Brighton's card. He dusted it off and stuck it on the refrigerator. His *"not that desperate"* seemed foolhardy. Everyone was one step from desperation.

A flash of light caught his eye. Karen's wedding ring, on the table, reflected the first rays of sun peeking through the glass doors of their balcony. Gordon was mesmerized. He stood that way for a long time, thinking how strange it was that life could change so completely in the span of a single flash of light.

CHAPTER EIGHT

PRESENT DAY

The address of record for Tasha Cunningham was a housing project in east Baltimore called Lexington Heights. Marty said he'd been out there a few times on wellness checks. Dana couldn't recall visiting before at all. Lexington Heights was the type of place that the Baltimore City Police left alone, one of the many projects where crime had dug in so deep that cops only heaped more trouble on themselves by doing more digging. It was similar to an old box of clothes that had become home to a nest of rats. One didn't dig in. One closed it up and walked away.

The deep cold had apparently cleared out most of the activity in the center yard, surrounded on three sides by brutalist towers that reached five stories high and housed more than five hundred people. Three young men sat smoking on a ratty couch in the center of the dirt, their feet up on rusted school chairs. They spotted Dana and Marty as soon as they turned the corner. One of them hastily put his cigarette out, turned around, and whistled once sharply through his fingers. His whistle was echoed again from a corridor between towers, then again out of a window somewhere a few stories up. Soon, whistles were echoing throughout the towers, then just as abruptly, they stopped.

"Subtle," Marty said as they walked past the pair, smoking again with their boots still up. "Real subtle. No need to get up on account of us, gentlemen. We ain't here for you anyway."

The smokers said nothing, watching them with blank expressions.

Dana could feel the weight of their eyes on her back as they made their way to the south tower. She could feel people staring from all over and had to make an effort to keep her pace steady and her hand away from her gun hip. People who lived in the projects were usually smart enough not to mess with the cops unless the cops messed with them. Usually.

Marty easily pushed open the door to the south tower. Whatever locks these entryways once had were long gone. Dana could see her breath in the hallway despite the hissing rattle of an old steam heater. Dirty cardboard and stacks of phone books gathered dust against the yellowing walls. One of the phone-booth-sized elevators was taped off. Marty pressed the call button for the other, but nothing happened.

"Stairs?" Marty asked.

"Probably smart," said Dana.

The stairwell was erratically lit, and the concrete flooring was stained by foot traffic and what looked like grease from leaking trash bags. The exit to the fourth floor had no lock either. The hallway was deserted, but Dana heard life teeming all around them, behind closed doors. Children yelling, babies crying. The shuddering of pipes. The steady murmur of humanity just out of reach.

They walked the threadbare carpet of the hallway until they found the apartment number on file. Dana knocked three times. The murmuring stopped in the bubble around them. Down the hall, a young girl peeked out from a doorway but shot back inside again as soon as Marty glanced her way.

Dana took another deep breath and knocked three more times. Just when she was about to pull out her phone to double check with dispatch, she heard a chain clasp slide into place then the bolt lock flip back. The door opened six inches, and a woman with the telltale pitted face of an addict peered out. Her hair was pulled back by a faded red kerchief. She might have been anywhere from twenty to forty years old.

"Tasha Cunningham?" Dana asked although she doubted it.

The woman looked them up and down. She didn't look like an active user. The scabs and scars on her face had faded to a soft purple in most places.

"Nobody by that name here," she said.

"I'm Dana. This is Marty. We're—"

"Cops. I know."

"We're looking for Tasha. She hasn't done anything wrong. We just want to make sure she's safe and ask her a few questions," said Dana.

"Safe, huh?" she said.

"Nobody's in trouble," Dana said.

The woman eyed Marty distastefully, but thankfully, he seemed to know when to take the back seat. He affected a blank face and said nothing. She found Dana again and snuffed a short breath out of her nose.

"Tasha hasn't lived here in years," she said. "She left not long after her brother got sent up. Going on five years now."

"Do you know where she lives now?" Dana asked.

"I wouldn't tell you if I did. But I don't, so all's the same."

Dana crossed her arms then thought better of it, wanting to seem as open and approachable as possible. "SNAP program still lists this as Tasha's primary residence," Dana said, keeping her voice calm.

The woman said nothing but narrowed her eyes.

"Have you been getting her mail? Maybe collecting her benefits?" Dana asked evenly.

As the woman moved to close the door, Dana interjected, "I'm not gonna report you. Looks like maybe the extra help is doing you good. But if you could point us in the direction of Tasha Cunningham, we'd appreciate it."

The woman paused and looked down at the floor as if ashamed. When she looked up again, her eyes were perhaps a shade softer. "I was homeless. She told me I could. Told me she was going to New Hope and they was gonna take care of her. That's all I know."

"Thank you," Dana said, but the woman was already closing the door.

Dana turned to Marty, and together, the two of them simply stood in the damp cold of the hallway and listened to the sound of hundreds of people barely getting by. Dana tried to picture Charlie living there with Tasha. Their father had never been in the picture, according to the police report, but for a time, their mother lived with them. She would have opened the door just like that. However, the scars and scabs on her face would have been fresh right up to the day she died, about three months after Charlie arrived at Ditchfield. Then the two kids were adrift.

"You think he's in there?" Marty asked.

Dana had initially wondered the same thing. They would need a warrant to enter without probable cause, though. And Dana didn't think they had it. She didn't think they needed to get inside, either. That place was in the dark and distant past for both Charlie and Tasha.

"No," she said. "But I think we need to pay New Hope a visit."

NEW HOPE COMMUNITY CHURCH, a simple and classic chapel with a bright white spire that shot into the sky, was a four-minute drive from Lexington Heights. The cross atop stood like a beacon amid the Bermuda Triangle of three of Baltimore's poorest and most dangerous neighborhoods. The sign outside was freshly painted. No graffiti marred the pristine walls of the church house. Nobody was working the corners anywhere nearby. Even the sidewalks seemed less cracked.

Dana and Marty pulled up to find another police car already there. Marty pulled in front and parked while Dana pulled in behind. The cruiser was one of the new super-charged Fords, which usually fell to cops in Duke's retinue. Sure enough, Victor Garcia was sitting in the driver's seat. Garcia and Packman were partners, but Garcia was the smarter of the two. He was less of a bully but more of a weasel.

He looked up from his dash array as they approached. If he was surprised to see them, he didn't show it. Eventually, he rolled down the window. "Can I help you?"

"You working my case now?" Dana asked.

"You want to sit in a church parking lot all day, be my guest," he said.

"Did Duke put you on this?"

Garcia paused for a moment to choose his words. "The

chief thought it might be a good idea to post a watch. In case."

Dana was unnerved that Duke seemed to be one step ahead—and keeping her in the dark about it. She seriously doubted he was using manpower to help her. Duke had never helped her in his life. His world was one of swapped favors and land grabs. Every decision he made had an underbelly.

"You see anything?" Marty asked.

"Nope," Garcia said, popping the word with his lips.

"Your rotation is patrol. Duke should have you and Packman following up on the truck," Marty said.

Dana knew he liked Garcia even less than Packman.

"Oh yeah? You speaking for the chief now?"

"Take it easy, Vic," Dana said, rolling her eyes. "We're all on the same team here, right? So, no sign of the truck?"

Garcia gave a sleazy half smile.

"What is it, Vic?" Marty asked, both hands on the open window as he leaned down.

Garcia's face fell, and he leaned away before stopping himself. Dana smiled. Apparently, Garcia also still remembered the way Marty had connected with Packman.

"We got a hit on the truck early morning. Security camera picked it up, abandoned at a long-term parking lot outside of the airport. No sign of the kid."

Dana couldn't believe it. The airport was the last place she expected Charlie to go.

"Did he try to get on a plane?"

Garcia shook his head. "Never went into the airport. We think he took another car. The security system at the lot shows the car count off. But it's a shitty system, so they don't know which one yet."

"And when were you gonna tell us about this?" Dana asked.

Garcia pouted his lips. "Chief wanted it kept under wraps until we know more about the new car."

"From his own detectives?" Marty emphasized. "Why would he do that?"

"Hell if I know," Garcia said. "Why don't you go ask him yourself?" He nodded in the direction of the church. "He's right inside."

Dana was caught flat-footed as Garcia's lip curled into that aggravating half smile again. He knew Dana didn't want to see Duke. Their relationship worked best when neither was near the other.

Warren Duke had been an oppressive hand on her shoulder for her entire career, but for her first four years on the force, he didn't even know her name. Dana knew he never consciously held her down, but his apathy proved just as effective. The cops in his circle kept moving up, while she stayed in the same place.

Then she started making waves with Gordon. Her cases got press coverage. Duke started paying attention, which only made things worse for Dana. Duke knew he would never get her in his pocket, and he needed his people in his pocket.

For a time, Gordon seemed to have Duke checkmated because Gordon knew a secret. Duke's family was messy. His sister was severely schizophrenic, his niece similarly disturbed. Gordon knew that kind of thing ran in the family.

Everyone knew Duke had his eye on being chief of police. Rumor had it that he was readying for a mayoral bid soon. That kind of position went to people who had others in their pockets—and no whispers of mental illness whirling about their heads.

Dana looked directly at Garcia. "You should have led with that. I wouldn't have had to talk to you," she said, throwing his curveball right back at him. She turned to Marty. "Let's pay the chief a visit, shall we?"

"If you say so," Marty said warily.

As they turned away, Garcia reached for his phone. Maybe they'd called his bluff. Maybe he was texting Duke right then. Duke hated surprises, always wanting the upper hand. Gordon had taken that from him, and for a time, he'd gone quiet.

But recently, Dana had been wondering if her ace in the hole, Duke's family secret, was all that much of an advantage when, in order to play it, she had to sit at the poker table with a psychotic.

"You're not really gonna ask Duke if he's sandbagging us, are you?" Marty asked, his voice low, as they approached the chapel entrance.

"Not in so many words, no," Dana said. "But he's been content to leave us more or less alone for almost half a year. Now we're running into his people left and right."

"Could be a coincidence," Marty said.

The front door was at street level but behind a thick concrete island where a row of young trees grew, their branches winter bare. That was perhaps a new addition, built after Charlie plowed a car through the front doors, to keep anything like that from happening again.

"No such thing as coincidences," Dana replied as she pushed open one of the heavy wooden doors.

The cold light of winter seemed to stop at the front doors of the chapel. Inside under soft lighting, wooden pews the color of dark honey sat empty but expectant, facing an altar that had the look of a ghost-lit stage. The cross behind the altar was tinged in red by light filtering through a stained-glass window high above, which depicted Jesus frocked in red with arms outstretched, ministering upon a small hill. The silence was soft and heavy.

A voice from one side, stern and loud, made Dana jump and Marty spin: "Can we help you?"

Two young men were seated in metal chairs against the wall aside the entrance. Dana and Marty had walked right past them. They stood slowly, and although Dana couldn't see any weapons on them, they had the confidence of men with firepower, as though they were perhaps better suited for the hard corners of the Bermuda Triangle a few blocks over. They were dressed in heavy coats, dark jeans, and stomping boots. They wore skull caps of thick black wool. One had an eye patch.

"We're looking for..." Dana paused.

They were looking for a few people at this point. *Who first? Tasha Cunningham? Charlie?*

"They're likely here with the chief," someone replied confidently from down the aisle, near the altar. A man walked their way with the slow confidence of someone who owned the place. He was broad, but his silhouette tapered, not unlike a coffin. "You'll have to forgive the extra security, but given our history with Charlie Cunningham, we can't be too careful."

He came to rest in front of them. He wore a fitted three-piece suit of dark wool as comfortably as Warden Abernethy had worn his track suit. His black skin was freckled at the eyes, his hair closely cropped and flecked a disarming gray. He held a fedora by the brim in one hand, and an overcoat hung over the opposite arm. He took one look at their badges and nodded to himself before shifting his fedora to his left hand and offering a handshake. "I'm Josiah Hill, senior pastor at New Hope. Warren and I were just finishing up. It's never a good day when your job suddenly becomes police business, but I'm not sorry for the extra eyes on our humble home here."

Dana considered rolling with it, playing like she was supposed to have been here all along, but a second shadow emerged from the door beside the altar, a tall man in a dark sports coat, with a golden ring on his pinkie that flashed in the low light. Warren Duke paused in the act of buttoning his jacket as soon as he saw them. The whites of his eyes narrowed, and his unnaturally tanned face darkened further.

Warren Duke quietly walked down the aisle as Dana shook Hill's hand. He stopped just behind the reverend and said nothing but simply watched and listened, head barely moving, like a rattlesnake emerging from its den.

Dana took a straightforward approach. "We're actually following up on a lead. Trying to get a location on Tasha Cunningham."

The reverend's face flashed with momentary uncertainty as he turned toward Duke, apparently waiting for some sort of confirmation.

Duke shook his head. "They aren't here with me, Reverend," he said, his voice even. "I told you that you should have a lock on that door."

Josiah looked at Duke a moment longer, during which Dana badly wished his back wasn't turned to them, so that she could see what passed between them. When he turned around again, his face was composed once more. "Who am I to lock the house of God?" he said by way of answer then waited in comfortable silence, as if expecting Dana's validation.

Dana felt strangely compelled to give it, finding herself nodding, even.

"These fellas look like a pretty good lock to me," Marty said, still eyeing the two men, who stared back unflinchingly.

Josiah looked upon them with pride and rotated his fedora slowly in his hands. "Brother Alonzo and Brother Dameon are here because of Tasha," he said. "You said you were following up on a lead, Officer..."

"Frisco. Sergeant Dana Frisco," she said, although without her usual vigor.

"Sergeant Frisco," he replied, nodding as if he'd known her for years. "I'll do you one better. Tasha Cunningham is here. We've offered her a home in the church house ever since Charlie was arrested."

Duke put his hands on his hips and looked up at the rafters, his lips a thin line.

"Wait, she's here?" Marty asked, pointing at the ground. "Now?"

"Yes," Josiah said.

"Can we talk to her?"

"No," said Duke. "She's fully aware of the situation with her brother. She hasn't been in contact with Charlie and has nothing more to say on the matter. We've questioned her thoroughly."

"That might have been nice for me to know, Chief," said Dana, "seeing as this falls under my jurisdiction."

"I tell you what falls under your jurisdiction, Sergeant," he said, his voice suffused with simmering anger. He stepped close enough that Dana could smell the sharp punch of his cologne like expensive leather. He ticked off on his fingers. "You missed the truck. You missed the car swap at the airport. You're just *now* following up with

Tasha? To the extent we know anything, it is because of *my* people."

Josiah held out his hat as if gently wiping the air between Dana and Duke clear. "Now, Warren. This isn't the place. I'm sure Sergeant Frisco is only trying to help."

For the first time since she could remember, Warren Duke did as he was told. He backed away, although the sound of him breathing through his nose seemed to echo off the altar.

"Warren is correct, though," Josiah said. "Tasha has always been... fragile. She doesn't know where Charlie is. She's scared. We just want to keep her safe."

"Safe from whom?" asked Dana.

"From Charlie, of course," Josiah said, looking down briefly, as if in suffering solidarity. "Tasha wanted out, all those years ago. Out of the hell that her brother was just getting into. Charlie didn't like that. She came to New Hope for help. Charlie didn't like that either. I'm sure you know what happened next."

"You got a new concrete planter," Marty said.

Josiah chuckled. "Yes, we got a new concrete planter. And a new bay window. Whole new entryway, matter of fact."

The reverend ushered them toward the door with the brim of his hat. "Why don't you walk out with us," he said.

And before Dana knew it, they were doing just that. She was walking out alongside Marty, following Josiah, with Duke just about pressing them from behind.

Josiah gestured at the dilapidation and grit painting the city blocks in the near distance. "If you have the misfortune to fall on hard times in this place, it's almost impossible to get your head above water again. Especially if you're a woman." He shrugged on his camel-hair overcoat and donned his hat, in no particular hurry, as if confident the world around him would wait. "Now you see, the young men, they end up in jail or dead. But the suffering of young women is prolonged. Lifelong. We try to help if we can."

He stopped them at the sidewalk and turned to face Dana fully. "We'll take good care of her. Don't worry. But the sooner you can get Charlie Cunningham somewhere he isn't a danger to himself and others, the better. Nice meeting you, Sergeant. You too, Detective. Wish it was under other circumstances."

With that, Josiah walked away, toward an old black town car parked on the sidewalk with REVRND on the vanity plate. Dana knew they'd been redirected, ushered out, and essentially told never to return, but Josiah had a way of doing it that made her feel as though she'd accomplished something and was leaving of her own accord. She'd been snake-charmed.

Duke, on the other hand, didn't give a shit about charming her or anyone else that got in his way. He came up beside her and stared her down out of the corner of his eye. "Josiah is a polite man. A man of God. I am not. I'll tell you this. You fucked up three times now, and I have it documented. When this is all over, your file will finally be big enough that no wrongful termination lawsuit in the world will hold up. And then I'll have you out on your ass."

He lingered.

"Or?" Dana asked.

Men like Warren Duke always had an *or*.

"Or you just let my people take over wherever Josiah Hill is concerned, while you go back to the midlevel bullshit you're best at," Duke said. "And maybe you keep your job."

Warren Duke walked away, toward where Garcia was

waiting. He paused by Marty and sized him up. "You backed the wrong horse, Detective."

"We're a team, right, Chief? One big, happy family," Marty said, not quite squaring him up but facing him fully.

Duke snuffed once like a bull then walked to Garcia's cop car and got inside. Neither man looked their way as they passed by.

Dana and Marty found themselves alone together on the sidewalk outside New Hope. A siren wailed somewhere in the distance. The throaty sound of cars revving through a part of town where nobody wanted to stop carried clearly through the cold air.

"That went about as well as I thought it would," Marty said.

"I'm not done with this," Dana said.

"I know."

"What's her name?"

"Who?"

"Your girlfriend."

Marty scratched at the five o'clock shadow already darkening his jaw. "Brooke."

"Brooke. Nice name," she said.

"She's a nice girl," he replied, and his genuine smile warmed her, a sip of hot coffee on a cold day—especially after New Hope. No matter how "open" New Hope claimed to be, she'd found no warmth there at all.

"I'd like to meet her sometime," Dana said.

"If things keep going strong, hopefully, you will," said Marty.

They crossed the street and parted ways to their cars. Dana wanted to do some thinking. Marty said he probably had enough time to do a full cycle at his home gym before Brooke came over for dinner. They were going on the paleo diet together. He said he'd hit a limit with his BMI and read somewhere that paleo might help him break through. Dana told him to have fun with that.

On her drive home, Dana thought about Marty and Brooke—who, in Dana's mind, was beautiful and probably a yoga instructor or personal trainer, maybe both—dancing around Marty's tiny kitchen, cooking plants and nuts and seeds, which made her smile. She kept her mind there in that place because she didn't want to think about Gordon not being at her home when she got there, maybe not being there for a little while. She tried not to think about how he'd wanted to do a little cooking of his own for her, a wonderfully odd thing for him to propose, and she had ushered him out.

She'd done so to keep Chloe and Maria safe, but still... it felt wrong.

Most of all, she didn't want to think about how Warren Duke was right. She'd missed the truck and missed the car swap, and she was slow on the Tasha lead, so slow that Victor Garcia had gotten there first. She was better than that. Or she used to be, anyway, before a sliver of shrapnel had slipped past her skull and put her in a coma.

Whispers of doubt crept closer, moving in like a cat when her head was turned. Whispers told her that piece of shrapnel had severed something integral inside, something that made her the good cop she used to be, the cop that had rescued that little girl from the dumpster and later carried her, battered but alive, from the old theater. Whatever it was that used to give her that quick jump off the line seemed to have deserted her.

She feared she was going dull at precisely the time she needed to be razor sharp.

So Dana turned up the classic-rock station in the

minivan and pictured Marty dancing in his kitchen with a girl he liked. Eventually, she was smiling again. She could still keep that fear—all too familiar now—at bay a little while longer. But she knew she couldn't shut it away forever.

CHAPTER NINE

According to Andy Bagshot, Maranatha High School wasn't very different from Ditchfield. Both were big brick institutions. Both held bunches of kids in little rooms and made them do stuff they didn't want to do. As a matter of fact, regarding looks, Ditchfield beat Maranatha High hands down. Ditchfield manor was a historic place. Maranatha was just big and squat and dirty, like an old airplane hangar.

Both places had another thing in common as well: They both employed Andy Bagshot. And for much the same job, keeping the boys—and girls—in line.

Andy picked up a shift a week at Maranatha on his day off for a little more drinking money. He'd been throwing a bit too much cash at the cam girls recently. Not that it hadn't paid off—after dropping two hundred on his favorite, he'd gotten her cell number. That was step one on the way to buying a night with the saucy little whore.

He knew her rates, though. If he wanted to do what he really wanted to do with the dirty bitch, he would need more cash.

His usual heavy hand didn't go over well at Maranatha. He'd nearly lost the gig when he slammed a kid against a locker for being out unattended and mouthing off when Andy asked to see a hall pass. He pressed the little shit up against the cold metal and held him there by the throat until some simpering teacher had threatened to call the police. Andy liked to hold kids up against things, by the throat. At Ditchfield, he liked to press with his baton. Often, he had to tuck a chub up under the band of his pants afterward.

Andy had a thing for throats in general—especially on his cam girls. Cam girl plus baton plus some throat and some pressing action? That was prime spank material. And expensive.

But they'd never fired him from Maranatha for choking that kid, with a chub in his pants. That was good, especially since Abernethy had put him on temp leave for blowing it on night watch with that shit stain, Charlie Cunningham.

No matter. They wouldn't fire him from Ditchfield either. They would dicker and wring their hands and whatnot, but he'd be fine. Nobody fired Andy, for one simple reason. At all those places—institutions that have to deal with creatures that will steamroll the public if they are allowed to—the top brass want someone willing to press on throats.

Never mind that the principal at Maranatha said he was a "visual presence only." Never mind that he was told to keep his hands in his pockets and baton on his belt. The people who ran these places often said these things, but they didn't mean it. Not really.

Still, with all the drama at Ditchfield, he needed this gig.

And even if he had to keep his hands to himself, it wasn't all bad. He was paid twenty bucks an hour to basically stand by the front door and try not to get caught staring at asses. *They certainly didn't make 'em like that back in my day*, he thought, watching a particularly perky gaggle of girls walk past and inside. As far as he could remember, all the girls at his high school had been fat. And even the fat ones wouldn't put out until he'd gotten them too drunk to see.

One of the little sluts turned and caught him looking. Her head zipped right back around, but Andy swore she gave her ass a little extra bounce.

Not bad at all.

The third time a certain car rolled by, Andy took notice. Part of his gig was rounding up the truants that screwed off in the surrounding neighborhoods and nearby park. The truant kids pulled this little trick where they walked in and through the metal detectors then right out of the gym entrance out back, where they'd parked their beaters—junk SUVs and rusted-out sedans they drove around until they could find a place out of the way to smoke weed.

Andy recognized most of the cars those kids drove. He knew the usual culprits. But he didn't recognize the one he'd seen roll by three times already, a boring white sedan that looked too clean to belong to any high school kid. He stepped out from under the eaves and followed it as it made its third pass, tracking the same square route, down the street out front, stopping briefly at the stop sign leading into the parking lot, then rolling around the corner and down Clifton Avenue, where it turned right.

Andy couldn't get a good look inside the car. He saw only an outline of the driver: thin, bald or shaved head, and tallish, judging by how close his head was to the roof as he looked out at the schoolyard.

He was looking right at Andy.

The guy's head scanned forward until it found him, and it stayed on him as the sedan made its slow way past the stop sign and around the corner.

Andy had the distinct impression that whoever was driving that car only stopped looking at him when he had to physically turn around in the driver's seat—basically at Clifton, where he turned right.

That meant he'd be coming around again.

Andy flicked his baton from his belt and walked slowly across the front entrance to where the parking lot started. He knew he was supposed to be hands off, but he didn't take too kindly to being mean mugged by some pussy hiding inside his car. All those kids were the same—hard-asses until they got punched in the face. He decided to walk out to the parking lot and wait for the kid to pass again, to let him know who was boss or, at the very least, to get a good look at him for later.

Andy's breath puffed and hung in the still, damp air, disturbed only by the lazy spin of his baton.

The car made almost no sound as it rolled around the bend into sight again, nothing like the rattles and chugs most of these kids' cars made. It looked like a rental—no plates, even. Maybe it was Andy's lucky day and the kid was driving a stolen car and he could finally put his baton back to use. He'd been itching twice as bad since Abernethy told him he had to cool it. Funny how that worked.

The car rolled to a slow stop at the stop sign. Andy stepped down into the parking lot and flipped off the driver. He was only mildly surprised when the car made a languid right-hand turn at the four way to move into the lot itself.

Andy smiled. So it was some truant kid after all. And he wasn't even putting up a fight. He squinted to try to see through the windshield, but the glare through the clouds above reflected right at the spot over the driver's face. Andy motioned with a single finger to tell the kid *get the hell over here if you know what's good for you.*

The car crept toward him as if the driver was just letting the automatic transmission do the work for him. Andy bade him come, peering as the clouds ran over the windshield, his finger hooking the boy forward until a break in the sky above finally gave Andy a decent look at the driver.

A boy, like he'd thought. Black kid. Thin and gaunt. Nothing special, save for a weird ear.

Even then, Andy didn't put two and two together. As soon as he clocked out at Ditchfield the day Charlie went missing and the cops were out of his face and the physical evidence of the kid running away wasn't immediately in front of him, Andy had set the entire ordeal out of his mind. He did know Charlie was out there somewhere, doing whatever it was degenerate kids like him did, but when Andy wasn't on the clock, Charlie wasn't his problem.

Twenty feet from where Andy stood, the car lurched forward, and in the two seconds it took the engine to rev to a roar, Andy remembered about Charlie Cunningham.

Andy folded over the hood like he'd been hooked at the belt and yanked on a line. His boots caught under the grill while his arms splayed over it. Charlie stared down at him like he was nothing more than a scrap of paper he was determined to blow off the car.

Andy recognized that look. He'd seen it a few times while looking in the mirror before paying another hundred for the cam whore. Charlie had made up his mind and turned off whatever part of his brain might see Andy as a person.

Still, Andy didn't think he was going to die, not even when Charlie barreled the car up and over the sidewalk and shattered both of Andy's ankles in the process. He was Andy Bagshot, after all. He was on the thumping side of the baton.

The roar of the engine was so loud, and Andy's face so close to it—mere inches of metal away—that he didn't even hear the earth-shaking cacophony as Charlie plowed the sedan through the double glass doors of Maranatha High School. His senses were thrown into such terrified confusion that he felt the forearm-sized shard of plate-glass window spearing his liver as nothing more than a needle of pressure—then his spinal cord was severed as he was slammed into a metal support beam, and he felt nothing at all below the neck.

Andy had the consciousness of a floating head for a few fleeting seconds, just long enough to see Charlie Cunningham looking down upon him before flipping up a hoodie and disappearing.

All Andy could do was blink. So he blinked as fast as he could... then slower... and slower until his eyelids stuck open and his eyes let go of their focus forever.

DANA WAS PEDALING the squeaky spin bike in her basement—trying to keep up with Marty in the workout department when she could—when she got the call. Dispatch described a potential attack at Maranatha High School. All available officers were requested. The suspect had slammed a car into the front entrance and was currently still at large. One casualty was confirmed—a security officer named Andy Bagshot.

She was out the door, sweat still dripping down her face, before the bike had even cooled down.

When she arrived on scene, Maranatha High was still in chaos. Dispatch said half of the students had fled to an abandoned parking lot across Clifton Street, while the other half was apparently still inside, barricaded behind classroom doors. They were awaiting an all clear from the Baltimore Police.

Three squad cars were there, junior officers from the northern district patrol division. They were trying to enter the building and fielding panicked questions from the staff in the parking lot at the same time, and they didn't look particularly happy about either job. She beat Marty to the scene, but he was on his way. That's what he got for living in his hip neighborhood across the city instead of in cookie-cutter suburbia up north like her.

Dana's hair was bunched up atop her head in a sweaty mess, and she wore a still-damp workout shirt from some police benefit years before over baggy sweatpants, and the cops looked blankly at her. When she showed her shield and rank, they visibly sagged, as if thrilled to have someone more senior to make the decisions.

She pulled her gun from her holster and left the rest of her rig in her car. "I'm going in," Dana said. "Who's coming with me?"

A pair of the patrolmen pulled away from the crowd and briefed her as they approached the wreckage.

"We were first on scene. After the initial attack, nothing. No shots fired," said one cop.

"Any sign of the suspect?" she asked.

"Car's empty. That's as far as we got."

"All right, keep your weapons out but down," Dana said. "I don't think this is an active-shooter situation, and we don't want to turn it into one."

The patrolmen looked at one another as they walked

toward the school, confused. One seemed about to press for further details, but then all three came upon Andy Bagshot's shoes at the lip of the sidewalk, and whatever questions anyone had went out the window.

They followed the thickening trail of blood.

The car door was open, the airbag deployed. Dana could see no blood inside the cabin. Charlie had likely prepared for the impact, but an airbag to the face hurt, no matter what. He would be smarting from the collision as well, but nothing like what had happened to Andy Bagshot.

Andy looked like he was in the middle of a particularly difficult wall-sit exercise, stuck between a metal column and the hood of the car. His head was back, mouth open, eyes looking blankly at the winter sun overhead. His hands were flat on the hood, as if he'd given it a big hug. From the waist up, he looked almost normal.

The space underneath the car looked like a red Pollock painting. Blood dripped in some spots and streamed in others. Andy's legs were splayed awkwardly, bent at unnatural angles. The skin of his exposed abdomen looked like a paper bag full of smashed strawberries.

A shoeprint marred the crisp edge of one spreading dollop of dark blood on the concrete near Andy's hip, a waffle tread, half in and half out. Dana pictured Charlie standing over his handiwork there, perhaps making sure the light fled from Andy's eyes, hoping that a bit of the pain the man had caused him might flee along with it. She wondered if he felt better after all this... or if he felt nothing at all.

More bloody shoeprints led toward the school.

"C'mon," Dana said. "Inside. Stay alert."

Glass glittered like sand thrown across the floor of the entryway. Dana stepped over the twisted metal of the doorframe ripped from the walls. The doors to the rooms immediately inside were locked and dark, but she sensed panicked bodies behind them. The hallways were permeated by the sounds of muffled crying and urgent whispering. She had a quick flashback to the hallway in the Lexington Heights projects.

"Baltimore Police!" she yelled then listened carefully.

Sometimes, the first callout flushed the birds from hiding—not this time. The frightened whispers redoubled.

"Stay where you are," Dana announced. "We will escort you out room by room once we're sure you aren't in any danger."

The bloody footprints ended at the far end of the front hall, where they blended into the everyday scuffs and smudges of a well-tracked floor. Dana walked over to the last remnants of the waffle print and pushed open a nearby door. She edged her way inside what turned out to be the gymnasium and looked carefully around the room before entering. No students were there. All of them had apparently fled out the open back doors.

Dana crossed the squeaky-clean basketball court, eyes down, scanning for anything. She saw a small smear, a bit redder than the other scuffs. Her pulse quickened as her gut told her Charlie had gone that way. She ran across to the open double doors at the far side, and there she stopped, her spirits instantly drained by the sight of hundreds of kids in the parking lot directly across the street.

She forced herself to slow, scanning the crowd for anything abnormal as she approached the tense crowd, but the whole scene was abnormal. She looked for a tall, thin black kid—maybe in a hoodie or a beanie cap to disguise himself a bit—but she found fifty kids that matched that description nearly enough in one glance.

She slipped her gun into the baggy pocket of her sweatpants and pushed through the crowd, trying to get a good look at as many faces as she could. She scanned for anyone that was limping or wincing or standing aside, alone.

"Charlie!" she yelled, but her voice joined the panic of all the others, blending right in.

And that's what Charlie had somehow managed— again. He'd blended his way right out of Ditchfield, and now he'd blended his way right out of a murder scene.

She should have known better. Charlie was a chameleon. He disrupted a scene then slipped right into the chaos with the practiced ease of a child who had lived within chaos his entire life. The Dana of six months before would have had the patrolmen follow up inside the school while she came right here, right off the bat. The old Dana might have had Charlie Cunningham in cuffs already.

Cars streamed in and out of the main lot and the side lot. Charlie was likely in one of them already, a flathead screwdriver jammed into the key block or spliced wires dangling from the console. Maybe he'd found one with a spare key up in the tire well. Maybe he'd scouted it hours before, to secure a getaway. She should have instituted a cordon around the entire school first thing.

She was disappointed in herself. She'd been sloppy. Sloppy and slow.

Camera footage would be more useful to her than scanning random faces. She wanted to see the school and the parking lot from the moment of the attack on and also earlier in the day. Charlie was likely in a new car, and she needed to know the make and model before Duke blamed her for letting him get away and used it as an excuse to get her fired. He was closing his fingers more tightly around this case, while Dana felt she was losing her grip.

She was right about one thing: Charlie was a killer.

Gordon's theory that he was simply a misguided kid with anger issues was shattered, along with the entryway of Maranatha High School and Andy Bagshot's spinal column. That didn't make her feel any better. Charlie would be considered armed and dangerous. Duke would likely brief his officers on the use of lethal force. He'd signed his death warrant the second he killed Bagshot.

More than anything, she wished she could talk to the kid and understand what he was thinking. Maybe all he'd ever wanted was a chance to kill Bagshot. Maybe he'd taken one too many hits from the asshole and decided to forfeit his own life to wipe the man from the planet. Given the life Charlie'd had, she wouldn't exactly blame him.

Or maybe this was part of something bigger.

Maybe the time had come to let Duke have the case, to move back under the safety of her little rock with Chloe and Maria. She could hit up Gordon for that home-made breakfast and let Packman or Garcia or any other Duke bootlicker take care of Charlie.

If she did, she wondered when she would forget the little keychain with Tasha and Charlie, smiling, together, holding each other before Baltimore ripped them apart.

Probably not for a very long time.

Marty's midnight black Charger roared into the parking lot. He hopped out and went immediately to work. People seemed to defer to him without even meaning to. That was the kind of cop she used to be. He didn't bat an eye at the hysterical crowds and didn't seem fazed by the car wreck. Before long, he was crouched by Andy's body, doing good cop work.

From where Dana stood, the car wreck looked surreal, like a jagged rip in the fabric of the reality of the school, a run in the stitching of things. Marty was a solid waypoint, something she could focus on and still feel sane.

She gave one last look around the crowd in the adjacent lot, not even really sure what she was looking for, but feeling as though she had to do something. Nobody seemed to be paying her any attention whatsoever. Her gut told her Charlie was gone.

She walked back toward the main lot, stopping at Clifton to make doubly sure the street was clear. She doubted she'd ever look at an oncoming car the same way again. What an absurd idea a car was, really—a thousand-pound metal box you could rev up to killing speed by pressing down six inches on a pedal.

Cars were weapons, all of them. Weapons were everywhere, and all of them in the hands of anybody over the age of sixteen with half a brain. It struck Dana that driving cars was one of the things everyone took for granted, part of the social contract of the working world, but that wasn't the type of thinking that was good to dwell upon. Otherwise, you'd see how crazy it was, blindly trusting complete strangers to stay in their lanes when one swerve this way or that could mean the end of everything.

Marty was directing an evidence shield to be placed around the car and body. Two officers were pulling a screen tight, creating an open-faced box around where Andy lay, still bleeding. *Smart*, Dana thought. *I should have done that. No need to expose these kids to any more trauma than they've already experienced.*

Marty stepped away and walked toward her as soon as he saw her, removing a pair of latex gloves. "I got the students and staff pairing up with their cars if they have them. I bet we find one missing," he said. "And I requested all security-cam footage for the day, yesterday too. We'll find him."

"He took off inside, but I think he just passed right through the gym and out back again in the aftermath," said Dana. "I lost him. Never really had him in the first place."

Marty tilted his head to get a better look at her, and she met his eyes only with effort.

"You all right?" he asked.

"I'm all upside down about this whole thing," Dana said. "I want Charlie in custody, but not for this," Dana said, gesturing at the screen. "I'm not even sure I'm mad he did it," she added, lowering her voice.

"I get it," Marty said. "I'm having a hard time blaming him too. Bagshot was a special kind of shithead."

"Maybe I'm wrong about the whole thing," she said. "Maybe he only wanted to kill Bagshot after all."

Marty cleared his throat, looked around, and nodded Dana over to one side, by his gleaming car. She followed wordlessly.

When they were out of earshot, he spoke. "About that. I found something on Bagshot. Something I decided not to log as evidence. Yet."

He reached into his jacket and pulled out a plastic baggie. Inside was a business card. He handed it to Dana. One corner looked like it had been dipped in red, but the rest was crisp and clean and looked brand new.

Reverend Josiah Hill – Elder and Senior Pastor
New Hope Community Church

On the reverse of the business card was the number one, hand drawn in pen and circled.

"This was tucked between the buttons of his shirt. Andy didn't put it there."

It was a message from Charlie, then, perhaps meant for the Baltimore Police or whoever else followed up on Bagshot's death.

"The start of something," Dana said, thinking aloud.

"Maybe. I can't help but think 'strike one,' like we're not getting something. And another fastball is about to come down the pipe," Marty said, looking back at the screen.

Rapid-fire camera flashes illuminated the outlines of the CSI squad within.

Point taken, Charlie, Dana thought. New Hope was at the center of this. That much was clear. Dana had felt as much since that unsettling run-in with the reverend and Duke the day before. Something was off about that place. *But if Charlie knew something they didn't know, why not tell the cops?* Hell, he could pick up the phone and get Dana on the line any time he wanted.

But he hadn't. Instead, he'd left a calling card at a murder scene. At great cost to himself.

For Dana, the first step toward figuring out what Charlie had to say about New Hope was understanding why he couldn't say it. And she needed to figure it out soon. If Charlie did have a list and if that list was somehow related to the cards in his possession when he was shipped to Ditchfield, the next person he targeted through his windshield could be Gordon.

CHAPTER TEN

When Dana told Gordon that Charlie Cunningham was most likely a killer after all, he did not take the news well. Gordon hadn't thought Charlie was capable of murder, maintaining that Charlie's assault with the car at New Hope was a cry for help. And he was dead wrong.

As soon as Dana finished detailing how Charlie had run Bagshot down at Maranatha High School, Gordon went over to his scotch cabinet and poured a finger of one of the crappy blends he had at the back—he thought he wouldn't deserve a single malt for a long time—and downed it in one go. He paced for a time, wondering where he'd gone wrong. One thing Gordon did know: Charlie had gotten to this point in large part because Gordon had failed him.

Then he found himself back at the liquor cabinet, with another finger of cheap scotch, which he downed in another go.

Things devolved from there until he ended up in his converted broom closet, surrounded by patient files from that public-school study—both Charlie's and others— burying himself in his past to try to find some blueprint to navigate his present. The files were remarkably thin. Soon enough, an empty bottle of scotch was sitting on the floor, with two pieces of his World's Best Doc novelty pencil beside it. He'd cracked it in half after his second drink.

Ethan Barret had given him that pencil after he helped spare the kid from Ditchfield. *Funny how quickly our wins are forgotten in the face of our losses*, Gordon thought drunkenly.

Time had gotten away from him. He'd missed two appointments with his regular, everyday clients. They didn't kill people with cars and actually helped pay his bills, but what had started with rehashing Charlie's case turned into falling down the rabbit hole of the last year of his marriage, and he didn't feel like seeing anyone just then.

The responsible half of his brain was psychoanalyzing the drunk and anxious side, which was likely in the middle of a minor breakdown. He had the odd sensation of sitting in his chair and scribbling notes about himself.

Hmm, yes. The scotch. That's always step one, isn't it?

You're thinking of your ex again, aren't you? You're fully capable of handling this yourself, but maybe you'll give Karen a call to talk this all out anyway? Step two.

You're a good psychiatrist, and you know it, but you snapped that pencil in half because you'd prefer to wallow, and now you smell like a dirty distillery. Attractive. And you know Dana loves you, but now you're wondering what the hell she sees in you anyway, aren't you? That's step three. And we've arrived at our final stop of the evening: Full-blown Self-loathing. Congratulations, Gordon. Punch your ticket on the way out.

Knowing the clinical roots of his own anxiety didn't make pulling himself out of a spiral any easier. Ten years at Hopkins then another ten of talking kids off ledges only

made his insights into his own neurosis crystal clear
—high def.

So he sat in his boxer shorts on a document box with
his laptop hot on his pasty thighs until the words of
Thomas Brighton from five years before danced to the forefront of his muddled head: *Did you know that Ditchfield is
a nonprofit? You oughta look at their public filings
sometime.*

The thing about falling down rabbit holes was that at
the bottom of them, one often found more rabbit holes.

He started with Ditchfield's 501c3 filing. The mission
statement front and center for the entity legally named the
Ditchfield Juvenile Rehabilitation Center made Gordon
laugh out loud: Empowering Youth to Live Productive and
Law-Abiding Lives.

The financials were sobering. Ditchfield had received
eight million dollars in donations in the last fiscal year.
Brighton wasn't kidding when he said the place was
connected.

New donor-disclosure laws allowed many nonprofits to
redact donor specifics—Ditchfield included—but Gordon
was a pro at navigating old city databases, and he managed
to find some older 990 filings that had been spared
redaction.

The documents weren't fully digitized, so the online
search function didn't work, but Gordon scrolled through
page after page anyway. He almost missed what he was
looking for because his hangover was well and truly set in,
and his eyeballs felt like they were scraping against his
eyelids. He left his closet to go the bathroom and get some
water, and when he came back, the answer was right there
on his screen: a list of donor organizations to the Ditchfield
Juvenile Rehabilitation Center circa 1991. First and fore-

most was an organization called the New Hope Foundation.

He slapped the screen with his thumb and held up his arms to signal a touchdown. New Hope Community Church—New Hope Foundation. The two had to be connected.

He checked his watch—barely three in the morning. *Plenty of time.* Gordon switched tracks and started digging into New Hope.

The going was much easier, almost too easy. Their most recent org filings spelled everything out clearly. New Hope Community Church was just one part of a much larger organization that included four community centers across Baltimore, as well as a small media company.

Also, Reverend Josiah Hill was more than just the senior pastor of New Hope Community Church. He was listed as CEO emeritus and the current chairman of the board of directors for the foundation.

Gordon felt as though he'd stumbled upon some dark secret—a twisted collusion that somehow validated his belief that Ditchfield was a blight, fed by some thread of poison that had its roots deep in the city... but of course, that was because he knew the truth about Ditchfield.

To anybody else, this paperwork would look like nothing more than a wealthy private foundation supporting an institution that rehabilitated juvenile offenders—responsibly and ethically. The mission statement of New Hope Foundation was suitably vague: Uplifting the Underserved of the City of Baltimore. Ostensibly, that aligned with Ditchfield's.

A simple search showed Josiah Hill front and center in the press, as well. A native Baltimorean—what locals called a "Bawlmer"—he'd been born and raised in the Monument

Street area east of Johns Hopkins Hospital, which was gritty and had been even grittier in the late seventies. Hill had worked as a community organizer, canvassing for some of the successful local politicians at the time before putting himself through divinity school on a scholarship.

He had an inspiring story, on the surface, at least. He came back to help clean up the neighborhood where he'd cut his teeth organizing. He lobbied for his people and pulled together enough money to buy property. He'd basically been offered the third congressional district in 1992—running against a banged-up incumbent—but he declined. The *Baltimore Sun* article quoted him as saying he "wanted to focus on grass-roots work with New Hope."

Gordon flipped through article after article.

"Rev. Josiah Hill Receives Honorary Doctorate from Hopkins School of Public Health"

"Hill Spearheads Record Grant for Baltimore Performing Arts Complex"

"Rev. Josiah Hill Breaks Ground on New Community Center"

"Office of Mayor Receives Crucial Hill Endorsement"

The pictures always showed a well-dressed man of presence, aging handsomely throughout the years, usually complete with a fedora. The camera's flash caught moments of deference to the man. People seemed to look up to him naturally. He was a man who didn't want to be the king but who seemed perfectly happy to name the king.

And he certainly seemed to know what his community

needed, from his centers to the church to Ditchfield itself. All to serve—all of it tied up with a neat little bow.

Except for Charlie Cunningham.

Gordon set the laptop down. It was nuclear-level hot on his thighs, and the fan was whining like a dentist's drill. He thought about another glass of scotch, but respectable scotch-drinking time was far in the past, and he didn't want to arm his future self with that shame bullet. *Coffee instead.*

Gordon stood too quickly and felt light-headed. He steadied himself on the wall and closed his eyes while the stars subsided. He wondered when he'd last had a glass of water and decided to get one... with the coffee, of course. When he felt like he could stand again, he opened his eyes and found himself looking at a dusty box labeled Tapes. That was odd because Gordon had stopped taping sessions years before, after concluding it negatively affected patients to know they were being recorded.

The connection had to slog through a thin layer of scotch, but it came, and all the more powerfully.

One stipulation of the consulting project with the Baltimore Public School system was that the sessions be recorded. The school board requested it so that they could audit if they wanted, and it was also a way to limit liability. Gordon was given a little microrecorder and about a hundred cassette tapes. Somewhere in all the paperwork, he'd checked a box asking for them back after a period of time.

He'd forgotten all about them, unsure when they were mailed back, even. He must have been in the depths of the divorce. A lot from that five-year time period before Dana was spotty. That wasn't just because of the booze, either. His mind had been trying to save him from himself by blacking out the details.

Gordon popped the box open and looked inside to find row upon row of tapes, stacked in alphabetical order—last name, first initial. They were dated too. He clasped his hands in thanks. *Credit where credit's due. Shout-out to Karen for being anal retentive.* The handwriting was all hers.

He flipped through the tapes with a rapid *clickety-clack* like a toy train running loops on a track. He stopped when he came to Cunningham, C. and pulled out all of them, five full tapes. Those he took from the dusty half-light of his broom closet into the pitch black of his office proper. He almost tripped over a Chinese takeout box on the way to his desk and had to clear the desktop of clean clothes he'd thrown there instead of folded.

Dana asks you to stay clear and you go into full-on bachelor devolution after barely four days, he thought. *Get it together, Gordon.*

There, in the back of the top drawer, sat his old tape recorder.

He spent the next fifteen minutes looking everywhere for eight AA batteries before finally stealing them from the remotes and all the clocks in the loft. Then he went back into the kitchen, set the recorder down in a sliver of moonlight by his pour-over coffee setup, and pressed Play.

"Hi, Charlie. My name is Gordon. Thanks for talking with me today."

A snort of laughter. The creak of an old school chair.

"I didn't have much of a choice, man. But okay. Sure."

The sound of their voices shot Gordon into the past. His was painful to listen to, weirdly reedy. Charlie's was so boyish that he couldn't believe it came from the same kid who would slam a car into a church mere months later and then, years after, run a man down in cold blood.

"*Do you know why you're here?*" Gordon asked.

"*You talkin' to the bad eggs,*" Charlie replied, and Gordon could almost hear the air quotes. "*Look, man, I was just checkin' handles. If someone leaves a car door open overnight in Baltimore, they oughta get robbed on principle.*"

"*I'm not here because of that,*" Gordon said. "*Well, I mean, I am, in a sense. But not the way you think.*"

Gordon shook his head as he poured coffee beans into the grinder. He sounded half as confident as the fourteen-year-old boy.

"*We're just trying to figure out if there's a way that BPS can help you and other kids like you that seem to have a lot of run-ins with the cops. That's all.*"

Gordon paused the tape and turned on his bean grinder, packed with nineteen grams of single-origin coffee beans from some shady spot on a hill in Guatemala that he wished he was sleeping on right then. As the burr smashed the beans to pieces, he thought about the interview. More was coming back to him. For a while, Charlie had deflected. Gordon was fairly sure Charlie was simply happy to have something to do. Bright children were like that.

Gordon fast-forwarded the tape. He would give the whole thing a listen later, but right then he was just trying to jog memories loose, to get a sense for the time and place. Quite frankly, he wasn't sober enough for a thoughtful listen. He stopped the tape randomly—a satisfying *thunk*—then set about filling up his electric gooseneck kettle, programming it to heat to 197 degrees. The temp readout glowed red in the dark of his makeshift kitchen, slowly climbing. While it heated, he pressed Play.

"*—suspended a few times for fighting. Quick and brutal stuff. Then you get picked up for the door-check thing,*" Gordon was saying. "*Were you trying to steal a car?*"

"*You think I'm gonna cop to an attempted felony on tape?*"

"*This is covered under patient client privilege. Nothing you say to me can ever be used against you.*"

That single laugh again. Then quiet. "*Yeah fuckin' right. That shit don't exist for people like me.*"

The electric kettle clicked off at 197, just before boiling. Gordon flattened a Hario filter in his V60 ceramic and set it atop a tempered-glass carafe. Then he wet the filter to wash it of its paper taste.

"*All right then, how about this? What's running through your head when you do this stuff?*" Gordon asked.

"*Nothing.*"

"*Nothing? Nothing at all?*"

Gordon tapped the ground beans gently into an even layer on the damp filter. The reasons Karen might jump to sociopathy weren't hard to see. But she'd only listened to the tapes. She hadn't been in the room. Gordon clearly remembered a pause, a moment before Charlie said "nothing" that told Gordon it wasn't nothing.

As Gordon recalled, Charlie dodged a bunch of questions then just got up and left not long after. He popped the tape and flipped it over. While fast-forwarding for a bit, he wet the grounds then let them sit. Steam wafted lazily in the filtered moonbeams passing through the skylight.

He pressed Play and started a slow pour from the kettle, keeping the hot water just above the grounds. Pour, stop. Pour, stop.

"*—don't you worry 'bout me, man. I ain't the one you need to worry about. I make my own help.*" Charlie was midconversation.

"*Who should I worry about then?*" Gordon asked.

"The people you don't see. The people that don't got the strength to help themselves," Charlie answered.

Silence. Then Gordon from three years ago was tapping faintly on a pad of paper. The sound mixed almost seamlessly with the slow drip of the coffee into the carafe. Gordon was on autopilot in both cases, thoughts surfacing, memories rising.

"You went to the hospital last month. Ended up on the wrong end of a fistfight with a kid named Alonzo Cook," Gordon said.

Silence *from* Charlie. Then he said, *"Can't win 'em all."*

"School report said you were silent on why it happened. But others there said it started on account of some words Alonzo said." The fluttering of Gordon flipping papers.

"They all start because of words," Charlie replied, flippant.

"About Tasha," said Gordon.

Gordon froze, the pour-over half done. The softly rising steam was the only movement in the kitchen. Charlie was remaining silent, but Gordon remembered that moment in all its clarity. He'd expected the boy to dodge the question with more flippancy, to keep messing with the peeling paint on the desk, but instead he stilled and looked directly at Gordon, right into his eyes. Unblinking, he just stared like that until Gordon was forced to speak to kill the odd silence.

"Is your sister one of the people I should be worrying about? Who can't help themselves?"

More silence—longer that time.

"No." Charlie said eventually. His voice was cold, flat. *"She got me, don't she?"*

At the time, Gordon thought the boy was angry with

Tasha, too, just like he was angry at everything. Karen maintained he wasn't angry at anything and that was the whole problem. He felt nothing.

Again, Gordon saw how she might have gotten that, listening to this without the perspective Gordon had. Those last words Charlie had offered him, sitting across the plexiglass at the Ditchfield visitor's room, rang in his head. He'd spoken them as if under duress, like a POW interviewed on camera in a hostile land: *find Tasha.*

He wasn't angry with Tasha at all. He was terrified for her.

Gordon looked down at the coffee as if surprised to find it there. He started his slow pour again, cursing softly. He'd exposed the grind too long, and it would be slightly bitter. But slightly bitter pour-over was still better than nothing at four in the morning when one needed to think. He was looking for that perfect balance of being loose enough to make the mental jumps he needed and focused enough to stay on target.

Charlie excused himself. *"I got no more time for this today. When are you done with your little experiment, anyway?"*

"Another two weeks, then we'll wrap up. Hopefully have enough to get funding for some more counselors in here," said Gordon, undaunted.

Charlie laughed again, that single soft note, a laugh that said another couple of counselors wasn't gonna cut it. At the time, Gordon had written it off as teenage attitude and a healthy dose of reality. The school had a single overworked counselor who also doubled as a case worker, and one man could never attend to the needs of all those kids.

Now, Gordon had a different read. Charlie was angry

with a system he knew could do nothing for him, because he had a big problem, one that threatened his sister.

Gordon sipped his coffee as quickly as he could without scalding his lips. He needed more information. His mind was tapping its wristwatch, saying they didn't have much time left. But so was his tired body, saying no amount of caffeine was going to save him from four heavy-handed pours of scotch on no sleep.

Gordon spent the next hour skipping through the tape, but all he got was that Charlie became increasingly distant as their sessions rolled on. By the end, he'd said very little. In their last session together, Gordon had asked Charlie if he was grateful for anything, a question spurred by Karen, who still classified the boy as a sociopath. At the time, Gordon had been doing research into the science of gratitude.

"Anything at all?" Gordon asked. *"Even if it's just one thing."*

The thinking was that a grateful kid couldn't be a sociopath, by definition. In fact, gratitude therapy was being tested as a method for rewiring the dormant areas in the amygdala of actual sociopaths.

He never got an answer, just that single-note laugh.

The question struck Gordon as particularly naïve now. Mere weeks after the end of the recording, Charlie Cunningham would be taken from the wreckage of the entryway of New Hope Community Church to a holding cell at the city jail, then straight to Ditchfield's Pod D.

Suddenly, nothing was standing between Charlie's big problem and Charlie's twin sister anymore.

CHAPTER ELEVEN

G ordon awoke to knocking at the front door of his office. He'd fallen asleep on his couch, holding limply onto his coffee cup, and when he startled awake, the dregs spilled on his crotch. He stood, and his phone fell from his lap directly onto the corner of the coffee table with a solid smack that made him wince.

The knocking continued.

"Hold on!" he yelled. "Just a minute!"

His contacts felt dry and tacky. He rubbed at his eyes and checked his phone. He saw he'd missed five calls from Dana and one from Karen. It was also two in the afternoon. He'd been dead to the world all day. Dana would be understandably pissed. The call from his ex-wife, though—that gave him pause.

"Gordon! Are you in there?" Dana was at the door.

"Coming!" he replied.

He threw on a robe and hastily tied it while making his way downstairs. He smoothed the frazzled remnants of his hair and opened the door. She was standing with her hands on her hips, staring at him as if dumbfounded by his general being.

"Why don't you *ever* answer your phone?" she asked.

"I was up late, going through Charlie's files," Gordon said. "And drinking a fair bit of scotch," he added guiltily.

Dana rushed in and slammed him into a hug. "Thank God you're safe. I thought you were dead. I mean, not really, but a little bit."

Gordon patted her on the back and took in the glorious smell of her clean hair. "A little bit dead?" he asked.

Dana pulled away, held him at arm's length, and tried not to crack a smile. She scanned him up and down once more, stopping at his crotch.

"That's coffee," said Gordon. "I promise."

Dana nodded and pushed inside, already on to the next. "This Cunningham case is messing with my head. Marty looked at the tapes and figured out that Charlie boosted a white SUV from the Maranatha lot. I kept picturing you half underneath every white SUV on the road, pasted to the hood like one of those Halloween decorations where the witch is wrapped around a tree."

Gordon followed her in, thinking he probably should've opened a window. "Sorry about the mess."

Dana went to the couch, tested the cushion, found it wet with coffee, then pushed over a pizza box and sat on the other side. She sank to the couch, huffing out and leaning her neck back, arms flopped and palms up. "I've seen worse. You should see what Chloe can get up to in three days. I'm just glad you're alive. That's my bar these days. Marty and I have been trying to piece together all these threads while crisscrossing the eastern district. Duke has every able-bodied cop on the lookout for this car."

"He's not gonna find it," Gordon said. "Charlie's too smart for that."

"I know," she said. "Marty found him on tape, casing the parking lot two hours before he hit Bagshot, checking handles, prepping his getaway. He has no intention of getting caught this time around."

"He has a bigger plan," added Gordon.

"Yeah, knocking off everybody he thinks is responsible for making him miserable at Ditchfield, which likely includes you. Then what? Disappearing with his sister, maybe?" She closed her eyes and rubbed at her temples.

"Hard to say." Gordon moved over to the sink and poured a glass of water. He took a big sip to wash down the fuzz of the morning.

"That's the story Duke is pushing, anyway. He had a press conference about the wreck this morning. Charlie is a 'dangerous criminal' who is 'out for revenge' and will be met with 'lethal force,'" Dana said, using air quotes.

Gordon took another drink. "Pretty cut and dry. Nothing more to see here. That's a Warren Duke special. Maybe that's why I don't like it," he said. *All wrapped up in a nice little bow.*

Dana held up a plastic sandwich baggie with what looked like a bloody business card inside. "I told you about the card from New Hope, but I didn't tell you that there's a number on the back. One. As in 'one of many.' And one of them could be you."

Gordon took another sip. He understood her point. He'd essentially given up on Charlie when he gave up on everything else after Karen left him. He didn't mean to abandon him, but that's what ended up happening. He wouldn't blame Charlie for holding a grudge against him.

And since Charlie was now a killer, by all rights, Gordon should be looking over his shoulder.

But he still had time, a small window of time, to maybe make things right. And that was overpowering his fear.

"I need to see Tasha Cunningham," he said.

"Marty and I tried. She's under lock and key at New Hope Community Church," Dana said.

"No, like *see her*. I need to see her with my own eyes."

"I told you we tried."

"You're a sergeant in the Baltimore Police Department, and Marty is Detective Beefcake. What do you mean *tried*? What happened?"

Dana looked squarely at him. "You know that's not how it works, Gordon."

Gordon held out a placating hand. He'd overstepped. "I know. I'm sorry."

"And you should give Marty more credit," Dana said. "He's a good guy. And a great cop. He saved your life."

"I'm sorry," Gordon said, absently rubbing at his scarred knee. "I know he is. That was harsh. But I'm feeling a little harsh. This shouldn't be this hard. We're missing something."

"What *happened* was Warren Duke. And Reverend Josiah Hill," Dana said, standing.

Gordon stood straight, his water forgotten. "They were together?"

"Yeah. Duke was his usual asshole self, but this Hill guy... he's a real piece of work. Had us out the door and basically apologizing for disturbing him before we really knew what hit us. He's that kind of man," Dana said, disappointment in her voice. Gordon knew she'd had her fair share of manipulation at the hands of powerful men and didn't much care for it.

Something was wiggling in the back of Gordon's mind, a sticky piece of memory from the night before. He drummed his fingers on the counter.

"The guy's some sort of powerful community figure," Dana said. "Makes sense that Duke would want him on his side if he really is planning a run for mayor. God help us," she added, crossing herself.

Gordon moved past the couch and back upstairs. He needed his laptop.

"Duke," he said. "I saw Duke somewhere. Not Warren, though."

He popped open the computer and plugged it in. It was mercifully cool after having worked overtime on his lap. His tabs were still open. He clicked through them and landed on the Articles of Incorporation for the New Hope Foundation. He scrolled wildly, the pages flitting by, trying to remember where he'd seen what he half remembered. That had been solidly into the fourth glass of scotch.

He slowed, blurring his vision a bit. He remembered big blocks of text, just like... *there.* He stopped on the Members of the Board. Rev. Josiah Hill was there, up top. But below him, Gordon found what he'd caught: Archibald J. Duke, member of the board of directors.

"What's Duke's dad's name?" Gordon called downstairs.

"His dad? I don't know. Probably some east-coast blue-blood thing like Higgledy-Piggledy the Third."

"He's the guy with the big-time shipping business out on the docks, remember?"

After a moment, Dana replied, "Archie, maybe? That sounds right."

Another puzzle piece clicked into place in Gordon's

mind. The picture was still blurry, but the edges were coming together. He had the borders.

Gordon walked back to the stairs and paused, forcing himself to take them slowly. His knee was already aching, and the day was way too early for that. He'd done himself no favors using it as a computer stand all night.

"He's on the board for the New Hope Foundation. Archibald J. Duke. They're all connected," Gordon said.

Rather than firing her up, that seemed to weigh Dana down. She deflated another inch into the couch. "Of course they are," she said. "They're all connected. It's been that way forever, and it's never going to change."

Gordon limped over behind her and put a hand on her shoulder. He thought about the ring still in the breast pocket of his old tweed blazer, hung on the rack upstairs. He'd patted the pocket every time he passed, as if it might somehow jump out and hit the road if he wasn't careful.

"You okay, Dana?" he asked.

"Not really," she said honestly. "Ever since the coma, I feel like I've been playing catch-up."

Gordon limped around to face her and eased himself into his chair. He said nothing, only listened.

"I'm not sure I can do this anymore," Dana said. "I've mostly slowed Marty down for this whole investigation. I think that explosion took something from me."

"It likely did," Gordon said simply, and before the hurt in Dana's eyes manifested into something too real, he added, "But not the way you think." He tapped his Frankenstein knee. "In medicine, this is what they call a *good* recovery. I can get around just fine, but you and I know I'm not going to be jogging to catch the train anytime soon. You had what they call a *full* recovery. It's possible that there might be some very mild cognitive dissonance every now and then, headaches and the like, but I saw the brain scans, and I took them to some of my colleagues, and every one told me the same story. Fully recovered."

Dana crossed herself again then dropped her hands to her lap. But she still seemed defeated. Gordon sought her eyes and found them.

"What I'm saying is the physical damage we've taken isn't gonna be what stops us. I've got a working knee. You've got a working brain. They'll do the job just fine if we let them. But the psychological damage is a different animal."

Dana's eyes glistened. Gordon knew how hard she had to be outside the walls they shared. He knew the toll that took on her. He wanted nothing more than to give her a space to be herself when she needed it.

"Life isn't often explosions and house fires," Gordon said. "Mostly, we fight little battles. Every day. Without even knowing we're fighting them. The world likes to chip away at your confidence whenever it can, like a horsefly looking for a place to take a bite. I let the world take big bites out of me for a long time until I was convinced I was a fraud, a nobody standing in the place of a licensed child psychiatrist. It's a real thing. Called imposter syndrome. You can look it up if you want."

"Are you gonna charge me for this?" Dana asked, but a hint of a smile flashed in her eyes.

Gordon kept going. "Then I met you, and we saved a little boy named Ethan Barret, and I thought to myself, 'That's weird. You're supposed to be a hack. But hacks don't help kids, so something must be up,' and I realized that there's no difference between the people who succeed and the people who fail. Not fundamentally. I've been both. It's not about who is *best* for the job, it's about who *does* the job."

Dana looked at him as if trying to see what kept him ticking. He didn't know how to tell her that he was running mostly on fear—fear that he'd sit down and find himself unable to get up again; fear that the man he'd been a year before—the man drowning—was just a few steps behind, ready to jump in and take his place again.

She looked over at his desk, where he kept the framed issue of his published work on sleepwalking, his first accepted article in a major journal. Beside it was one picture of his mother and one of him and Dana, both taken at Waterstones. Gordon thought he looked a bit pallid in both, but he smiled nonetheless every time he looked at them.

"Where's your World's Best Doc pencil?" she asked.

"Oh. I snapped it about two drinks in, last night."

"Why?"

"Because I'm not the world's best doc, obviously. Although I'm working on it."

Dana laughed. "You know that's not how those novelty things work."

"It is for me," said Gordon.

"That's why I love you," she said.

Gordon just took that in for a moment.

"I need to see Tasha Cunningham," he said again.

"Then let's go see Tasha Cunningham," replied Dana. "But first, can you make me one of your fancy coffees?"

"On it."

He started measuring out the beans—nineteen grams for an eight-ounce pour. No more. No less.

∽

WHEN DANA PARKED her minivan just off the street of the eerily quiet New Hope block of the eastern district, it was already dark. Marty's Black Dodge Charger was already there, quiet, like a pocket of darker black, waiting to pounce.

"Marty's here?" Gordon asked.

"Of course Marty's here. He's my partner. He's gonna be almost everywhere I am for what is hopefully a very long and fruitful career in law enforcement," Dana said, her tone letting Gordon know quite clearly they didn't have time to press bullshit that didn't matter.

Gordon nodded.

Marty stepped from his car when they emerged. Gordon noted he was sporting his regular look, dark on dark on dark. He had to admit the leather jacket did look good on the guy. It made Gordon rethink his own slightly stained ski jacket, still sporting a lift ticket from a fairly crap day of skiing out in Claysburg, years back.

As he gave Gordon a once-over, Marty looked like he wanted to make a quip of some sort but held his tongue. "Hey, doc," was all he said, his voice low.

Gordon nodded at him, slightly ashamed. Of the two of them, Marty was clearly coming across as the adult, and Dana looked like she knew it.

Marty turned to her. "I'm assuming the warrant for this is in the mail?" he asked cynically.

"Don't need a warrant," Dana said. "According to the good reverend, the house of God is always open, is it not?" Dana spread her arms in mock benevolence.

Marty put his hands on his hips and looked back at Gordon. "This sounds like your idea."

Gordon was about to defend himself, but Dana spoke first.

"My idea too," she said, sliding her firearm into its

holster at her side. "And your idea, Marty. You showed up tonight for a reason."

Dana pulled her coat over her gun, and the three of them took in New Hope Community Church, sitting like a silent white monolith in the dead of night. Despite the soft lighting inside, something about the building, about the whole block, made Gordon's eye want to just pass it by. Someone could easily pass the whole block by. All around them, the eastern district teemed—even in the darkness, the expectant, fraught hush of a living, breathing community was still there. But on this particular block, Gordon felt like he was looking at a set piece.

Marty seemed to sense the unnatural quiet as well—he unzipped his jacket a bit and tapped the slight bulge of his shoulder holster as if to reassure himself. "Well, if we're going, let's go."

They walked across the street and around a concrete island with evenly spaced, bare trees that creaked softly in the barely there breeze of the night. Gordon tried to picture Charlie smashing the front door to pieces, looking for evidence of when a car hung half in and half out of this place, but everything had been patched, all of it carefully and cleanly redone.

At the door, they paused. Dana and Marty seemed reluctant, either professionally or personally, and Gordon understood both. He also understood the need for action.

"I'll do it," he said, gently pushing at the doors. They swung open easily, spilling weak light onto the sidewalk. Marty sidestepped him and entered first, his right hand resting lightly on the teeth of his zipper, inches from the gun inside. Dana held Gordon back with a gentle but firm grip on his shoulder.

After a moment, Marty relaxed, but he still scanned the room with a wary eye.

"Looking for someone?" Gordon asked low.

"Two guys were at the door last time. They didn't exactly strike me as the church-going type, if you know what I mean," Marty said. "But I don't see 'em." He didn't exactly seem relieved about it.

Marty walked in, and Gordon followed. Dana brought up the rear, closing the door behind them with a soft click that felt strangely final somehow. Yet in front of him was a chapel that looked like nothing more than a peaceful and open place of worship. Neat rows of pews sat there, each with a soft accent light at the aisle. A centerpiece of stained glass cast a faint red glow on the cross and altar below. To either side were alcoves where rows of votive candles were lit, their singular flames swaying slowly.

Nothing else moved. Still, Gordon felt an ominous undercurrent to the silence that tugged slightly at him, like the surf sliding back from shore.

"Kind of bizarre, all this just wide open in an area of town where if it ain't bolted down, it gets boosted," Marty whispered.

"Maybe the junkies know better than to mess with this place," Dana replied.

"And where is everybody?" Marty asked.

That, to Gordon, was perhaps the more pressing question. From everything Gordon knew about Reverend Josiah Hill, he was constantly surrounded by the community. His other community centers were always busy, day and night.

"Maybe they know to stay away too," Gordon said. "Right now, at least."

"This way." Dana led them down the left aisle, between the pews, down to where she'd seen Hill and Duke emerge at the side of the altar. She pointed at a small wooden door adorned with an upraised crucifix that read Staff Only.

Marty stepped up and tried the handle. It didn't give. He jiggled it again then leaned on the door. "Guess not every door in God's house is open," he said.

"Want me to kick it down?" asked Gordon. "I mean, I've never done that before. But I don't want to get either of you in trouble."

"Kick it down?" Marty replied. "Gord, your leg would blow up."

"Well, maybe I could kind of shoulder into it or something," Gordon said. "That might not cause permanent damage."

"Shh," said Dana. "Someone's coming."

Gordon froze. He heard it, too, footsteps somewhere behind the door and getting louder. He and Marty stepped back. Gordon stared dumbly at the door until Dana pulled him quickly aside, and the two of them pressed flush against the right side of the altar. Marty withdrew further to the left, blending into the shadows gathered beyond the reach of the votive candles.

They waited.

A young hard-looking black man emerged, ducking through the door and into the sanctuary. He wore dark jeans and a dark oversized jacket that swished in the silence. He was followed by a second man in an all-black sweat suit with a flat-brimmed Ravens baseball cap and a black eyepatch over his right eye.

"Van's about packed. I'll call the reverend and get going to the barn," said the first. "You watch the door while I'm gone."

The first kept walking up the aisle, but the one with the patch paused as if he forgot something then turned around and opened the door again with a key. He reached inside and around and pulled out a dull black nine millimeter.

Gordon squeezed Dana's hand, and she squeezed back. He looked over at Marty across the room. He knew Marty saw it too. Their options were running out. With every step these men took, another path out of this place disappeared. Dana shook her head furiously at Marty as if she could read his mind, but Marty stepped forward anyway.

"Good to see you fellas again. Dameon and Alonzo, right? I was hoping you might help me out," he said, his tone friendly, his hands out and palms up.

Alonzo brought the gun up and fired twice. The sound punched Gordon's ears, obliterating the silence of the church. The fire of the muzzle painted itself on the inside of Gordon's eyelids, and when he opened them again, Marty was down.

"Shit," said Alonzo, looking down the muzzle of the gun as if surprised to find it there.

"Drop the weapon!" Dana shouted, stepping out and in front of Gordon, leading with her handgun.

Alonzo turned to Dameon, already halfway down the aisle. "Go!" he shouted.

Dameon ran, and Alonzo took that moment to spin around and aim again. Gordon saw the dark metal of the barrel twirl around as if in slow motion. In the reddish light, it cast a shadow that looked a bit like an accusing finger.

Dana fired twice. Alonzo's nine millimeter loosed one more round, as if in animalistic response, but the bullet went high. Alonzo dropped into a moaning heap on the ground, and the gun clattered down afterward. Dameon was already out the front door. Gordon saw him hook left before passing out of view, running full tilt.

Dana ran up to Alonzo, still leading with her gun. He

was clutching his right shoulder and seemed to be having trouble breathing, but he was very much aware. Dana kicked the gun away and pushed him down with a hand planted firmly on the other side of his chest.

He moaned again. "You know what..." He took another breath. "You fuckin' done?"

Gordon ran past both of them to where Marty was pushing himself back against the nearest pew. He was hitching for breath that didn't seem to come, pawing wildly at his chest.

"Marty, please," he said although he didn't know where to go from there.

Marty's jacket was in tatters, still half zipped. Blood was running from tiny black specks above the V-cut of his T-shirt, and when Gordon unzipped his jacket, he fully expected to find a ruin of ground meat.

Instead he found a vest of body armor.

Gordon dropped to his other knee and almost collapsed on the man. "Oh, thank God."

Marty grabbed Gordon's arm with one hand, and with the other, he popped the vest open at the buckle underneath his shoulder holster. It came free, and he took in a huge breath.

"The key," Marty said, squeezing Gordon's arm hard. He pointed at the little door.

Gordon looked at the handle of the little door, where the key still dangled, then back at Alonzo. Dana snapped up to them.

"Marty?" she asked, her voice brimming with tremulous hope. "Marty, are you—"

"Go!" Marty said.

Gordon pushed himself up like an old dog and limped over to Dana. He looked down at Alonzo, who was clenching his jaw against the pain—and likely against a string of words he would've liked to fire at all of them. But he'd been trained well, it seemed. Silence was golden.

"He had a vest on," Gordon said, and as he spoke, he still couldn't believe it himself. Somewhere out there in the floating cosmos was a timeline where Marty Cicero got blown to pieces in a church in east Baltimore, and it had almost been their timeline. But it wasn't. And it wasn't their timeline because Marty was a hell of a lot smarter than Gordon had ever given him credit for.

Gordon squeezed Dana's arm. "I'm going in," he said. He hoped his eyes conveyed everything else. He hoped they even conveyed all he wanted to say about the ring tucked safely away in his jacket pocket back at his flat, stupidly unused. But he doubted she saw anything more than the man she'd always seen.

He hoped that was enough.

"Be careful," she said. "I love you."

Gordon turned around without another word, clicked the key into place, and opened the door with his shoulder. He stepped in and left the acrid gun smoke behind, but the ringing in his ears followed him as he made his way down a narrow, dimly lit hall. He heard frantic movement ahead. Heavy things were dropping, and what sounded like a table's worth of metal gear was being shoveled somewhere.

Gordon picked up the pace to what he might call a fast lurch. A door sat open ahead, heavy and steel. Dameon was flitting in and out of view within, shoving things into a bent cardboard box filled to the brim with papers and computer parts. He knew he was in no shape to confront a young man, terrified and possibly armed. If he tried to analyze him with impromptu therapy, he'd get beaten senseless at best. But maybe he could bluff his way through.

"Police!" he shouted. "Get on the ground! Face down, hands on your head!"

That sounded about right. It checked out with the few times he'd seen Dana in action and the hundreds of cop shows he'd watched.

Dameon froze, and Gordon pressed against the far wall, hoping he'd think a burly city cop was barreling down on him and not a forty-six-year-old psychiatrist with a bad knee. Apparently, Dameon didn't care to see either. He grabbed the box and bolted out the back door without so much as one backward glance.

A crunching sound was followed by the slamming of doors. Gordon followed as quickly as he could, navigating a harshly lit office in disarray. When he pushed open the steel double doors after Dameon, the man was already peeling away in an unmarked white van. Tires screeched as he took a corner hard. Gordon waved his way through a cloud of exhaust, limping down the alleyway after the car without really knowing why. Then he remembered the steel doors and reversed course, sticking a leg out just before they closed. He hissed in pain as his shin became a doorstop, but the way back remained open.

Gordon heard sirens in the distance as he pulled open the doors and went inside again.

The office looked like it had been hit by a tornado. It seemed to be a stripped computer lab, with dangling cables and hastily unplugged wires. Dead monitors spread out evenly along a series of desks that faced a blank brick wall. The only other door was whitewashed nearly the same color as the brick. Gordon might have missed it if the lock hadn't caught his eye—a big, industrial-grade thing with a throw bolt the size of a ruler. Gordon slid it aside and pulled the door open.

He was met again by the sounds of the night and a small enclosed patio that extended out from the secret doorway. At the far end was a small window leading into what looked like a budget apartment. He pushed through the bones of an overgrown bush and crossed the small, open courtyard as quickly as he could to reach the front door. He tried the handle, fully expecting it be locked, but it was open—his first welcome surprise of the night.

He hesitated even as the door swung easily inward. He caught it and pulled it back then knocked. "Hello? Anyone there? I come in peace."

Silence. Darkness.

He pushed open the door and found a dorm-like living quarters that had the empty echo of fresh abandonment. A common space attached to four rooms, all doors open. A few papers lay on the floor, with some cables and wires strewn about. A heap of what looked like baby monitors was piled in the corner.

Gordon's gut told him Tasha had lived here. Maybe others had lived there too. But they were gone. Gordon popped his head into the nearest bedroom. The walls were dark red, with no windows. Most of the space was taken up by a sagging twin bed, stripped down to a yellowed mattress. More baby monitors sat on the floor. The smell of old sweat mixed with dust raised the small hairs on his neck. The entire area had an air of oppressive sadness, not unlike Pod D at Ditchfield. The longer he looked, the more it glommed on to him. He felt a powerful urge to run.

The sirens were very close, and one wound down, clipped. He heard car doors opening and slamming shut.

Nothing was there any longer but the ghosts. Gordon turned back, crossed the courtyard, and entered the office once more. He saw the computer lab for what it was now: a surveillance station. They'd recorded things there, things those monitors showed.

He eased himself down onto his knees and looked flatly across the floor. Dameon had been hurried. The place probably wasn't as stripped as they wanted it to be. Papers were strewn across the floor. Maybe Gordon could still salvage this operation and glean some tidbit of info that might help Tasha and Charlie.

He flipped a piece of paper near to hand, a grainy print of a photograph. When he saw the picture on it, his resolve redoubled. He picked the rest of the papers up, all of them, not even looking, only gathering. He jammed papers into his pants pockets, scrunching and folding. Underneath a small pile of receipts in a corner, he found a thumb drive. He pocketed the drive and the receipts, thanked God for small miracles, then left the way he'd come.

Gordon was halfway down the narrow hallway when he heard someone approaching from the chapel side. A series of scenarios flashed through his mind of what might happen if he was found there, and none of them were good.

He about-faced again. A wonky soft-shoe trot took him quickly to the double doors through which Dameon had fled. He pushed them open just as he heard the inner door slam shut. He flipped around outside the doors and closed them as quietly as he could, then he pressed himself up against the frigid bricks of the outer wall of the church.

Gordon took three deep breaths and wiped the sweat from his brow. The freezing night air turned him from hot to cold in an instant. He stepped softly down the alleyway and turned the corner just as he heard the double doors open. He wanted badly to look and see who emerged, but he would've been spotted in an instant. So Gordon kept walking.

He hooked a left then another left then one more until he was nearing the front of the church again. At no point did anything he pass give any indication that a horror-show dorm and an oddly quaint courtyard lay somewhere within. Nobody passing by would ever know, which was exactly how Josiah Hill had likely designed it.

Not for one second did Gordon think the good reverend wasn't completely aware of everything that happened under his roof. Or on his block. Or in his city.

From a shadowed vantage point just around the corner, Gordon watched the scene unfold.

Four police cars and one ambulance were outside. Marty Cicero was being wheeled out on a stretcher, but the head was elevated, and he was sitting up, talking to the medics. Dana came after, followed closely by Warren Duke.

She held up a hand in stoic farewell to Marty. He gave her a thumbs up and pushed it farther out as if to impress it upon her, then the rear doors of the ambulance closed after him.

Dana turned around and faced Duke. He was a good foot taller than she was, and he used all of it to tower over her. Gordon couldn't hear what he said—he knew Duke preferred the low growl—but he got the gist when Duke held out his hand and Dana unclipped her gun and handed it over. She followed it with her badge.

Through it all, she stood with her shoulders back and her head held high, unflinching, even after Duke turned away and stalked off. Gordon had never been prouder of her than at that moment. He had half a mind to run up and propose to her right there, ring or no ring.

The other half of him, the one not soaked in fading adrenaline, told him right then probably wasn't the best time.

He texted Dana: *Around the corner. Meet at car?*

Her phone lit up with the text, and she exhaled into the night. Some of the tension left her shoulders. He realized that, up until that moment, she'd thought he was still trapped somewhere inside that madhouse of a church. *I really do need to get better at the phone-communication thing.*

Gordon waited until the cold from the brick started to seep through his jacket, then he set off toward Dana's mini-van, keeping out of the pools of white light thrown by the streetlights. When he got there, Dana was already inside, looking blankly out the window. When he tapped the glass, she started then quickly reached over and lifted the wonky lock on the passenger-side door.

He sat down and put his hands in front of the heating vents. His nose was running. Dana looked at him expectantly, grabbing one of his hands in both of hers. She seemed to be processing, looking for words while her brain raced back and forth over the events of the past half hour. Gordon had no doubt she was in shock.

"Okay," he said. "I'd say that went pretty well."

Dana snorted once then started laughing. Soon, she was crying with laughter. At least, Gordon hoped that's what was happening. She was still holding his hand in a way that suggested a fair number of other tears were in there as well.

"Pretty well?" Dana asked when she was composed enough. "My partner got shot in the chest. Twice."

"Yes, that did happen, but—"

"I'm on unpaid leave. No badge. No gun. That's the first step toward removal for dereliction of duty," said Dana.

"I saw that. And I'm not saying there weren't some hiccups—"

"And for what?" Dana continued, undeterred, her head in her hands.

"For this," Gordon said, taking the picture he'd found and floating it down to rest on the center of the steering wheel.

Dana lifted her head and looked at the print. Then she looked harder, picked it up, and turned it sideways.

"This looks like a glamour shot gone wrong. Is it Tasha?"

"No, I don't think it is," Gordon said.

He'd been looking at it in the cold light of the night while he waited for a clear exit. The woman in the picture was made up heavily—big eyelashes and lips painted as red as apples. Her cheeks sparkled with a blush that was many shades lighter than her skin. But Gordon had seen the pictures Dana had of Tasha—up until almost a year ago— and that was a different woman.

In silence, Dana looked at the picture for such a long time that the weak light of her cell phone clicked off three times, and she clicked it back on again each time.

"I saw cameras," Gordon said after a minute. "And beds."

"How many beds?" Dana's eyes were getting that sheen that came over her when she saw things that struck her deeply—grave things that affected children.

"Four," Gordon said quietly. "They were... bad. The place smelled like fear."

Dana whispered a prayer in Spanish that Gordon couldn't make sense of, but he felt it was a prayer of lament, one that spanned dialects and languages. Her voice was hoarse and broke at the end. She had probably known since the beginning somehow that Tasha Cunningham was being taken advantage of. She was a lost woman with only one place to turn, and that place had been New Hope.

The tears she cried then—quietly into her hands then into Gordon's shoulder as they sat side by side on the darkest block of their city—were entirely tears of sorrow.

CHAPTER TWELVE

SIX YEARS AGO

Four of the lightbulbs in Thomas Brighton's outdoor chandelier were burned out. Gordon counted them while he waited for Brighton's secretary to answer the door. The chandelier was up high too. He doubted the bulbs would get changed any time soon. He couldn't imagine Brighton in his shiny oxfords and his double-breasted suit fifteen feet up on a ladder. Nor could he imagine the buxom secretary up there in her red heels.

"I don't see a Pope," she replied through the speaker.

"Try Plop," Gordon said, rolling his eyes.

"Oh! Here you are!" she said, buzzing the lock. "Come right up."

The lock snapped back, and Gordon stepped inside. The entryway had been spruced up with a gilded mirror and a vase of fake flowers since his last visit. A small space heater rotated in one corner and smelled faintly of burning plastic.

As he approached, Brighton's receptionist looked up from a gossip rag and smiled around her gum. Her hair looked freshly blasted, so blond it was almost white.

"Water?" she asked. "We got some bubbly water too," she added proudly.

"No, thanks," Gordon said, taking a seat in the same chair as before.

He put his head in his hands before realizing that might make him look as strung out as he felt. For the first three weeks Karen was gone, he'd held out half a hope that the phone would ring and she'd say she'd changed her mind. For two weeks after that, he just hoped the phone would ring at all. Then, the previous week, the phone did ring, and it was Karen, and she asked him how he was holding up.

He said not great.

She spoke of the difficulty of processing trauma while within it. She told him to give himself time. Then she said, in a very clinical tone, that she was beginning divorce proceedings.

Gordon said he wasn't surprised. Even though he was. The unraveling of his married life over the past month and a half still occasionally hit him with the jump scare of a jack-in-the-box.

Brighton slid open the doors with as much flair as ever, although his smile seemed a tad forced. "Dr. Pope! Thought I might be hearing from you again. Come on in."

Gordon moved from chair to chair, resituating himself in one of Brighton's faded wingbacks with a bit of a grunt. Brighton's receptionist picked up her reading again as Brighton closed the doors behind them.

"I'll save us both some time here," Brighton said, walking back to his cracked-leather desk chair. "No, I haven't looked further into criminal negligence at Ditch-field, and no, I don't plan on it."

Ditchfield. He'd gone almost a month without thinking about Ditchfield. That might have been the only silver lining in this whole mess. But that meant Charlie Cunningham was well and truly institutionalized. His support systems were almost completely broken down.

A flash of anger surprised Gordon, bubbling up from somewhere within, tapping emotions he thought had gone cold over the past few weeks.

"You know where I got your card, Thomas?" he asked. "Where I first found it?"

"Courthouse?" Brighton replied, looking idly out the window, his tone humoring. "Maybe the Fells Point bars? Some strip club on The Block? I drop cards like candy everywhere trouble finds people."

"Ditchfield," Gordon replied.

Brighton came around again and met Gordon's eyes then looked away. "That must have been a long time ago. I don't go up there anymore," he said with none of his usual swagger.

"You did though, once. There's a whole stack of them on the intake desk. A few here and there in the administration building too."

Brighton cleared his throat. "Early on, I was trying to build my client list," he said. "That's all it was, drumming up business."

"Were you working for Abernethy?" Gordon asked softly, genuinely curious. The anger was already dying down again, and with it went all his drive to care.

"All I did was follow up on a few tips for potential representation. Kids that were already on the fast track, understand? I just... I basically filed the paperwork. That's all," Brighton said, his eyes darting around the room, looking at everything but Gordon.

Brighton was just short of pleading, but Gordon didn't know what for—a crack in the slick-lawyer persona. Maybe if he pressed, he'd open that crack a bit wider and peel off some of the patina, to see more of the man underneath.

But pressing took energy. And while he was surprised that Brighton was being as genuine as he'd ever known the man to be, what didn't surprise him was that Ditchfield's reach extended to an attorney that walked a blurry line on Bail Bond Row. If anything, it gave him more reason to shelve Ditchfield.

Brighton seemed to take Gordon's silence for further probing.

"Did you look at the filings? Do you see what I mean when I say *connected?*" Brighton asked, his voice a harsh whisper.

Gordon hadn't dug into the Ditchfield filings. He'd planned on it, but then he got punched in the heart. He was too busy trying to bail out the capsizing boat that was his own life.

"Last time, you mentioned an expert-witness gig. I need some extra cash," Gordon said. "I'm having some marital troubles," he added lamely.

Brighton seemed confused by the sudden turn of topic. Then, relieved, he laughed and steepled his fingers again. The polished veneer returned.

"That's why you came?" he asked. "To ask for a job?"

"Just a gig every now and then, if you have it," Gordon said, and it was his turn to avert his eyes from the conversation.

"Marital troubles? You need a lawyer? Not my specialty, but I know a guy—"

"No," Gordon said. The word came out like a sigh.

Brighton leaned forward on his elbows. "No offense, Doc, but you have the look of a guy that's gonna get run over in a divorce."

"I don't want to fight for anything," Gordon said, rubbing at his temples. "The clients are all basically hers anyway."

"That's exactly what I mean," said Brighton.

"Look, do you need an expert witness or not?" Gordon asked.

Brighton held up his hands. "Yeah, yeah. Sure." He dug around in his desk, opening and closing drawers until he found a little black address book. "Fill out your info here: full name, email, occupation, credentials, and all that."

Gordon stood and took the notebook and flipped quickly to an empty page in the back, half afraid of what he might find within if he looked too closely. He figured any little black book Brighton owned was best held like a hot potato.

When he handed the book back, Brighton looped it closed with a tether and tucked it away. "I'll send over court documentation when we need you," he said.

On his way out, Brighton's secretary waved cheerily at him, and he made a nearly herculean effort to muster a smile so that he didn't look so pathetic. Nobody wanted to put an Eeyore on the stand, no matter how expert his testimony might be.

Walking back to his car, Gordon thought vaguely about all the things he needed money for. The flat he and Karen shared... that would have to go. He couldn't pay the mortgage solo. He might have been able to keep up the rent on the office if he cheated on code and figured out how to live there too. He'd slept on the couch plenty of times before, and it had a small washroom and shower. That was doable.

He could keep up appearances if he put himself out there more, establishing himself as a solo act. But he'd been a part of Jefferson and Pope for so long that he wasn't sure he could do it alone. Karen was the funding part of their duo, while he was the client part. He would need a lot of clients—new clients.

And he didn't care enough anymore.

He was drowning in apathy. He would say he was a textbook case for moderate-to-severe depression, the hallmark of which was complete lack of feeling, were it not for one thing: he felt very strongly that he never wanted to treat kids again.

He knew his sterility wasn't his fault. He knew that Karen was, in all likelihood, the bad actor here. None of that mattered to Gordon.

The most terrifying outcome of the entire mess wasn't that it had ended in divorce. The relational implosion of Jefferson and Pope had taken away something even more special.

Whenever he thought of kids, he now thought of personal failure.

And he didn't see how anyone, anywhere, could ever make it right again.

Gordon walked along the cold concrete sidewalk, past winter-stripped trees and the rattling bones of bushes, caught trash twitching within as the wind picked up off the bay.

And scotch, he thought. He cared about scotch too. Strongly.

He thumbed the edge of Brighton's card in his pocket as he wrapped his coat more tightly around himself. He hoped the little snake had some work for him soon. Gordon's liquor cabinet was looking rather pathetic.

CHAPTER THIRTEEN

Thomas Brighton settled down for lunch in his office and sipped on a glass of iced vodka. He was feeling fairly pleased with himself. He'd just snagged a big client in a carbon monoxide poisoning case with a long tail—the woman's son had gone hypoxic after a furnace in their apartment leaked in the middle of the night a little over a year before, and he was having mental issues. The kicker was that the detectors had no batteries. They had proof too.

Best of all, it was a civil case—people vs. money, not people vs. people. The criminal stuff was weighing on him of late. The last time he felt really accomplished in the criminal-defense arena had been with Ethan Barret, almost a year before. And that had been a bright spot. Brighton had no problem taking cases where the innocence of his client was suspect—everyone deserved a fair trial, after all—but recently, he'd been feeling strange. This Charlie Cunningham stuff, along with Ditchfield, all brought back memories that made him feel... not guilty, of course, never *guilty*. But not *great*.

That day, though, he felt pretty good. He felt pretty good

because of the civil case he'd bagged, and he felt pretty good because he'd been able to decline the offer of representing a juvenile criminal case that didn't sit right with him. Also, he was halfway done with a glass of vodka and had a famous crab-cake sandwich from Darrow's Barrel in front of him, ready to chow.

He topped off his vodka, turned to his crab cake, and just as he was about to take his first bite, the front door buzzed.

Annoying. Probably a package, though. Brighton purposely kept his lunch hour free every day. He fought for it. Meeting-creep was real even though he was essentially a one-man show, no offense to Natasha.

He tried not to listen in as he ate—he often tried to will his office to be bigger than it was—but he couldn't help it.

Natasha was being her usual semi-helpful self. "Who?" she asked. "I don't see any reverend on the schedule today."

Brighton stopped chewing.

He didn't quite catch the reply, but he recognized the deep voice. His first bite of crab cake felt like it dropped another six inches into his gut.

"Mr. Brighton is at lunch right now. And like I said, he's booked all day." One bright-red heel was bobbing up and down with increasing vigor past the glass doors. "Next time, I suggest you call ahead first—"

For a span of moments, Brighton wondered what would happen if he just sat there behind the glass in his little office with its big desk. He could let Natasha turn away his troubles at the door while he spun his old leather chair toward the window and ate his lunch.

Likely, he'd get another visit, a little less friendly than the first, perhaps. Some things—and some people—just wouldn't be put off. Some handshakes stain. Some choices that seem small at the time can reverberate. One might think the noise had quieted, but in reality, the echo was just bouncing off the rocks on its way back.

He pressed the button on his intercom, cutting off Natasha. "This is Thomas Brighton," he said. "With whom am I speaking?"

"Hello, Thomas," came the reply, like an old friend. "It's Josiah."

Brighton closed his eyes for a moment. When he opened them again, Natasha was turned toward him, arms out in question.

He waved her off. "Hello, Reverend. What a nice surprise," he said, trying desperately to sound like he meant it. "Come on up."

He pressed the lock's button and buzzed up Reverend Josiah Hill. After looking longingly at his crab-cake sandwich and gingerly rolling it up in its paper wrapping, he set it aside. He finished his vodka in a shot and slid the glass next to the wrapped sandwich, then he stood and straightened his suit.

Brighton opened the double sliding doors reservedly. Hill emerged from the hallway, along with another young man, an acolyte or a bodyguard. Both were dressed in dark suits, and Hill had his wool fedora in hand.

"Sorry to bother you at lunch, Thomas. Unforgivable, I know. I'll be quick."

He nodded to the young man, who took a seat in the waiting room and rested his hands on his knees. Somehow, Brighton found himself following Hill into his own office. As he closed the doors, he caught a glimpse of Natasha watching the big young man, wide-eyed.

Hill took a seat, crossed his legs, and set his fedora

neatly over his knee. He waited until Brighton rounded the desk and settled himself before speaking.

"How have you been? It's been a little while," Hill said kindly.

"Good, good," Brighton answered. "I've been exploring the civil side of law recently..." Brighton said then trailed off. He wondered if his professional pivot might have had something to do with the reverend's little visit.

"I saw that." Hill looked around the office. "New ventures, new clients, I'm excited for you," he said, although he didn't sound particularly excited. "This place hasn't changed a bit."

"New chair," Brighton said. "Fixed the chandelier too. The wiring was shot for about a year. Turns out Baltimore winters aren't good for outdoor chandeliers. Summers neither. But the rest of the place... I like it the way it is."

Hill laughed, low and slow.

"Always thought that chandelier was tacky," Hill said. "Tried to get the previous tenant to take it with them when I bought the place. They politely declined."

Brighton's uneasy laughter drifted off to a heavy silence. Hill just watched him with a look as though he was about to break out into a smile even when he wasn't.

"This place has treated you pretty well, hasn't it?" Hill asked. "You've made a bit of a name for yourself. Got a decent reputation."

"You gave me a place to call my own," Brighton said. "I've tried to pay back that first year's rent several times—" he began, fidgeting with the vodka glass.

"I don't want your money, Thomas," Hill said, and that smile went across his face, sad and slow.

Brighton nodded. Hill had no shortage of money. What

he needed was more lawyers in his pocket—specifically, Brighton and Associates.

Brighton wet his lips. He felt he should say something, apologize for something. But he didn't know what.

"There was a young man caught selling stolen phones. Bit of a rap sheet. I believe you were supposed to represent him?" Hill asked, furrowing his brow as if he didn't know exactly which young man and exactly which case were in question.

It was the one Brighton had just declined to take up, the one he was celebrating passing on with the glass of vodka and crab-cake sandwich, now lukewarm and congealing in its wrapping paper to his left.

"I was offered a fairly big civil opportunity—"

"The young man was supposed to go to Ditchfield, Thomas, and you were supposed to see to it that he did," Hill said, as if reminding Brighton of something very obvious, like where he'd parked.

Brighton began to sweat under his collar as he saw flashbacks from years before of the boys he'd sent there, almost all of whom probably deserved it. At least, he'd told himself that over the years, especially at three in the morning, when he often woke up and had trouble finding sleep again for reasons that eluded him at the time but were becoming clearer by the second.

"I was under the impression that Ditchfield is a little... precarious at the moment?" Brighton said. He meant it as a statement, but it came out as a question.

"Ditchfield's never been better," Hill said easily. "In fact, we're investing heavily in it as we speak." He shifted his position, recrossing his legs and settling his fedora. "Old knees," he said offhand.

"Charlie Cunningham's been found?" Brighton asked.

For the first time since he'd arrived, a slight shadow of a cloud passed over Hill's face. But it was quick. "I'll take care of Charlie," Hill said. "You just concern yourself with the criminal trial I handed you. Fair? Otherwise, there are a few people on the Maryland Bar Association that owe me a few favors."

Brighton took his meaning clearly but tried not to let his creeping fear show.

"Why do you care that the kid who stole the phones ends up in Ditchfield?" Brighton asked before he lost all courage. *That kid and all the others over the years*, he wanted to add, but he faltered, suddenly aware of a headache creeping forward from the back of his skull.

Hill looked directly at Brighton. "Do you really want to know?"

Brighton looked down at his old desk, with its cracked leather writing table and its seamed wood, lacquered again and again over the years.

"Because I'll tell you if you really want to know," Hill added, and he seemed genuine. Then again, Hill always seemed genuine.

A lot of words ran through Brighton's head. Chief among them was the phrase *plausible deniability*.

"No," he said quietly. "I suppose I don't."

Hill smiled and eased himself to standing. "Smart man," he said. "That's why I like you, Thomas. I look forward to seeing our new young ward at Ditchfield soon. I do apologize about butting in during lunch."

"Not a problem," Brighton said, dazed.

"I'll be in touch," Hill said over his shoulder, helping himself through the doors and walking out in step with the young man he'd set as watch outside.

In short order, both were gone and the office was quiet, as if they'd never been.

But Brighton's lunch was cold. And he felt he'd just agreed to dive deeper into a deal he'd been trying to side-step out of for the past five years. Somewhere, he'd made a wrong turn. He'd been bewitched again.

He needed to think.

He pressed his comm. "Natasha, please clear my schedule for today," he said.

"But—"

"I'll make it up to them. Whoever they are," Brighton said forcefully. "Please," he added, calming himself. *No need to bring Natasha down too.*

"Fine," she replied flippantly.

Brighton topped off his vodka and spun his chair toward the window and sat for a long time.

At five on the dot, Brighton saw Natasha's blurry visage through the clouded glass as she stood, smoothed her skirt, and set her hair. She picked up her purse and called, "I'm leaving!" unnecessarily loudly.

"About time," he replied, their standard friendly parting.

Brighton's words were a bit slurred. A fair amount of the vodka was gone from the bottle, but he was no closer to figuring a way out of Hill's pocket, not without ending up disbarred. He wasn't sure how Hill could do that, but he knew he could. Hell, Hill could probably get him disbarred for the work he'd done for Hill. He had no doubt the man could incriminate him while staying above the fray. Above the fray was Hill's specialty.

Natasha's heels clicked evenly on the creaky wood as

she left. The glow of her phone was visible through the glass. She was totally checked out. *Must be nice to set aside your work like that. Be on when you have to be then forget all about it.* Sometimes, Brighton thought he should have just gone to work at a bookstore. He liked reading. That was the only reason he got through law school passably. If he was at a bookstore, he'd just clock in, talk about books, sell a few here and there, and clock out.

The problem was that selling books didn't buy suits. Books didn't buy watches or sedans. Books didn't buy fine vodka or nice dinners out or an office of one's own.

Right then, though, Brighton would have swapped all the nice things, including the suit right off his back, to be out of this mess with Hill. Whatever Hill did with these kids, whatever he needed them for, it felt bad. And if it felt bad on the surface, it was likely evil at the core. That's how those things worked.

He heard Natasha coming back down the creaky hallway. *Probably forgot her keys*, he thought. Or her jacket. Or her head. She was a good woman but totally scatterbrained, and in hindsight he likely should have called a few more references, but she had managed to keep the place from burning down for years, and that was enough for Brighton.

She was walking heavy, though... and slow.

"Natasha?" Brighton asked. "Everything okay?"

Thomas Brighton did not scare easily. He was street savvy enough to avoid most trouble and had the legal chops to save himself from pretty much anything else. Even Josiah Hill didn't make him *scared*. Hill brought on a sense of existential dread, perhaps, that was vague and ephemeral and all-consuming, but he wasn't a scary man. That's precisely why he was so dangerous.

But when Brighton called out for Natasha and was met

by nothing but the creaky sound of heavy footsteps on old wood, he became very afraid.

He kept a gun in the office. Bail Bond Row wasn't in the greatest area of town, and the people that frequented the establishments there weren't often of the highest caliber. He'd shoved the weapon somewhere in his locked desk drawer four years before and promptly forgotten about it until right then. He had a mild distaste for guns. They didn't go well with double-breasted suits. But he dug furiously in the top drawer of his desk for the key to the bottom drawer.

A man stepped into Brighton's waiting room. And even though his view through the clouded glass of his sliding doors obscured any defining features—pretty much all he could see was that the man was skinny and black—Brighton had no doubt at all about who'd come in.

Charlie Cunningham was paying him a visit.

Busy day, Brighton thought darkly, fumbling with the stupidly small key to his bottom drawer. *Lot of drop-ins.*

Charlie opened the sliding glass doors slowly, one in each hand, almost theatrically slow, in a way that struck Brighton as a macabre reversal of what he'd been doing to clients for years.

Brighton paused, key in lock. He couldn't help it. He had to get a good look at the kid giving the city such fits.

Brighton knew he'd represented Charlie poorly. But he was ashamed to find he didn't recall him, not specifically—no details that he could place and think, *Aha! That's him!* What he saw was a rangy young man with a ragged left ear and a singular, driven look in his eye. Brighton was old hat at picking out emotions through eyes. He saw furious anger inside Charlie, barely kept in check by a deadly purpose.

While Brighton was frozen, Charlie kept moving,

constantly, fluidly. By the time Brighton's hand was in the drawer, grasping for the gun, Charlie had come around the desk. Without a second's pause, Charlie lifted a boot that looked two sizes too big for him and planted it right in Brighton's chest like he was trying to kick open a door.

All the air left Brighton in a huff, and he collapsed forward, still seated. His chair hit the window behind him hard, and his head popped backward, bouncing against the puffy leather. The glass window cracked with the sound of a stick snapping.

Brighton tried to speak. His words were his best weapon, but the air was maddeningly slow in coming. By the time he got half a breath, Charlie Cunningham had reached in and pulled out the handgun—a snub-nosed .32 revolver—and turned to face Brighton. He looked carefully down at him and idly picked up a mechanical pencil off Brighton's desk with his free hand.

Charlie looked very much like a man caught between two paths: a gun or a pencil.

In the eternity it felt to get air back into his lungs, Brighton had chosen his words carefully.

"I'm sorry," he said.

Charlie brushed off the apology with a faint twitch of his upper lip. "You knew?" he asked. His voice was curiously childlike. Not high, but not yet shed of the reedy timbre of youth. The contrast between his appearance and his voice was disorienting.

"Sort of," Brighton admitted, defeated. "I knew Hill needed to keep the inmate count up. He had specific targets. Kids he wanted."

Charlie's eyes narrowed, but the emotion was still there. Brighton felt that if they went blank, if Charlie stepped away and let whatever else was inside take over, he'd be dead.

"I didn't want to know why. So I didn't ask. But I knew enough. Knew it was wrong."

Charlie advanced slowly. The gun wasn't pointing at Brighton yet, but it wasn't pointing at the ground anymore either. As Brighton watched it rise slowly, his vision grew blurry. He found himself crying—a stranger sensation than getting kicked in the chest. Brighton couldn't remember the last time he'd cried for any reason. And he found he wasn't even crying for himself, not totally. He was crying for all those kids he'd sent to that godforsaken prison.

"Did they abuse you?" he asked, barely getting the words out.

That seemed to give Charlie pause, and his eyes narrowed. "This ain't about me," he said. "But you knew that, right? I saw Hill come in here. Saw that pig come back out, lookin' pleased with his shit."

"Not about you?" Brighton asked, confused. "Then it's about all of you. All those kids I helped send up there. Hill got me by the balls early, and he kept squeezing, but that's no excuse. I got no excuses left."

Charlie's eyes flashed, his brain almost humming audibly. "Man, fuck them other boys," he said. "This ain't about them neither."

Charlie stepped forward, and Brighton instinctively pushed backward. The window creaked ominously. Brighton got the sudden impression that he was being tested somehow. And his life depended on if he passed or not.

"Who is it about, then?" Brighton asked.

"Tasha." Charlie's eyes bored into Brighton. "It's about Tasha. And how Hill's gonna pay."

Brighton's mind raced. He checked the name against

everything he had, inside and out. Gut reactions, old cases, new cases, bad cases, good cases—nothing.

"Who the hell is Tasha?" Brighton asked desperately. He didn't want to die because of somebody he'd never known.

"Where is she?" Charlie snapped. He raised the gun until it was pointed squarely at Brighton's chest, an angle that seemed past the point of any return.

"I have no idea who you're talking about, Charlie," Brighton said, his voice jittery. His words were deserting him, fleeing his head and abandoning ship. Obviously, he'd failed whatever test Charlie was giving. He had an acrid taste on his tongue like licking a battery and somehow knew he was tasting his own fear, so acute that it was a real thing in his mouth.

Brighton's day in court had come, and Charlie Cunningham had found him guilty. But the worst part—the part Brighton knew he'd take to the grave and be forced to dwell upon forever—was that he probably deserved what was coming to him.

CHAPTER FOURTEEN

Dana felt strangely exposed without her badge and gun. She kept tapping her hip out of habit as she sat in an uncomfortable plastic chair against one taupe wall of Marty's room in the bustling Hopkins ER.

The weightlessness of the empty spot on her hip where her gun should have been unsettled her. It was a microcosm of the general free-falling sensation that had taken over her entire life, as though she'd reached what she thought was the bottom of the stairs only to find one more surprise step.

"What are you gonna do?" Marty asked, sitting up without the need for the hospital bed at his back.

The Kevlar had absorbed both slugs, barely. The blasts, clustered top left, would have blown right through his heart. Instead, he had a monster bruise on his chest and a cracked sternum, along with a lot of shirtless recovery time that Dana knew he would secretly enjoy—the shirtless part, anyway.

"You just got shot, and you're asking me what I'm gonna do?" she replied, smiling wearily.

"I only got shot. You're getting axed," Marty said, wincing a little as the nurse rewrapped his trunk of a chest.

"We got a comedian over here," Dana said.

"Sorry," he added. "Bad joke."

Dana waved it off with a fleeting smile.

She'd been placed on leave before but never suspended without pay, never told to hand in her hardware. Next came a token internal review, likely headed up by Duke, then she'd be fired. Firing a cop was hard in Baltimore, but Duke had basically done it. He'd been gunning for Dana since the day he realized she wanted to succeed in his department despite him, and she was about to be out of the way.

She could fight the suspension. They hadn't trespassed at New Hope Community Church. There was no illegal entry of any sort. They'd been fired upon first, and Dana only returned fire when she thought she was in mortal danger. Theoretically, she had a case, but if she wanted to stand in front of Internal Affairs and look Duke in the eye and tell him she still deserved to be a sergeant in the Baltimore City Police—if she really wanted to pick that fight—she needed to believe it herself first, one hundred percent.

She wasn't even at ninety percent. She was hovering somewhere near fifty and losing more faith in herself every day the Charlie Cunningham case went on.

Duke would chew her up and spit her out.

"Duke'll probably come for me too," Marty said, testing out some deep breaths and gritting his teeth a bit. "I didn't discharge my weapon, so it's less of a whole thing, but it's only a matter of time. Hill will make sure of that."

"Maybe," Dana said. "Or maybe this is a good time to..."

Marty looked carefully up at her. "Good time to what?"

"Move on?" Dana offered tentatively.

Marty started to say something then stopped himself,

calmed his demeanor, and turned to thank the nurse, who said she'd notify the doctor for discharge papers. When the door closed behind her and the two of them were alone, he turned back to Dana, who was patiently waiting. She wasn't sure what she expected. Yes or no, either answer would chip at her heart.

On the surface, Marty had everything Duke liked in a cop. He had a healthy respect for authority and process. He was also, crucially, not a woman. He would do better without her. In fact, the only thing Duke likely held against Marty was his steadfast loyalty to his uppity partner who kept breaking rules.

Dana was about to say so when Marty interrupted her.

"You don't get to tell me to move on," he said with forced calm. "The first time, with you and me and you and Gordon... I got that one eventually. It's been hard, but I'm doing it. And it's working, I think. But this, about how I get to be a cop, this is different."

She found herself stammering, at a loss for words. "I was just thinking that—you know—you've been doing so well. Personally, professionally. We sort of switched. You're the grown-up now, Marty. We're on different trajectories. I thought maybe you ought to cut me loose. Chuck the dead weight."

"You're not dead weight," he said, exasperated.

"You know what I mean," Dana said. "I asked the impossible of you with me and Gordon. To show up and do your job with me *and* to let me go? And you did it. And you're better for it. Maybe it's a sign."

"A sign?" he asked. "I don't do signs. I do cop stuff." He tapped his chest and winced again but gamely recovered. "So do you. And what *I* need is to be able to have you in my life in a way that we can both live with."

He got up slowly and went to the coat rack, where his badge hung on its chain next to his tattered Kevlar vest and his destroyed leather jacket. He shook his head sadly at the jacket but patted the vest like a good old dog and flicked his badge affectionately.

He paused and moved back to the vest. He stared at it so long that Dana started to take a second look. The impact zone was clearly delineated, the protective layers of Kevlar warped and crumpled. She knew he'd specifically left instructions that it be kept close to hand because he needed to log it as evidence. But the sliced-up top quadrant was new.

He turned to Dana. "Did you take the chest camera out?"

Dana shook her head. A look passed between them that said everything without saying anything at all. Hill had gotten to it somehow, likely through one of Duke's lackeys while he was in surgery.

Marty took another pained breath and shook his head, exasperated. "These assholes are good. Thorough. But we're better. So long as we keep working together."

His continued friendship and dogged loyalty warmed her heart, but she felt he wasn't facing the facts. Charlie had been two steps ahead of her since the beginning. She'd risked the lives of the two most important men in her life in a barely legal raid for a bunch of papers that Gordon was still sifting through and that could realistically be of little evidential support. And to top it all off, she'd gotten her partner shot.

A sane cop would run screaming for the hills. But Marty was stubborn and loyal to a fault. And somehow, he still thought she could do her job.

"What about *suspended* don't you understand, Marty?"

"If we can crack this case, who knows what might change," Marty said, keeping his voice low and glancing at the door.

Dana took his meaning. Hill was a sterling monument in this city, but they both knew that if you tipped him over, a lot of squirming bugs would be exposed underneath. Ditchfield was one of them. The Duke name was another. All of them were tied together.

"What can I do?" Dana asked helplessly.

Marty tapped his shield again. "You'll figure it out. I'm going to go do cop stuff like file the incident and ballistics reports as best I can and try to avoid getting fired. But first, I'm gonna try to explain all this to Brooke."

Dana got up to go. She didn't want to intrude anywhere Brooke might take offense. Marty seemed to understand.

On her way out, he called after her softly. "Dana, this is a heavy piece of metal," he said, holding up his shield. "But it's still just a piece of metal. It doesn't make you a cop. That comes from somewhere else. Somewhere deeper."

Outside the room, a young woman was nervously pacing by the intake desk. Brooke was as pretty as she'd imagined but more genuinely so. She was obviously giving them time, and Dana felt an overwhelming sense of gratitude to the woman. She walked right up to Brooke and hugged her by way of introduction, knowing no other way to thank her. She was a little surprised to find that Brooke returned the hug completely.

"Will you watch out for him?" Brooke asked.

"He's the one that watches out for me these days," Dana said.

"He's a softie, you know. He needs watching too," Brooke said.

"I got his back," Dana said. She didn't feel like she did,

but she knew that was the right answer, the one Brooke wanted to hear, anyway. "We'll all get a glass of wine one day, once all this dies down. I promise."

Dana concentrated on putting one foot in front of the other as she walked out of the ER. She felt aimless and tired, as if she'd been the one admitted. She needed to eat some real food and to hug her daughter. She needed the substance of her life around her.

She needed Gordon. Maybe he'd found something in the meager haul he'd scooped from the back rooms of New Hope.

She picked her phone from her purse and froze. He'd flipped the script on her: she'd missed five calls from him.

CHAPTER FIFTEEN

Gordon called Dana the first time once he'd spread out everything he'd stolen from New Hope on the floor of his loft. Each document lay side by side between his big chair and the little therapy chair he kept for the kids.

Only two pictures were among the documents, but they were more than enough to cement his suspicions. The second one was very similar to the first he'd shown Dana in the car: a young black girl—maybe fifteen, probably younger—heavily made up. She sat awkwardly on a small bed in a bikini that was far too big for her. She had an expression like she'd been asked to look sexy and was trying her best but wasn't quite old enough to know how.

Gordon had to take a break then. He called Dana and tried to swallow his low-level nausea. When she didn't answer, he got a drink. That helped a little.

The rest of the documents proved less immediately abhorrent. Spreadsheets had lines of numbers in one column and dollar figures in another. Other spreadsheets used abbreviations Gordon couldn't make heads or tails of, each associated with more dollar figures. Receipts for random, everyday things like paper towels and Clorox were there, along with other receipts for stranger things Gordon had never heard of—things like video borescopes, FLIR cameras, and T30 servers, all paid in cash.

He tried to open the thumb drive on his computer, but it was encrypted. He hesitated to guess at passwords too long for fear that some self-defense mechanism would rewrite the drive after too many failed attempts. He went back to the paper trail.

Gordon called Dana two more times when he recognized that some of the numbers on the spreadsheets were repeated. He saw the vague outline of a pattern weaving through the documents on his floor, but no matter how many times he shuffled them around, he couldn't quite grasp it. Dana had cop-fu. She was better at evidence, not to mention paperwork.

He realized he'd unconsciously set the pictures of the girls aside. He found them physically hard to look at. He almost went to get another drink, but he stopped himself when he realized the only reason he wanted to drink was to try to blunt the fact that the girls looking up at him from those photographs were very likely being sexually abused. Maybe right now. Another scotch might help him to avoid that, to hold more tightly to a false thread of thinking that, while these pictures were certainly in poor taste, maybe they weren't blatantly sexualized. Maybe this was all one big mistake.

He put the bottle back. This wasn't one big mistake. This was a horrendous reality. He dialed Dana again—still no answer.

He picked up his keys. He didn't need a scotch right now. What he needed was a lawyer.

. . .

GORDON POCKETED his phone and rubbed at his eyes. Five calls, three texts, and no answer from Dana. *She's right*, he thought. *It really is incredibly annoying.*

He knew she was with Marty, and Marty basically got a free pass for a good long while on account of having been shot in the chest with a nine millimeter, but still, *answer the phone!* His stolen evidence was sitting in a banker's box to his right, on the passenger's seat of his rattling coupe. He was sitting at a red light at the intersection of Madison and Broadway, willing his heater to hold up.

The last time Gordon had gone down this road with Brighton, the man had basically escorted him out of his office. But this wasn't just about Ditchfield anymore. This was about New Hope and about Hill. Even Thomas Brighton had to take a side on this one. Nobody could just wash their hands of the matter once they dug into that box.

Finding parking was difficult even in the early evening. Bail Bond Row was a twenty-four-hour operation, with people coming and going regardless of working hours. Gordon knew Brighton often stayed late—he'd hit the man up for work several times in the evening, back in the dark days, and once for an advance, which Brighton had laughingly denied. Gordon hoped to catch him in that sweet spot after all his appointments but before he packed up to go home.

By the time he approached the offices of Brighton and Associates, the time was almost six. At least one light was still on in the back, which was a good sign. Gordon walked up the creaking outdoor staircase and stood underneath the chandelier. He had his hand on the buzzer and was about to press when something crunched underneath his shoe, a large splinter of painted wood. He looked up at the chandelier, thinking maybe the dodgy thing was finally pulling away from its old wooden moorings, but it looked as stalwart and out-of-place as ever.

When he dropped his gaze again, he noticed the door had been forced.

Gordon took this in abstractly. The break-in was clean. Something had snapped the bolt side clean off. The front door, like the rest of the place, was old wood. It probably hadn't even protested much.

He pressed the comm. "Hello?"

Nothing.

He pressed the comm several more times but got nothing in return. The buzzer didn't even seem to be working. The doorknob didn't turn, but the door pushed open easily. Gordon let it swing inward until it bumped on the backstop.

"Thomas? Natasha?" he called.

Silence from within.

Just a break in, Gordon thought. *They're long gone home.* But his ears were ringing, faintly, in a way that told him the blood was racing through his body.

Just a break in, he repeated because if this was only a smash-and-grab for whatever fancy baubles Brighton kept in his office, that meant Dana was still wrong about Charlie Cunningham's "list." It meant Karen was still wrong all those years before when she said Charlie was a sociopath, pure and simple, and would never be understood.

With each step down the dusty wooden hallway, he felt less and less sure of himself. Nothing was disturbed in the outer room, where Natasha sat. Her desk was tidied up, pencils and pens all in a row, a rainbow of highlighters ready for another day.

Then he turned toward Brighton's office, dreading what he might find. The sliding glass doors were open. The desk lamp was on. The intercom was smashed, the cords cut. Drops of what looked like spilled ink flecked Brighton's old wooden desk, but Gordon knew they weren't ink.

Brighton's chair was turned around, facing the big window at the back of his office. A nasty crack split the pane from corner to corner, feathering out around an impact point in the center.

Gordon licked his lips. "Thomas?" he ventured.

No answer. Gordon really, really didn't want to turn that chair around.

He could smell the blood in the room and something else, too, a strange whiff of ozone, like burning plastic, that some ingrained, ancient response locked deep within his brain told him was the lingering smell of fear. Strong, animal fear.

The ringing in his ears was a high keen as he grasped the old leather and spun it his way.

Nobody.

"Just a break in," he said aloud to himself. *Except for a decent spattering of blood.*

Gordon allowed himself a few deep breaths. The ringing had receded, and in its place, a sound like running water was coming from somewhere in the back of the house. He turned around to follow it and found himself face-to-face with the bloody ghost of Thomas Brighton.

"What's this now?" asked Brighton, wild-eyed.

Gordon yelped like a rat had run across his shoes. He dropped the box, spilling papers all over the worn wooden flooring. He scrambled to gather them then felt the best thing to do was deal with this fresh hell first by putting Brighton's desk between himself and the apparition.

"Gordon?" asked Brighton in a very alive tone. "What are you doing here?"

"I thought you were dead!" Gordon said. "You're not dead, right?" he added. He felt far too fragile in general to deal with ghosts at the moment—real or imagined.

"Not yet," Brighton said, "although it was a damn close thing." He was pressing a wad of paper towels to the right side of his face, and it was sopping wet and running with red. His pristine white cuffs were pink. "I thought he was gonna kill me. But all he did was slice me up with a pencil then bash my head with my own revolver. My lucky day."

Brighton took the wet red mess away from the right side of his face to reveal a jagged rift in the skin of his face, starting just below his right temple and ending about halfway down his chin. It looked black in the low light but wept blood evenly and consistently.

Gordon took an involuntary step back, cringing. *That's gonna leave a mark.*

"Who?" Gordon asked.

"Who do you think?" Brighton asked, applying pressure once more.

"Charlie was here?" Gordon asked, looking around as if he might jump out from behind the wingback chairs at any moment.

"Yes, he was here," Brighton said.

"What did he want?" asked Gordon. "What did he say?"

"He asked me if I knew. I said yes. But I think what he knows and what I know are two different types of knowing." Brighton flipped his compress and steadied himself against the doorframe.

Gordon's mind raced over and around Brighton's words. *But first things first.* "Maybe you should see a doctor, Thomas. That's a bad gash."

Thomas shook his head, the whites of his eyes visible all

around. "I'm not going anywhere. I deserved this—deserved worse, to be honest. You can patch me up. Come on, I got a first-aid kit back here somewhere. Natasha made me buy it, God bless her."

Brighton turned on his heels and walked back around the corner toward the rear of the office. Gordon stood blinking for a minute before he realized half the papers were still scattered across the room. He hurried to gather them all back into the box.

"Come on, Pope! I'm bleeding here!" Brighton called.

"I'm not that kind of doctor!" Gordon replied, following with the box in hand. He turned a second corner and came upon a little half bathroom that looked like a small animal had been sacrificed and swung around by the tail.

"Good Lord," Gordon said, stepping back out again.

"Here." Brighton shoved a small red plastic suitcase into his arms and turned back toward the sink. He tossed the old soaked wad into an overflowing trash can and wet a new, partially bloody wad.

Gordon set his box down and reluctantly popped open the first-aid kit. "What do you mean *knew*? What do you know, Thomas?"

Brighton looked at Gordon in the mirror then turned off the faucet and braced himself against the lip of the sink with his free hand. He looked down, watching the slow and steady drip of his blood as it spattered against the white porcelain.

Gordon waited. If Brighton was in deep in all this, too, Gordon didn't know what he was going to do—certainly not help the man stop bleeding.

"In the early days, when I had no money, no clients, nothing, I made a handshake deal with Josiah Hill."

Gordon closed his eyes.

"I made sure certain kids went to Ditchfield, kids he tapped. In exchange, he got me under this roof."

Gordon waited for more. Brighton shook his head, watching the blood fall. He looked genuinely disgusted with himself. That was a new look for Brighton.

"That's it?" Gordon asked after a moment.

"Isn't that enough?" Brighton replied. "Some of these kids... they maybe didn't deserve Ditchfield."

"Nobody deserves Ditchfield," Gordon said, "but that's beside the point. Is that all Hill asked you to do? All he asked you to cover up?"

"Yeah, why? Is there more?"

Gordon blew out an enormous breath, feeling that he could finally breathe for the first time since having seen that splintered door outside.

"Yeah. There's more," Gordon said.

Brighton dabbed at his face, looking about as lost as Gordon had ever seen him.

"Do I want to know what it is?" Brighton asked.

Gordon said nothing. This was a decision Brighton would have to make for himself.

Brighton looked down at the banker's box pressed up against the wall then back up at Gordon. He nodded. "Patch me up first, as best you can."

"I'm not that kind of doctor," Gordon said again.

"You'll do better than a hack lawyer," Brighton said, and he tilted his weeping cheek toward Gordon. "Blast it with rubbing alcohol first. I want to feel the burn."

BRIGHTON SAT in his big leather chair, holding his head in his hands, Pope's papers spaced evenly across the dark wooden desk in front of him. An hour before, he'd thought he was going to die in that chair. But as the full weight of what he was seeing in front of him pressed upon his heart, he wondered if perhaps he should have.

Gordon sat in a wingback across from him and downed two ibuprofen with a slug from one of Brighton's water bottles.

"Just so we're clear," Gordon asked, "what do you see here? I've been up for a while, and I've had a lot of coffee and a little scotch, and I want to be sure I'm not crazy."

Brighton looked at him. Gordon had patched him together with five Steri-Strips like little railroad ties spaced evenly down the right side of his face, but it was starting to feel really swollen. He wondered if it was medically possible for a cheek to burst. "You said you saw the rooms? And camera equipment?"

Gordon nodded, grimacing slightly, as if those memories were going to stick with him for a very long time.

"These receipts, they're for hidden cameras and private encrypted servers," Brighton said.

"They managed to take off with all that stuff by the time I got back there," Gordon said.

"He was whoring these girls out from inside a *church*?" Brighton asked.

Gordon set his head back on the chair, apparently vindicated. Brighton knew what he was seeing. He also knew what he wasn't seeing, which was enough to convict Hill of something that would put him away for life.

"At least online," Gordon said. "Maybe in real life too."

"My God," Brighton muttered, trailing off. He picked up the photograph of the particularly young-looking girl in the bikini and tossed it down with disgust. "What is she, thirteen, maybe?" he asked.

"It's a lot to take," Gordon said.

"It's a goddamn horror show," Brighton said, looking up at Gordon. "You gotta believe me when I say I had no idea about this mess," he said.

"I do," Gordon said. "Evidently, so does Charlie. That's why you're alive right now."

Brighton stood and looked over the desk, hands on his hips. "But it's still just pictures and numbers. There's nothing linking them. I'm sure that whole place has had a bleach bath by now and looks nothing like what you saw. This won't hold up in court, certainly not against New Hope."

Gordon held out the thumb drive. "There's this too. But it's encrypted. I can't get in."

Brighton quickly walked around the desk, his shoes tapping lightly on the hardwood. He plucked it from Gordon's fingers and turned it around in the light from his Tiffany lamp. "It's a USB drive," Brighton said, smiling.

"I thought maybe you knew somebody who could hack it," Gordon said.

"Of course I do," Brighton said. "Me."

Gordon looked skeptical. Brighton knew he must be a sight: a middle-aged fop with limp hair plugs and a puffy face, soaking wet and slowly bleeding. But he didn't care anymore. Somehow, when Charlie had spared him, he'd dug out a hole in Brighton's heart where a bunch of junk had been. Then Gordon had come by and ripped it wider but also planted a seed of something like hope.

Maybe he could redeem himself somehow in all this mess.

"You don't work for years on Bail Bond Row without picking up a few tricks when it comes to accessing evidence," Brighton said, rummaging around the bottom drawer of his desk. He paused when he saw the empty place where his revolver had been. Charlie had it currently. *Problematic*, Brighton thought. *But one thing at a time.*

He found what he was looking for, a small electronic box with a USB port and a digital display. He held it up and attempted a smile before gingerly patting at his wound to make sure nothing had popped.

He flipped open his laptop and logged in, then he plugged the box into one of the ports on its side. The box blinked on. After a moment, the digital panel said Ready in retro red lettering.

"It's called a USB sniffer," Brighton said, taking the thumb drive and inserting it into the port on the opposite end of the box. "I bought it off a shady software developer a few years back. He was getting sued for intellectual property infringement and needed some cash."

With the drive inserted, the box whirred softly. The panel showed a rotating stylus. "I don't claim to know how it works. Something about listening in on the conversation between the drive and the computer, a security flaw on almost all USBs, where the password gets passed right along with the request. I don't really care."

The sniffer beeped once, and a string of characters appeared on the panel, nothing recognizable at all. They could have guessed for years and never hit it.

Brighton smiled. "It worked," he said. He ripped a sticky note from a pad on the desk and wrote down the password then popped the sniffer out and plugged the USB directly into the laptop.

By that time, Gordon had come around behind the chair and was holding onto the leather for dear life. Brighton shared his trepidation. He entered the password at the prompt and was brought to a file explorer screen with just two folders. One was named Contact and the other Sample.

Brighton swallowed a sickly-sweet wave of nausea. He looked over his shoulder at Gordon, who nodded grimly. He clicked on Contact. Within was a spreadsheet that, at first glance, looked very similar to the paper copies he had on his desk.

The disappointment was clear in Gordon's voice. "More numbers," he said.

Brighton scanned the document quickly: two columns and forty-five rows. The first column contained combinations of two letters and two numbers. The numbers were sequential, while the letters seemed random: AC01, RY02, LB03...

The second column was names: first name, last initial. A quick scan showed all of them to be male.

"Client list?" Gordon asked, squinting.

"Maybe. Looks like it."

Brighton hovered over the second folder, the one labeled Samples. He kept having to swallow acid indigestion down. He double-clicked before he lost all nerve.

Inside the folder were four video files, each labeled in the same style, two letters and two numbers. Gordon was breathing with forced calm behind him. Brighton clicked on one labeled BY39.

The video opened on a view of a room with bare white walls and a maroon bed. A young girl was adjusting the camera. Her smooth black skin was smeared with gold rouge at the cheekbones. Her lips were a candy-apple red.

"Her pupils are dilated," Gordon said evenly, clinically.

The girl sat back down on the bed. She wore black underpants and a lacy black bra with one strap falling off at the shoulder.

The purring voice of a man came from off-screen. "Hi, Brianna. How are you feeling?"

The girl didn't respond, only stared at the screen for a time.

"She's in shock," Gordon said, pain noticeable in his voice. "And likely drugged."

"I'm fine," said Brianna, slowly and slightly slurred.

"I want you to do some things for me. Okay, Brianna?" asked the man.

Brighton tried to place the voice but couldn't. It sounded like it was coming from elsewhere, outside the room, over a speaker.

After another long pause, the girl nodded.

"I want you to take your clothes off, okay?" the man said.

Gordon let go of the chair and turned away toward the window, breathing heavily. "Shut it off," he said.

Brighton was only too happy to oblige. He'd seen many things in his years in criminal defense, many bad things. At first, he'd insisted nothing could get to him, but then, gradually, as he started to shake hands with people like Josiah Hill, he wondered if perhaps each terrible thing he'd seen had taken a piece from him after all, without him noticing. He was happy to feel disgust welling up within himself. Disgust was a defense mechanism, after all. Maybe he wasn't completely lost.

He closed the video, feeling strongly that if he watched the whole thing right then, with everything and everyone still up in the air, he would lose a piece of his soul through his eyes.

He flipped back to the spreadsheet and found the entry for BY39, the same label as the video file. The date next to the initials was from the first week of January.

"I think it's safe to say the letter-number combos are designations for the girls," Gordon said. He seemed to have recovered and was back over Brighton's shoulder. "The names have to be a customer list."

"First name, last initial for the men," Brighton said, shaking his head. "Not much to go on." Although a few of the names struck Brighton as vaguely familiar for some reason.

"Wait a second," Gordon said, stepping around. "Go back up. To the top."

Brighton flicked the track pad back to the top of the spreadsheet.

"There," Gordon said, pointing.

Beneath the gnawed tip of his fingernail was a name: Charlie C. The corresponding code was TC09.

"Charlie Cunningham?" Brighton asked.

"Maybe," Gordon said. "And TC for Tasha? It fits."

Brighton highlighted the row, and when he did, a date appeared next to each name in the formula bar. Charlie C.'s was 02-24-15.

"That ring a bell to you?" Brighton asked.

Gordon scratched at the scruff on his chin. "That would have been around the time he ran the car into New Hope, I guess. But the day itself, I have no idea. I wasn't in a great place then."

Brighton highlighted the cells and scrolled down, exposing all the dates behind the names, then he leaned back and crossed his damp sleeves over his chest, taking everything in.

"Some of these are in the future," Brighton said. "Look, that's in four days."

Brighton was struck again by a sense of familiarity, but this time because of the dates. He knew that date, the one from the future. He clicked out of the cell and brought back the name on top: Jamal M.

The two came together with a nearly audible click in Brighton's mind, and with that click came a new wave of terrible understanding—and more questions.

"Jamal Martin is the defendant I declined to represent in a criminal case set for four days from now," Brighton said wearily. His face throbbed fiercely in time with his racing heart. "Josiah Hill visited me this morning and told me that declining wasn't an option."

"Wait, Hill was here?" Gordon asked.

Brighton felt a stray rivulet of blood coming from the bottom of the gash. He dabbed at it with his cuff. *Shirt's ruined anyway*, he thought. "I hadn't heard from him in years. I thought I was rid of him, but I should have known. Hill wanted to bring back the old business. Said he was *expanding*."

"Did Charlie see him?" Gordon asked.

Brighton nodded. "He said he followed him. I think he might have killed him if he knew where Tasha was. But that's the missing piece for him."

Brighton closed out of the hacked drive and opened up the BCDC Court Records database, wanting to double-check Jamal's court date. Sure enough, the date on the court record matched the date on the decrypted spreadsheet.

Brighton's shattered resolve was piecing back together, shard by shard. If it had been a mirror, it would be reflecting a very different man than the one who'd walked into the office that morning.

Just to make sure, Brighton looked back at the latest date in Charlie Cunningham's court records. The final hearing that sent the boy to Ditchfield was held on February 24, 2015, another date match.

"These are court dates," Brighton said. "They're the day these boys got shipped to Ditchfield."

"And also the day that Tasha Cunningham was left alone," Gordon said, moving back over to the desk, to the pictures. "The day New Hope could close in on her and all the other girls like her."

Brighton spun back around to Gordon. "You think they're related. The girls and the Ditchfield boys."

"Most likely. Dependent on each other, at least," Gordon said, picking up the picture again.

Brighton was struck by the depth of the pain on Gordon's face. The good doctor looked like he wanted to reach through the grainy ink and pull the girl out of that room himself.

Until that night, he'd always thought of Gordon as a desperate sort of person, a man barely treading water in the world around him and, regarding the expert-witness stuff, a man he could use to further his own agenda. For the first time, Brighton considered that maybe the reason Dr. Gordon Pope always seemed barely above water was because he was the type of man that kept throwing himself back into the deep end every time he managed to climb out.

"I think the boy and the girl are a package," Gordon said. "Hill gets one then gets the other."

Brighton flipped back to the court appointment of Jamal Martin, set for four days hence—the first half of Hill's next twisted package deal... if his pet lawyer followed instructions.

But Thomas Brighton wasn't feeling much like following instructions at the moment. He knew what he had to do, and he knew what it would cost him.

"I'll stand up to him in court," Brighton said. "I'll go after him."

Brighton was surprised—and relieved—to find that the good doctor did not look shocked. Perhaps Gordon saw something inside him that was still worth redeeming. He was a shrink, after all. He probably had more than an inkling of what was going on in Brighton's head.

"But none of it sticks unless we have a girl on the stand, testifying," Brighton said. He knew which girl too.

Gordon looked down at the photo again. "That's a hell of an ask," he said. "Even if we somehow find Tasha, she may be too damaged to testify."

"Without her, we've got a bunch of disgusting movies, creepy pictures, and old receipts," Brighton said. "Even child-porn charges won't stick if there's nothing tying the computers specifically to Hill, and the computers are gone. Right now, it's your testimony about what you found while borderline trespassing on private property."

Gordon inhaled then exhaled. Brighton knew he understood what would stick on Hill and what wouldn't. Brighton also felt that charges of possessing child pornography was too lenient by far, and Gordon would surely agree.

"So we're back to where we started," Gordon said. "Chasing Tasha Cunningham."

"Except now I got a gash down my face," Brighton added.

"And Dana is about to get fired," Gordon said, raising a finger.

That was news to Brighton. He knew Dana Frisco tangentially, mostly through bumping into her in the courthouse. But he'd always thought she was good people.

"And Marty Cicero got shot," Gordon said, ticking the two off on his fingers. "He'll be fine, just bruised up," Gordon added after seeing the look on Brighton's face.

"Who shot Cicero?" Brighton asked.

"One of Hill's men," Gordon said offhand. "A man named Alonzo." He was looking at his phone, distracted. "Dana had the *audacity* to fire back," he added, heavy on the sarcasm.

Brighton had a flicker of an idea. "Did she kill him?" he asked.

Gordon shook his head. "He's at Hopkins."

The flicker caught. "He knows where she is."

Gordon furrowed his brow. "Maybe. But he's almost certainly under Duke's watch. And I doubt he'd talk to me, not after all that mess. Not with Hill on his side."

Brighton checked his watch, already moving. He counted back the time since the shooting at New Hope. Depending on how bad the wound was, the surgery could take four, maybe five hours. Then another hour in step-down recovery.

Maybe nobody had seen the guy yet.

"He's not gonna talk to you," Brighton said, taking off his suit coat and rolling up his bloody sleeves to pass for clean. "He's gonna talk to his lawyer, the one with years of experience shoveling Hill's shit for him, the dutiful lapdog."

Brighton shrugged on his camel-hair overcoat, picked up his leather suitcase, and spun back toward Gordon with a flourish. "He'll talk to Thomas Brighton, Esquire, of Brighton and Associates."

CHAPTER SIXTEEN

Gordon Pope looked at Thomas Brighton across his desk as if seeing an entirely new man. Getting his face misaligned had realigned something else inside him, something Gordon sensed had been slowly breaking of its own accord, incrementally weighing him down for some time. Five years before, the guy wouldn't advance Gordon twenty bucks to get a sandwich and a few beers. Now he was talking about walking into the lion's den on behalf of Charlie and Tasha Cunningham, two people that, as far as Gordon was aware, stood to gain him nothing, financially or otherwise. They could, in fact, spell the end of Brighton's career.

"Isn't impersonating an attorney illegal?" Gordon asked finally.

"Well it's not exactly what I'd call *best practice*. But I'm not looking for admissible testimony from the guy. I want a location. That's all. Hopefully, you and your cop buddies can do the rest. It's our best shot."

Brighton was right. Not only was it their best shot, it was likely their only shot. Tasha and the other girls held in those horrendous rooms were the key to bringing down Hill's castle.

"I gotta go. Time's ticking." Brighton looked around at his disaster of an office as if seeing it for the first time. "Yikes. Uh, how about you get all of this together and lock up on your way out? I'll be in touch."

Gordon blinked. "Lock up? The door's busted."

"You'll figure it out!" he called over his shoulder, already down the hall. "You're a doctor!"

The front door creaked halfway shut, and Gordon found himself alone in the offices of Brighton & Associates. Everything had happened in such a whirlwind that the sudden silence was heavy. The roughed-up office, the creaky old repurposed house, the smell of wet blood mixed with old plumbing—all of it brought home what he had to do.

He set about gathering the evidence as quickly as he could while he listened to his messages. Two were waiting for him, which he hoped were from Dana.

"Gordon, it's Karen..."

Gordon froze, phone pressed between his ear and shoulder, his hands full of papers. He had completely forgotten he'd missed a call from his ex-wife sometime during his drunken record diving in the broom closet.

"Listen, I know it's short notice, but I'm coming out to Baltimore tomorrow to speak at a Hopkins APA dinner, and I wasn't even going to tell you, but then I thought how childish that was, so I thought we might meet up for dinner at Waterstones. My accountant's been on me for years to finalize the split of the business, so I thought maybe we could kill two birds with one stone. Catch up over a Cobb salad and get some paperwork signed. Anyway, call me."

Gordon dropped everything in his hands and grabbed

the phone. He looked at the time stamp just to be sure. Karen had called at 8:15 p.m. the night before. That meant she was in town already, and for some reason, the thought of Karen coming at this time, with all these knives still being juggled, made him deeply uncomfortable.

Then he saw a business card.

He'd missed it before because it was on the far corner of the desk, where the comm system used to sit, before Charlie destroyed it. Gordon had seen the card a hundred times over the years, at the courthouse, around Baltimore, and of course, up at Ditchfield... where he'd seen it first.

Brighton and Associates
Thomas Brighton, Esq.—Founding Partner
Mental Health Attorney | Psychiatric Defense Specialist
Illuminate. Enlighten. Brighton & Associates.

Nothing unusual about the man's business card being on the desk in his place of business, Gordon thought. Yet something about that card struck him as different. For one, it was older, frayed. The font looked outdated, the design different from the stack Brighton kept neatly situated in a crystal cardholder on the opposite side of the desk.

Gordon recognized it as an older model, one might say, the kind still kept out at Ditchfield, the place that time forgot. It was from an era when Thomas Brighton was a different kind of lawyer.

Gordon realized he was shaking slightly as he picked it up. He flipped it over, already dreading what he knew he'd see there.

The number two was circled in pen, hand drawn, like the crooked bullseye of a target.

Dana's words echoed in his head, underneath the slow

and steady return of the ringing: *He has a list. And like it or not, you're on it.*

He recalled her imploring face on that cold morning that felt like a million years ago, when she said she had to keep Chloe safe by keeping him away. He remembered the strange weight of the engagement ring in his breast pocket and the question unasked.

That was not Thomas Brighton's business card. It was Charlie Cunningham's business card, or rather, it was a calling card of unfinished business.

Dana had said three cards were in Charlie's possession when he took off. The first was for New Hope, which he'd left on Andy Bagshot's ruined corpse. The second was for Brighton and Associates, which he'd just left on the bloodspattered desk of Thomas Brighton.

The third was the business card for Jefferson and Pope.

His phone buzzed and startled him nearly to jumping. He snatched it up. A reminder was indicating a second voice mail, also from Karen Jefferson.

The ringing in his ears picked up a notch. He had a feeling of impending collision, like he was parked on the tracks at a crossing, stuck between the closed crossbars, with trains careering toward him from both directions.

He listened to the voice mail.

"Gordon, it's Karen again. You're still terrible with the phone. Good to see some things never change. Anyway, I'm at the office. I let myself in with my key. I'm going to wait here for a bit, grab a few things I'd always been meaning to pick up. If I still can't get hold of you in half an hour or so, I'll just leave the papers. Call me."

He looked at the time stamp. She'd called him a mere ten minutes before, when he and Brighton had been knee-deep in all the darkness from Ditchfield.

Gordon had an awful feeling, distinct and clear, more a premonition than anything, that Karen Jefferson was about to meet Charlie Cunningham.

He threw everything back into the box as quickly as he could and tried to recall whether Charlie would have any cause to remember Karen specifically. He had a vague memory of mentioning her in a session or two, and not favorably. Something like:

"My wife deals better with red tape than she does with patients."

That wasn't bad, not damning. But then, like dominos, one memory felled another. He'd dropped little seeds in their weekly meetings about how he and Karen had totally different views about how to help the boy. And then, at Ditchfield, the first time he'd seen him:

"Charlie, my wife says you're a sociopath. Help me prove her wrong."

Gordon felt sick to his stomach. He yanked the USB drive from Brighton's computer then turned toward the door and was reminded that it was nonfunctioning. He cursed and looked around for some way to lock up.

He dropped the box, grabbed a wingback chair, and dragged it to the creaky hall. It was a tight fit. *Good.*

Gordon got behind the wingback and pushed it down the hall. The wing tips scraped along the paint, leaving dark little trails of crushed red felt. At the door, he tipped the chair back and jammed it under the knob.

He trotted back down the hall as fast as his knee would allow, picked the box up on his way, and headed toward the back. He passed the bloody bathroom, where the sink was still dripping. He left out the back door, stopping only to make sure it latched behind him before quick-limping down the outer stairs on the way to his car.

CHAPTER SEVENTEEN

The drive from Brighton's office on Bail Bond Row to Gordon's loft in Mount Vernon was normally fifteen or so minutes, but he was hoping to make it in ten. Gordon dialed Karen as he sat, sick to his stomach at a red light on East Biddle. The phone rang and rang and rang. The light turned green, and he almost pitched the cell against the passenger door. Karen always answered her phone. Even during the divorce when he was drunk and pitiful, she answered. It's what she did.

Gordon dialed Dana again. She picked up on the first try. *Small miracles*, Gordon thought. Then he was immediately confronted with how to frame the fact that his ex-wife might be in serious danger on account of him.

"Dana, I think you're right," Gordon said, speaking quickly.

"Gordon, thank God," said Dana. "I miss five calls from anyone, I assume the world is ending."

Gordon got caught first in line at another red light. He inched forward by degrees.

"The world's always ending," he said. "It's all about how we live in it."

He looked both ways then gunned it, with a small prayer that Dana was the only cop he'd end up speaking to on his drive.

"Charlie broke into Brighton's place. Slashed him up. He's alive. Doing better, actually, than I think he's been in a long time," Gordon said as he took a hard right and gunned the coupe up to a rattling sixty miles an hour on Hartford.

"What? Gordon, slow down, what are you talking about?"

"The business cards. Charlie left one of Brighton's behind. It had the number two written on it."

Silence from Dana.

"You there?" Gordon asked.

"Yeah, I'm here," said Dana.

"You were the one that said it. He had three cards on him. He's dropped two of them. That leaves one."

"Where are you?" Dana asked.

Gordon's mind was racing. "He was listing. Ordering. Planning his approach. I dismissed it initially because I had an idea of who this kid was, but I think I'm wrong. I think we're all wrong."

"Are you in the car?" Dana asked. "Focus, Gordon."

"Yes, I'm on my way to the office. And get this: Karen is there," Gordon said, holding his outspread fingers to the windshield as if he wanted to squeeze his frustration out of the orange clouds in the evening sky.

More silence from Dana. Gordon could picture her leaning back on the counter, one hand holding the phone to her ear, the other stroking an eyebrow as she thought. That was a tic of hers.

"You want me to call this in?" Dana asked. "Marty is

out on recovery, but there's a handful of other good apples
on the force still—"

"With the rap sheet Charlie's got? They'll kill him. You
know it, and I know it," said Gordon. "I need you."

"Gord, I'm not technically police right now," she said,
her voice wavering.

"Bullshit. You're every bit the cop you always were and
more," said Gordon, leaning into a hard right that made his
tires squeal softly.

He got a long honk from someone and didn't care.

"I don't even have a gun," Dana said.

"Good," Gordon said.

More silence. Gordon pictured her nervously fussing
with her eyebrows. "Dana, please."

"My whole fear with this business card theory was that
you would be placed in danger. I wanted you to stay *away*
from all this," Dana said, helplessly.

"You know I can't do that. Especially not if Karen is
walking into some kind of trouble she knows nothing
about."

"Okay," Dana said. "Okay." She sounded as if she had
to rev herself up, give herself an internal pep talk that she
wasn't quite buying. But she was coming.

"I'm five minutes out," he said.

"I'll be there in fifteen," she replied. "I'd say be careful,
but I'm not totally sure you know what that means."

As Gordon was trying to think of a witty reply, she
hung up.

FOR A FEW FLEETING moments on the awkward run from
his car to his loft, Gordon thought perhaps he was overreact-
ing. Nothing he'd thought about the case, neither the crim-

inal case nor the psychiatric case, had turned out even remotely the way he'd predicted. Maybe his instincts here were wrong as well.

Then he saw neat slivers of his doorjamb sprinkled across the entryway. *Of course,* he thought grimly. *The one thing I get right.*

The door opened easily. More shards of wood lay on the floor inside. A stab of fear mixed with sickly sweet nostalgia at seeing Karen's bag and coat in the foyer, just like they always used to be, way back when, before everything.

His place was still a mess and smelled vaguely of old Chinese food. He couldn't see anyone right away, but he felt them. The darkness inside was expectant.

"Hello?" Gordon ventured.

He flicked on the lights and heard a shuffling from around a corner, as well as heavy, panicked breathing.

"Charlie?" he asked. "It's just me, Gordon. I'm coming in alone."

A man cleared his throat somewhere inside, a soft sound that was still somehow a violation. Gordon worked to unclench his teeth. If he hoped to get out of this encounter alive, he would need to be at the top of his game, to find that space where he could glide, effortlessly working in both his own mind and that of his patient.

Then he turned the corner and saw Karen bound to his desk chair with an ethernet cable, a strip of duct tape slapped over her face, her eyes wide beyond the whites and into the reds at the far edges. He took a step toward her, and as if on cue, Charlie stepped out from behind the stairway and pointed a gun at him.

All his training fled him in an instant.

He didn't know what he was expecting Charlie to look like, but it wasn't that: a skinny pole of a young man in a baggy black hoodie and a loose pair of jeans that fit like he'd stolen them off the line in a hurry. His hair was bushy and unkempt, his cheeks hollow, and even his ragged ear looked different, more lived in, like the old war wound of a street cat. He held the gun awkwardly, at a bit of a lean, like he could barely support its weight.

Only his eyes were the same, piercing and steady, simmering just before a boil.

"Charlie, what did they do to you?" Gordon asked, his voice barely above a whisper.

"You know what they did," Charlie said, eyeing Gordon up and down as if squaring away the sight of him with whatever memory he had. "What they still doin'."

"Trying to crush you," Gordon said.

The words simply came out, but they rang true. From day one, everybody wanted to squeeze the life out of that kid—his parents, who never gave him a shot; the teachers who couldn't deal with him; the court system rigged against him; Ditchfield, quite literally. The city itself was set against him from the very beginning because he lived in the projects, hustling to survive with the added weight of responsibility for Tasha.

Everything and everyone seemed designed to hold him down... everyone but Gordon. Somehow, Gordon had to make him see that.

Charlie pulled a business card from his baggy front pocket and held it up. Gordon could see the even black lettering of Jefferson and Pope LP on one side. He flipped it to reveal the number three in a scrawled circle.

"Last stop," he said, and he flicked it at Karen, who let out a muffled whimper.

"You don't have to hurt her. You don't have to hurt anyone, but especially not her. She isn't even supposed to be here," said Gordon, willing himself not to sound as desperate as he felt.

"Two questions," Charlie said, all business. "First, did you know?"

"No!" Gordon exclaimed. "I mean, I knew Ditchfield was horrendous, but I had no idea Josiah Hill was involved in any of it. Especially not when it came to those girls."

"Two. Did you find Tasha like I told you the last time I saw you, through the glass?" Charlie asked.

"No," Gordon said again, but without strength. "I should have. But my life sort of fell apart, and..."

"And you gave up, same as the lawyer," Charlie said. "Let me get sent up to that hellhole and then went back to your lives." He shook the gun at Gordon and spoke through gritted teeth. "You gave me no choice! This is what I gotta do to get through to you!"

"You're not a killer, Charlie," Gordon said.

"I sure as shit killed Andy Bagshot," Charlie said. He looked like he was trying for a merciless smile, but it came across as a grimace of pain.

"This is different, and you know it," Gordon said. "Andy was torturing you. Karen and I were just bad psychiatrists."

Charlie's eyes seemed to go unfocused, which Gordon thought was a bad sign. "You don't know the half of it," Charlie said.

"Then tell me," said Gordon.

Charlie came back a bit, finding the room again. "Dirty Andy's been fuckin' with me for years, sayin' he buys black girls on camera. Talkin' 'bout how he's gonna step up his game, maybe buy one in real life. Maybe somebody I knew. Then he showed me a picture on his phone, right before they came in with the needles. I recognized Tasha."

Gordon could picture it: Andy pulling out a greasy cell phone as Charlie lay strapped to that dentist's chair from hell and flipping through his filthy pictures, just like the ones Gordon had in the box. A brother would recognize his twin sister no matter what she'd been turned into. He wondered if Charlie screamed at him, straining against the four-point restraints to get to him as long as he could. Or maybe the fast-acting benzodiazepine had paralyzed him already.

"I put most of it together after I popped that bitch Alonzo's eye for saying he'd already taken her down. After he got out of the hospital, he tried to swagger back. Got a message through to me about raping her at New Hope like it was a walk in the fuckin' park. Like they let it happen."

"That's why you stole the car. Why you ran it into the church," said Gordon. He remembered seeing Alonzo, eyepatch and all, the night Marty was shot. He was the man that got away. Gordon understood finally. Charlie wasn't going on some sort of spree. He was looking for help.

Charlie's gun trembled slightly, and he looked like he wanted badly to squeeze the trigger. "New Hope was supposed to help her," he said, his voice cracking slightly. "Instead, they let Andy and Alonzo and whoever else use her like a rag. Then Brighton was supposed to help me. But he got bought off. Then you two were supposed to help me, but you gave up, and *this one* never thought I could be helped to begin with!" He stepped forward and pushed the stubby barrel of the revolver against the back of Karen's skull so hard that he bowed her head until her chin touched her chest.

"Charlie, I only see this going one of two ways. Either we help you tell your story, or you pull that trigger and Josiah Hill and Alonzo and half the Baltimore Police who are out there right now, trying to paint you as nothing more than a sociopathic killer, win."

Karen looked up at him, and he truly met her eyes for the first time, her focus wholly on him.

"Sometimes Karen is thoughtless. She has a thousand-foot view in a world that requires seeing eye to eye. But she's not the one that failed you. She never promised to help you in the first place. I did. And that is something I'll live with for the rest of my life."

As he spoke, all the conversations he'd had with the boy came back in one fire hose blast, snippets of conversations layered over one another in one big synaptic firing squad of memories. One, in particular, struck him.

"I asked you one time if you were grateful for anything," Gordon said calmly, evenly, with the kind of clarity that can only come when someone quite literally has a gun to their head.

Charlie's eyes glanced up and away, but the mania he'd been showing receded a bit. He was recalling the conversation.

"That was a dumb question to ask. Lazy too. I was trying to build a plan of care around making you reassess your past, thinking maybe you'd overlooked something wonderful, some beautiful memory you could hold on to. But your past was brutal. Sometimes, no amount of reframing can fix a shattered picture. Sometimes, you've just got to start painting again. I should have worked with you to paint something new. So how about we start right now? Give me a chance to find Tasha. If I can't..." Gordon didn't want to say it, but some contracts needed to be signed in blood. "You can take what you feel you're owed from me."

Karen's cries were muted, but her tears were real as

Charlie pulled the gun back from her head and pointed it squarely at Gordon once more.

"You know where she is?" Charlie asked, his voice deadly calm.

Gordon thought it a particularly ridiculous bit of irony that his entire life was now in the hands of Thomas Brighton, probably just then waltzing into the secured ward of JH Emergency in his fancy leather shoes with a freshly jagged smile. But that was the hand he was dealt.

"I think we may have a lead," Gordon allowed.

Charlie looked carefully at him then back down at Karen. He put the gun inside the baggy double-sleeved pocket of the hoodie. The snub nose was still there, but the immediacy of death seemed a mile away.

"You got one night to prove it," Charlie said. "And you and I do it together. Let's go."

Gordon cleared his throat. "Well, I'm not one hundred percent sure where to go just yet," he began, stammering a bit. "I was hoping we could just take a seat here. Maybe get a cold glass of water? Think through our options?"

"We're going now," said Charlie. "We take your car."

"My car? It's a piece of junk. Really. Our chances of getting killed go up substantially as soon as we sit down in that thing."

The revolver pressed through the fabric of his sweater like a pointing finger. Dana was about five minutes away. Gordon wondered how he might stall. *Offer the guy a cup of coffee?* That would take a good five minutes to make, easy.

"How about if—"

"Go," Charlie said.

Gordon took one last look at Karen. Her eyes pleaded with him, trying to convey something he couldn't quite grasp: anger, fear, but also gratitude. From kissing under the

Christus, to being in and out of a divorce, all the way to getting bound and gagged. What a ridiculous ride.

"All right," Gordon said, clapping his hands together lightly. "You say go, we'll go."

When Gordon pulled the keys back out of the front-door lock where he'd left them, he thought about that flash of light he'd seen on the coffee table all those years before. The roll of duct tape was sitting where she'd left the ring.

Charlie followed him out and closed the door softly behind them. On the walk to his car, Charlie kept the distance between them to within a step.

CHAPTER EIGHTEEN

Thomas Brighton was a man who lived by a handful of tenets. One of those tenets was "Never forget a favor." Another was "Get the shit you dread done first." A third: "Drink twenty ounces of water for every ounce of vodka."

But by far, his most sacred tenet was "Fake it till you make it."

That sacred tenet was what allowed him to walk, briefcase in hand, right up to the security desk at the Emergency Department of Johns Hopkins Hospital, looking like he was born to be there. He pulled out one of his cards, flashed it to the officer behind the desk and said he was there to see his client.

The officer eyed the card perfunctorily, barely even looking up from her computer. "Who is your client?" she asked.

"Alonzo Cook," Brighton said, as if it was obvious.

Of course, it wasn't. Up until about ten minutes before, he hadn't even had the man's full name.

He'd called Natasha on his drive over and begged her to

tap one of his contacts at the records department inside BPD. He needed a full name. At first, she demurred, saying she was on a date, but he must have sounded a special kind of desperate because she eventually agreed. It was a crap date anyway, she'd said.

So Brighton flexed one of his tenets and called in a favor. In fact, Marty Cicero had just filed the ballistics report for a recent shooting at New Hope Community Church. Two were wounded. One was Cicero himself, and the other was a man by the name of Alonzo Cook.

A quick cross-reference with the county courthouse told Brighton that Alonzo Cook had quite a rap sheet—right up until he didn't. He'd been arrested five times in his teens, everything from drunk and disorderly to assault. He'd entered a probationary program at seventeen as part of a plea bargain to stay out of Ditchfield, a reform program run by the venerable New Hope Foundation. He'd been squeaky clean ever since, at least on paper.

Brighton knew better.

"Alonzo Cook is in step-down under guard," said the officer, looking up for the first time. Her eyes widened slightly at the jagged new addition to his visage.

Still, he never let his smile waver. "That's exactly why I'm here," he said. "He's expecting me."

But of course, he wasn't.

The officer eyed him a moment more then pulled out an electric-orange sticker badge marked Visitor. She wrote the room number in the top right: 102.

Brighton pulled the sticker off its backing and pressed it above his gold chrysanthemum lapel pin. He tapped it a few times for good measure then thanked the officer and walked inside.

No matter how orderly an emergency department was

—and the ED at Hopkins was among the best—Brighton still cringed inwardly every time he walked inside. He'd been in and out of hospitals all his career—on behalf of others, for the most part—but it never got easier. He could sense a consistent undercurrent of panic, along with the sounds of pain, both heard and unheard, because even the guys that suffered in silence seemed to emit a kind of dog-whistle keen just too high to hear. All of it made Brighton slightly nauseous.

The important thing was that Brighton cringed *inwardly*. His exterior was as stalwart as ever as he pressed the button to unlock the heavy double doors that would take him to the step-down rooms, where patients fresh out of surgery awaited transfer to the recovery floor.

Brighton saw a police officer right away, a beefy fellow in full uniform, standing beside the door and unabashedly gawking at the asses of the nurses as they came and went. Brighton pulled his shoulders back to present as confident a front as possible. He slowed his stride until he was walking the hospital hallway as assuredly as he would his own living room. A glance at the officer's badge gave him the man's name before the cop even realized Brighton was approaching him.

"Officer Packman, right?" Brighton said, nodding as if in answer to his own question. "The chief told me you'd be here."

Who "the chief" was, Brighton couldn't be sure. But that hardly mattered. He knew that type of cop. The dolt would be flattered that "the chief" was thinking about him and probably a little amazed that Brighton knew his name, despite it being stitched right there on his shirt.

"Duke sent you?" he asked.

That was the guy, Warren Duke. Brighton knew of him

—total asshole, the kind of guy that the Thomas Brighton of a few days ago might have admired a little.

"He did." Brighton nodded sagely and pulled a card effortlessly from the breast pocket of his eight-hundred-dollar camel-hair overcoat. "Thomas Brighton of Brighton and Associates LLP. I'm Mr. Alonzo Cook's defense attorney. Warren sent me himself with instructions to speak with him and only him as soon as he wakes up."

He hoped the first-name familiarity would also cement his persona, and evidently, it was doing the trick. Packman was nodding slowly while he looked at the card, eager to have been in on the decision the entire time, eager to make it look like he knew what was going on.

Brighton decided to take a gamble. "Feel free to call it in if you want," he said offhand, as if such a thing was an absolute waste of Packman's time.

The gamble paid off. "No, that's all right. Go on in. He's been out of surgery for a few hours now."

Brighton nodded thanks and stepped past Packman, who was already uninterested in everything but the nurses' asses once more. He flicked down the handle of the door and walked inside.

Alonzo Cook was attached to all sorts of machines. IV lines trailed from both inner wrists, leading to what looked like a coatrack sporting bags of liquids. A tube was running out from under the covers at his side, draining thin red liquid into an evil-looking hazmat box on the floor. Brighton counted three monitors, each displaying a different set of numbers.

Alonzo was also wide awake, tapping a fingertip clipped tight with a heart-rate monitor slowly on the top of the covers, and staring straight at Brighton with one good eye.

"Who are you?" he muttered. His voice wasn't strong,

but it was crystal clear, not the voice Brighton would associate with a man fresh out of surgery that had a bullet removed from his chest.

The other blockers on this mission—front desk security, the officer on duty—those were nothing compared to what he'd have to pull off next. Alonzo was Brighton's true test.

He felt oddly elated. "I'm Thomas Brighton, your attorney."

"I don't know nothing about any attorney," Alonzo said slowly, pausing every few words but never taking his eyes off Brighton.

"Hill sent me," Brighton said, returning gaze for gaze.

Alonzo didn't bite. "This is the first I heard."

Brighton looked around, found a rolling stool, and pulled up a seat. He situated his empty briefcase carefully at his side and looked squarely at Alonzo. "That's because you were in surgery, Mr. Cook. Because you got shot. By a cop. For shooting another cop."

Alonzo leaned back on his elevated bed and took in Brighton through hooded eyes.

"Hence, your need for an attorney," Brighton said, holding out his arms in a mock welcome.

"I didn't shoot nobody," Alonzo said.

"Good," replied Brighton. "That's good. That's exactly what you're gonna say in court. And with any luck, that will be the end of it."

The tapping stopped. He'd gotten Alonzo's attention. *Time to set the bait.*

Brighton leaned in and lowered his voice. "What you certainly will not be saying is anything remotely related to the New Hope Foundation, especially New Hope Community Church and what you may or may not have been doing there on the night in question. Nor will you mention the

Reverend Josiah Hill's name anywhere whatsoever. In fact, once I leave this room, you will remain silent."

"Where you goin'?" he asked, wary but less confident.

"I have to clean up my second mess of the evening, concerning a certain acquaintance of yours on the night in question, caught running a red light in an unmarked van at midnight, who subsequently mouthed off to the officer and ended up in holding."

Alonzo's eyes went wide at that. Brighton had struck a nerve.

"They caught Dameon?" he asked.

"Yes, they did," Brighton said, affecting a tried-and-true note of disgust as he stood, which had proven particularly effective in court. It wasn't hard. He picked up his briefcase and made a show of getting ready to leave but slow played it a bit by checking his phone. He'd set the bait—time to wait for the bite.

"What about the van?" Alonzo asked quietly, in confidence.

"Thankfully, the reverend has friends in the department. We were able to swap the driver, but it was tricky," Brighton said, leaving the statement open to interpretation.

"But it made it to Ditchfield?"

Bingo.

"Yes, Mr. Cook. It made it to Ditchfield. If it hadn't, we'd be having a very different conversation right now," Brighton said.

Brighton had it. All the cameras, all the computers, all the recording equipment was now up at Ditchfield. That made sense. A big place like that, a lot of refurbished old buildings, some left derelict over the years—anything could be hidden up there, even a bunch of terrified young girls.

Brighton paused at the door and looked back at the man

who had almost killed Marty Cicero, a cop that Brighton knew only tangentially but who nonetheless felt like a guy that played on his team. "Remember what I said, Mr. Cook. Speak to nobody. And for God's sake, try not to shoot any more cops. It really taxes the reverend's legal team."

He let those words hang in the air as he pushed open the door and left Alonzo's darkened recovery room for the antiseptic white of the hall. Saying nothing to Packman as he passed, he only walked away, already dialing Gordon Pope.

CHAPTER NINETEEN

The slow rattle coming from somewhere under the hood of Gordon's coupe sounded like a lazy castanet as he sat in the darkness with a white-knuckle grip on his steering wheel. From their vantage, the sharp steeple of New Hope Community Church shot high into the sky, but the rest of the place was obstructed by a shuttered auto-parts store and a ratty off-brand gas station.

"I'm telling you, Hill's not there. Nobody is there," Gordon said. "They cleared everything out."

"Go around the block again," Charlie said. Brighton's revolver sat crosswise in his lap, the muzzle pointed right at Gordon's liver.

Gordon eased the coupe out. Traffic was sparse, both foot and automobile. People that weren't working the corners were walking quickly from one to the other, keeping to the shadows. Or they were buying and bolting.

Crime scene tape crisscrossed the big white double doors of New Hope just beyond the concrete island. No light could be seen through the windows, not even weak candlelight. Despite his guarantees otherwise, Hill's house of God appeared to be temporarily closed by the power vested in the Baltimore Police, likely by order of Warren Duke, specifically, until he could get things under control his way.

When they swung around the back, Charlie gazed intently at the high brick walling off the inner courtyard and that miserable inner sanctum. Gordon felt like he could still smell the place.

"This used to be the only spot Tasha and I could get food, back in the day," Charlie said, his voice distant.

Gordon said nothing.

"I remember Hill handing me a bologna sandwich when I was ten years old. He gave Tasha an extra chocolate milk that first time and every time after." Charlie seemed lost in the memory, as if he was trying to examine it from every angle in his mind. "You think he was whoring little girls out then too?"

For a moment, Gordon didn't realize he'd been asked a question. He was still grappling with the fact that he was being held at gunpoint in his beat-up two-seater by a guy that he'd spent the better part of the entire week and much of the end of his married life trying to connect with.

When Gordon found Charlie looking at him, waiting for his answer, he couldn't do anything but speak the first words that came to mind. "Probably. Men like Josiah Hill don't just wake up one day and decide to prey upon children. His setup might not have been as sophisticated, but he was likely grooming his next victims even then."

"With chocolate milk," Charlie said softly, almost a mumbled whisper. "How the fuck does a grown man..." He trailed off, eyes on the church again. He seemed to have gone down that line of questioning before, probably hundreds of times, knowing he'd find no answers.

"Likely, Hill was sexually abused himself," Gordon said simply. "That's almost always the case with sexual predators. Especially pedophiles."

Charlie sneered. Gordon could tell he didn't like hearing that. Anything that made the monster look like more of a man likely didn't align with Charlie's worldview right then. But to Gordon, that was simply a medical fact.

"It's no excuse," Gordon added. "There is no excuse for what Hill did, what he continues to do. I'm just saying that these cases are vicious cycles. You and Tasha were pulled onto a runaway train that was a long time coming. It probably left the station before you and I were ever born."

Gordon's eyes drifted down to the gun and wondered if they'd reached the part where the runaway train rounded the bend, one side lifted, wheels barely touching the steel, only to find that the track is out ahead.

He felt a vibration in his pocket and reached for it out of instinct then paused as the gun dug into his side.

"My phone is ringing," Gordon said quickly. "It could be the lead I told you about."

Charlie considered it and nodded once. "You say one word about me or where you are, I'm gonna end that call real quick."

Gordon squirmed to get the phone out of his pocket and answered it without even looking at who was calling.

"Hello?"

"I got it out of him, Doc," Brighton said, a bit breathless. He was walking somewhere, the tapping of his shoes audible. "Ditchfield. It's all up at Ditchfield."

Ditchfield. The word settled itself in his stomach like a stone at the bottom of a lake.

"Hello?" Brighton asked, his voice tinny and distant. "Gordon?"

Of course it was all up at Ditchfield. He felt the truth of that as surely as he felt the cold of the night closing in around him. It was as inevitable as the deepening winter. In some ways, perhaps, he'd always known.

All roads eventually lead to Ditchfield.

"You hear me, Pope? I think it's all there. The cameras, the equipment, even the girls."

Gordon's voice came out slightly panicked. "Yeah, I hear you. Makes sense."

"What's the plan? Where are you?" Brighton asked.

Gordon felt the barrel push in slightly, like a probing finger. "Uh, I'm... around."

Brighton paused. "What?"

"Tell Dana," Gordon said suddenly and cringed a bit, half expecting to get shot for it.

But Charlie held his fire. He'd likely heard Brighton too. Maybe his mind was on a crash course with Ditchfield, just like Gordon's.

"You're being weird, Doc. What's going on?" Brighton asked.

"I'm fine. I'll take it from here. You start building a case."

"Okaaay—" Brighton began.

But then Charlie snatched the phone and hung up.

Gordon turned toward him. Charlie had heard, all right. Gordon could see in him a mute fear that filled his hollow eyes and made them look more ancient, as if the word had triggered a primal flight response he was trying to wrestle back into its cage.

Maybe this was where their story ended—in Gordon's beat-up coupe idling on a run-down street outside New Hope. Charlie couldn't possibly have the strength to return willingly to the prison from which he'd fled, to waltz right back in to the scene of what was likely almost ritualistic abuse, day after day, for the most formative years of his life.

Gordon certainly wouldn't blame him if he put an end to it all right there. One way or another.

"We're gonna need gas," Charlie said.

Gordon cocked his head, not quite sure he'd heard correctly. "Excuse me?"

"You're almost empty. It's a long way to Ditchfield," said Charlie.

Just like that, the young man's decision was made. Gordon had no choice but to act it all out with him. He tried to think of where the nearest gas station was. Charlie returned the gun to a cautious rest in his lap, like a cat eyeing Gordon with a one-eyed stare.

As soon as Dana saw the evidence of forced entry at Gordon's front door, she reached for the spot on her hip where her gun should have been, and her fingertips lightly brushed her pocket. She muttered a curse. *Time to improvise.*

She pushed open the door and grabbed the first thing that came to hand: a cheap plastic umbrella from the stand just inside. She flattened against the near wall, using the angles of the entryway to limit her exposure while maximizing her view. Most importantly, she kept moving. The last thing she wanted was to get caught in a standoff with Charlie Cunningham while holding an umbrella. He would close in on her from one end while her own self-doubt closed in from the other, and she would be a sitting duck.

She was about to announce herself as police but thought

better of it. First, it wasn't technically true, and second, that might spook Charlie into doing something stupid.

"Anyone here?" she asked instead.

A muffled scream came from somewhere inside. She took the roundabout way, skirting the main room by dashing across the waiting room to the right. She hugged the far wall and peered into the back of the main floor.

A woman she'd never seen before was tied up to a chair, her hands bound behind her, forcing her shoulders square and jutting her chest out. A strip of duct tape was wrapped around her head and covered her mouth. Another, longer strip wrapped her tightly to the back of the chair around her waist.

"Where is he?" Dana asked before realizing the woman couldn't answer. "Nod if he's here."

The woman shook her head furiously. Wisps of perfectly dyed blond hair fell over her face.

"Is anyone else here?" Dana asked, looking up the stairs, back toward where Gordon's cave was.

Another furious shake preceded muffled speaking that Dana couldn't make sense of. She let the umbrella fall to the ground and moved to the woman. The tape was triple wrapped around her head and arms. She tried to pull it down off her mouth but got nowhere.

"Karen?" Dana asked, more hesitantly than she would've liked. The woman finally nodded.

"Hold up," Dana said and moved quickly to Gordon's desk to rifle through the main drawer until she found a pair of scissors.

She came back and carefully slipped one shear in the gap just behind her jaw and cut the wrapping apart. One quick pull opened up the front and exposed Karen's mouth. She took in a deep, gasping breath.

"Charlie took him," she said raggedly. "Took Gordon at gunpoint. They left in his old coupe."

Dana paused in her unwrapping and plucked out her phone. She hadn't missed any calls. She dialed 911 but held off on pressing Send at the last second. She couldn't be sure who would get the call on the other end. If she gave Duke a description of the car Gordon and Charlie were in, he would do anything to silence the kid. She could imagine Duke calling in some sort of SWAT intervention that treated Gordon as irrelevant collateral damage.

She had to trust that Gordon was handling the situation as best he could and take a second to think.

"Where did they go?" Dana asked, moving down to Karen's bound wrists.

She slit the tape neatly and pulled it off in a single motion to limit the pain. Still, she winced. Since neither of them was in immediate danger, Dana took a second to look at her fully. Karen Jefferson. Right there. In the flesh.

"I don't know. He didn't say," she said, pulling her arms slowly in front of herself and rubbing at the wrists. "Thank you," she added.

She was quite pretty, nicely dressed in a billowy pants suit that looked expensive. The light jacket looked tailored, and a tasteful diamond pendant around the neck had notably been left undisturbed by Charlie. Her diamond studs, too, looked like they cost a small fortune.

"Karen Jefferson," Dana said, as if the name was the punchline of a particularly flat joke.

"Are you a colleague of Gordon's?" she asked.

"I'm his girlfriend," Dana said.

Karen assayed Dana in a new light. "Dana Frisco?"

"You know me?" Dana asked.

"Of course I do. I know *of* you, at least."

Dana stopped cutting. She stepped back and sized her up again. After a moment in which Dana simply held the scissors and looked at the woman who had almost irreversibly cracked the foundation on which Gordon had built his life, she spoke again, mistaking Dana's shock for confusion.

"Yes, well, in addition to being Gordon's ex-wife, my name is one half of that shingle out front. Which is actually the whole reason I came here. I was waiting for him to return so I could discuss full divestiture, but I got Charlie instead."

"I know all about you," Dana said flatly.

Karen looked about to speak, but then she paused. A clinical look came over her, which Dana recognized as the same that struck Gordon when he went into doctor mode. "Am I not what you expected?" Karen asked evenly.

In the old pictures Dana had seen, Karen was always a somber figure, pretty but conservative. She'd expected a severe woman, a shrew, a type-A monster. This woman was striking and colorful and surprisingly calm, even for having been taped to a chair.

"You destroyed him, you know," Dana said.

Karen eyed the scissors briefly then settled her gaze back upon Dana. "Evidently not. Gordon turned the tables here. He talked Charlie out of killing me. He certainly didn't seem destroyed to me."

So he'd bargained for her life with his own. *You loveable fool,* she thought. Then again, frantic self-sacrifice always was one of Gordon's strong points.

Dana's heart panged. She missed him terribly, and not just because he had thrown himself into immediate danger... again. She'd actually missed him from the moment she told him to stay away for the safety of her family.

What an idiot she'd been. Gordon *was* her family. She never should have pushed him away, never mind that he went willingly, that he probably thought that was a smart idea. She should have pulled him in tighter with Chloe and Maria in their happy little home at the first sign of danger to any of them. Because that's what family should do. Family drew in. Family did not push away.

Karen was feeling around the tape stuck firmly to her fresh haircut. She pulled a bit and winced then took a deep breath and held the tape at the base before yanking the first wrapping off. Chunks of blond came with it, and Karen hissed in pain.

"You're a police officer, right?" Karen asked after gathering her composure. "Can't you get people out there on the streets to find him?"

"It's complicated," Dana said. "Not something you can just drop in on and get up to speed."

Karen looked at Dana sidelong while grasping at the second wrapping. "That's fair," she said.

Dana knew she had to decide right then and there whether or not to hate the woman. She had a right to hate her. She knew how toxic Karen was to Gordon, the man she loved more than anything else in her life save, perhaps, her own daughter. And she wasn't toxic in a clean and simple way where the wound could just be cauterized. She was insidiously toxic, having struck at Gordon where he was most vulnerable, by turning his love for children into a personal failing he was just managing to overcome.

Yes, she could hate Karen Jefferson quite easily. But she wouldn't... for one reason: Gordon didn't hate Karen. He knew her better than anyone, and he didn't hate her.

She snipped the shears once in the air. "I can help you get it off. Might have to cut a little bit."

Karen looked carefully at Dana then nodded. "Thank you," she said again. "Cut whatever you need. I was planning on going short anyway."

For the next minute, the only sound was the snip of shears. Dana worked quickly and surely and only had to snip off real length in a few areas. Soon, Karen was free. She stood and looked back at the chair as if offended by it. When Dana's phone rang, both women started.

Dana didn't recognize the number, but she scrambled to answer anyway. "Hello?"

"Is this Dana Frisco?" came the reply, a voice she recognized but couldn't place.

"Who is this?" Dana asked.

"Thomas Brighton. You may remember me as the asshole lawyer that paid Gordon Pope by the hour as an expert witness. Paid pretty poorly, actually."

"Yeah, I know you," Dana said, failing to keep disappointment from her voice.

"Anyway, long story short, I'm pretty sure Tasha Cunningham and all the rest of this mess is up in Ditchfield right now," Brighton said, as if it were the perfectly ordinary progression of things.

Dana didn't trust that she'd heard him correctly. "How do you know—"

"Gordon and I had one hell of a late-night working session," Brighton said. "This was the last piece of our puzzle. I called him and told him, but he just told me to tell you for some reason. I think something's up. He was being weird on the phone. Even for him."

"Charlie's got him," Dana said. "They went for a drive."

Brighton was silent on the other end of the line for a moment before coming back with surprising calm. "I figured something like that," he said. "The kid doesn't quit.

But I don't think he wants to hurt Gordon. Not if he can get around it."

"Oh? And you know this how?" Dana asked, fully recognizing that she was getting defensive.

Somehow, she was the last to know about everything recently, the last to get hit by whatever bolt out of the blue seemed to smack everyone else regarding Charlie and Ditchfield and everything. She was tired and scared for Gordon and under no illusions that things were going to end well, no matter what come-to-Jesus moment Brighton had gone through.

"Charlie and I had a nice little chat last night," Brighton said. "I think we're all straight on who the bad guys are. Plus, now you know where he's going with your boyfriend."

The full weight of his words hit Dana, and she had to lean against Gordon's ring-stained coffee bar for a moment to process. His sprawling coffee setup rattled in warning.

"You think they're going to Ditchfield? Now?" Dana asked.

"From what I've seen, Charlie's not exactly the hurry-up-and-wait type," Brighton replied.

Dana's mind felt like it was buckling. *A kamikaze run at Ditchfield in the dead of night?* She tried to think of the myriad ways that might end. None of them were good.

"I got some work to do on my end. I'm gonna leave the cop stuff to you. Listen, though, we got a hell of a case brewing. It'd be nice if Gordon lived to see it through."

Dana muttered thanks and hung up. She found Karen looking at her, waiting. She realized that the woman was expecting her to move immediately—she knew Gordon was expecting her to take charge right then too. He'd told Brighton to call her, after all. Right then was the time to do what she supposedly did best. Whether or not she thought she could do it anymore no longer mattered.

For so long, Dana had maintained that all she ever wanted was to rise up in the Baltimore Police, to lead. But the longer she lived around Gordon Pope, the more things changed. Recent promotions, future accolades, more money, more chevrons—they were all false gods.

Gordon mattered. Righting wrongs mattered. She might never be a sergeant in the Baltimore Police again, might never be a cop again at all, but she could be the kind of person that Gordon was proud to stand beside.

She zipped up her coat and checked her pocket for her keys.

"I'll clean up here," Karen said. "I was never very good in these types of situations. The trench work was always Gordon's specialty."

"I know," said Dana.

"Please keep him alive," Karen said with every ounce of pretense dropped.

All Dana could do was nod.

Her hurried walk to the minivan was surreal. She felt as if everything was converging. It only made sense that things would come to a head at Ditchfield. The place had mocked her for years from its ancient nook, embedded like a tick in the foothills. Dared her to return.

And so she would return. But she wasn't going all by herself—not anymore, not if she could help it.

MARTY CICERO COULDN'T SLEEP. After gingerly rolling from side to side for the fourth time that night, he knew he was keeping Brooke awake, so he got up. At first, he thought he might just pee and get a glass of water, but after he peed he thought, *Why the hell not pad around a bit downstairs?* Maybe Brooke could get some sleep if he wasn't fussing around. She certainly needed it. He'd told her right off the bat that being a cop's girlfriend wasn't easy, but he'd never thought she would be picking him up from the hospital that early in their relationship.

He stood for a while in the darkened kitchen, surrounded by the lingering smells of the meal she'd cooked him: organic chicken breast, grilled, on a bed of spaghetti-squash noodles. It was delicious, and he didn't have the heart to tell her that swallowing hurt, so he ate it all and gutted the pain. His discomfort didn't matter, not when the rest of his life felt so good. Even his kitchen felt good, lived in. No longer was it some distant part of the house, used only for blending single-portion protein shakes and microwaving lean single-serving meals.

He took a few more ginger sips of water and wandered to the garage, where he'd set up a small gym next to his Camaro. It was nothing special, just a small weight rack, bar and bench, and some handholds bolted into the wall, enough to do whatever cycles he needed. He looked wistfully at the bench press—his favorite lift. He was well aware of his meathead tendencies, but even he wasn't going to power through lifting seventy-five on either side with a cracked sternum. Not for a while, at least.

Bye-bye, sweet gains.

Funny thing, though. A year before, he would've been devastated. Now, he was happy to be alive. *Turns out getting clocked broadside with two slugs from a nine has a way of reordering a guy's priorities.*

Brooke was the one who'd made him promise to start wearing the Kevlar vest when he went out. She was the one who held it out to him before he left the house and watched as he buckled it on. Without her, he would've been a dead man, a pretty corpse lying in a casket and not seeming quite right in the middle because there was chicken wire in spots where his chest should be.

He sat down on the bench and watched the moonlight cut a white knife across the liquid black of his car. He wondered what a more practical car might look like in this garage, something with some room for more than Brooke and her purse. *Would a minivan like Dana's fit in here?*

His heart started beating a little too quickly. "Don't worry, baby," he whispered to the Camaro. "You know I'd never do you like that."

But still... that girl had him thinking thoughts—that girl and the two slugs. Another couple of inches north, and one of them would have slipped through his trachea and out his spinal column. No ambulance would have been fast enough then.

He thought he would've been angrier at being shot in the line of duty, like he'd want revenge. But then it had happened, and he was so happy to be alive afterward that all he could think about was preventing the people he loved from ever feeling that kind of fear—the kind after the slug hit but before he got a chance to check if the vest held up, and he didn't know if what he was feeling was pain from his chest getting a good thump or pain from his insides being scrambled.

Revenge didn't matter. If what Dana had told him was true, whatever was happening at New Hope was about a lot more than a crooked pastor and a few bad cops. It was a deep evil, the kind that didn't care if a few of its branches were snipped here and there. It had lived too long and dug too deep.

He wondered what it would've been like if the tables had been turned, if the great dice roll in the sky had sent Dana's wonderful daughter, Chloe, to grow up in the projects in East Baltimore—spitting distance from the darkness at the core of New Hope—and put Tasha and Charlie in Dana's comfy little house up north in suburbia, each with a room of their own. And the twins got home cooked meals every night instead of stringing out a food stamp card as long as they could.

What if Chloe was the one Hill forced to perform on camera, all painted over and drugged up?

Marty found himself balling his fists and clenching his teeth until his jaw trembled and the tightness in his chest fired a warning shot of pain across the bow.

The house whispered movement upstairs. Brooke was padding around in their bedroom on tiny feet. She hardly made any noise, moving with a dancer's grace. When she first told him she was a professional dancer, he'd thought she meant stripper, which was all the same to him. In fact, she'd meant the Baltimore Ballet. She laughed every time she remembered that conversation.

He felt bad for waking her. He'd spent enough late nights to know that once someone got out of bed, they were pretty much giving in to the insomnia. But truth be told, he wanted to be with her, wanted to sit with her and know she was there. By holding her, he could be reassured that he was not, in fact, lying dead on the ground in a false church. Whenever he wasn't with her, he was only ninety percent sure, sometimes less.

He walked back into the kitchen and set down his empty glass and waited for her to find him. She padded around the corner like a little white fox. Even his tight tees swam around her frame.

"You okay?" she asked.

"I am now," Marty said.

"Your phone's been buzzing," she said, seeming reluctant as she handed it over.

He felt some reluctance, too, to look down and see who was trying to get hold of him this soon and this late... and this many times.

Dana.

She called again, and the phone vibrated in his hand, the screen glowing brightly in the dark kitchen. He picked up.

"What's going on?" he asked.

"Ditchfield," Dana said. "They're all at Ditchfield. Tasha, the other girls, all the gear. Charlie too. He took Gordon. They're on their way in Gord's car."

Ditchfield. The dark heart. Maybe this was their chance to shed some light.

"I wouldn't ask you if I..." Dana said but trailed off.

"I know," Marty replied.

He looked up at Brooke. She knew. She could hear every word Dana said too. And what was more, he'd shared with her just earlier that night that he was worried about Dana. She hadn't been herself lately.

He wasn't worried that Dana was physically incapable or somehow mentally damaged or anything like that—she was just too much in her own head. She needed him to help nudge her straight again.

He looked questioningly at Brooke. If she shook her head, pulled him closer, and whispered that they should just return to bed, he would probably do it. He could call in the few good cops he had left on his side and bring them up to speed as best he could. Maybe by the time they formed a bigger plan and got more people involved, the girls would still be there.

Or maybe not.

And then he would try to sleep in his own bed, in the peace and quiet of his little duplex, with Brooke's warm body beside him. But the whole time, he knew he would be thinking of what his night of peace cost those girls that night... and every night thereafter.

Instead, Brooke nodded. But when she did, she dropped her head a bit, and her eyes were swimming in tears. Marty knew she would nod, knew she would never keep him from finishing this one way or another.

"I'll come pick you up," Marty told Dana. "Just hold on."

Dana thanked him in a half-choked voice, then she hung up. He pulled Brooke gently against himself. She was small and soft and warm, like a kitten against his chest. She was crying, little quiet tremors that shook her even though she hardly made a sound.

"Wear a vest," she whispered.

"I will," he promised. And he meant it. He had a spare in his trunk, right next to the one Alonzo had destroyed. This whole affair had a charged air. Things were primed to blow. If lightning struck twice, he wanted all the protection he could get.

He had a lot more to live for.

CHAPTER TWENTY

Gordon had been to Ditchfield eleven times over the course of his career. He remembered each visit and each patient clearly and wore each of them on his heart like a notch carved in the crumbling concrete of a cell wall.

The first time he rounded the soft bend on I-70—the one just after the Patapsco River crossing—he'd been in his twenties. A short-coat doc fresh out of school, finishing up a clinical rotation with the prison system, he'd been shadowing a psychiatrist who had to sign off on a transfer and was reluctant to do so. Watching her dicker over the paperwork, he wondered why. When he caught his first glimpse of Ditchfield in the distance and his heart sank without warning, he understood why she'd balked.

The place just had a bad air about it.

Rounding that soft bend never got easier over the years. In fact, the more he went out to Ditchfield, the more he felt like the Patapsco River marked some sort of barrier. It was an invisible toll booth beyond which hope started to bleed from the body, slowly but surely, the same way a car sips gas. He was reminded of the old wives' tale about running water keeping vampires out. But at Ditchfield, the vampires were already inside.

When Gordon and Charlie crossed the Patapsco late that night, the water below the bridge was ink black. The crescent moon above looked like a shard of ice, and the shadows of the forest pressed down all around them. Charlie sat silently with his gun still trained on Gordon. He'd been diligent about it the entire trip, diligent enough that every time Gordon's crappy suspension hit a broken section of Maryland's crappy roads, Gordon held his breath.

"There it is," Gordon said grimly.

Charlie didn't respond. Gordon glanced over and found the kid staring numbly at the compound. The main manor was lit like a gothic mansion, windows for eyes, the big double door a toothy mouth. The pods were arrayed to the right and left like little Monopoly houses, hemmed in by chain-link fencing topped with razor wire. The entire length of the property was lit up at intervals by banks of spotlights.

"How the hell did you get out of there, anyway?" Gordon asked. Strangely, that question had never occurred to him. At the time, it wasn't important. Now, though, it could be very useful to know.

"Swapped places with Jarvis," Charlie said.

"No, I mean physically. How did you get through the fence?"

"Hop's truck. He's the groundskeeper. I'd been watching him for a while from the yard. Knew where he parked it. Knew when. Knew he had all sorts of shit in the back, too, including clippers—the big two-handed kind. And I figured I could hotwire it. Turned out I didn't even have to. The ol' man kept the keys above the visor," Charlie shook his head, but he smirked, almost smiling.

"You clipped the fence?" Gordon asked, impressed.

Charlie nodded slowly, still watching Ditchfield as it grew in their view. "Clipped a big door, left one side whole. Took all of five minutes. Scraped the shit out of the truck, but I got it through. Then I shut the door again."

Gordon cleared his throat and wiped his sweaty hands on his slacks for what felt like the hundredth time. "I take it we aren't going to just waltz up to the front gate, then?"

Charlie shook his head. Gordon had figured as much. He'd had a nagging premonition ever since Charlie had made him fill his gas tank to the very top, back in Baltimore. Gordon never filled his gas tank to the top. Ditchfield was far, but it wasn't that far.

"You can't possibly think the break in the fence is still there," Gordon said, feeling clammy all over.

"You better hope so," Charlie said. "The front door'll be a whole lot messier."

They were almost at the turnoff. Up ahead, just visible in the weak lights of the coupe, a sign read State Prison Next Exit in reflective white on official turf green. Below that, it said Do Not Pick Up Hitchhikers.

Charlie sniffed at the sign as they turned off. Gordon had been carefully watching him for any signs of erratic behavior, something that might tip him off that he needed to take drastic measures like crashing the car in order not to get shot. But Charlie was vacillating between youthful bravado and an almost robotic calm. He guessed Charlie was running through scenarios in his head, psyching himself up to do something terrible, perhaps, then running through a sort of advanced postmortem of his actions.

When Gordon took the exit to Ditchfield, the clock on the dash turned to midnight.

"It's my birthday," Charlie said, as if in passing, like he was pointing out a particularly interesting rock.

"Are you serious?" Gordon asked.

Charlie nodded minutely. "Eighteen today. An adult in the eyes of the law. Likely, they'd be prepping to ship me to North Branch or some other max lockup," he said. "If I hadn't busted out, I'd just be leaving Tasha to the wolves when they transferred me."

"You know, if they catch you—I should say *when they catch you*, you'll be tried as an adult too," Gordon said. "You'll likely end up at North Branch anyway if you go through with this."

"I'm not going anywhere. This is my last stop," Charlie said.

"What does that mean?" Gordon asked, and a bit of the emotion he'd been trying to tamp down during the whole car ride bled through in his voice. "What's your endgame here?"

"I'm gonna take as many of the fuckers with me as I can," Charlie said, and his voice cracked involuntarily, breaking Gordon's heart a little.

"That's not going to save Tasha," Gordon said.

"You still don't get it, man," Charlie said, turning toward him. "Ain't nothing can save Tasha. Nothing can save me neither. Not against this place. But maybe I can see her one more time, show that I didn't abandon her. That I ain't forgot." Then Charlie recognized some turnoff. "Hold up."

Gordon's brakes squeaked as the coupe skidded to a stop. For a split second, Gordon thought maybe he'd changed the boy's mind, and strangely, he felt a pang of disappointment.

I'm going to need to unpack all this in therapy when all

is said and done. Maybe have a chat with Mom about it, he thought. Then he reminded himself that when all was said and done, he'd likely be leaving Ditchfield in cuffs. Or in a body bag.

But he'd thought about it, thought and thought. And unless he was willing to risk those girls' lives, they had to strike against Ditchfield right then, however they could. Gordon was far more aligned with Charlie than Charlie was likely aware—not about killing anyone, of course, but about making a big bang, maybe the kind of big bang that got attention and lifted up this poisonous old rock to expose the wriggling filth underneath.

"You gotta cut left," Charlie said. "There's an access road that runs 'round the back side, where D is."

Gordon cranked his window down and peered out into the night. The land was dark, a no-man's zone before the floodlights where everything looked like prickly shades of black. His headlights seemed to die about fifteen feet out, but he was pretty sure he saw an overgrown two-stripe dirt road in the near distance.

"You know, if my car falls apart out there, this is going to be pretty awkward for both of us," said Gordon.

Charlie allowed a quick snort that might have been laughter under different circumstances. "Too late now. Just drive."

Gordon eased his way forward, picking a route that avoided the biggest rocks. Then he heard something in the distance. At first, he thought trucks might be downshifting on the highway, but the throaty roar seemed to be coming their way, increasing in volume, and what was more, he recognized the sound of that engine.

Only one car was that overpowered, that obnoxiously loud at full throttle.

Charlie was listening, too, his head cocked to the side, out the window.

"What is that sound?" Charlie asked, wary.

"I think that's a Dodge Charger, Hellcat edition," Gordon said, a bit embarrassed that he remembered the whole title.

"Your people?" Charlie asked, and he pointed the gun at Gordon with real intention again. "Kill the headlights. Out of the car. Now."

Gordon did as he asked, put the coupe in park, and fumbled with his seatbelt. He stepped out and held his hands up. Charlie kept the gun trained on him until they were both standing in the ratty grass just off the main road.

"Likely it's Marty Cicero, the cop that Alonzo shot. If we're lucky, he's with Dana Frisco."

"Who's she?"

"She's my girlfriend," Gordon said. "And she was a cop, a very good one. Until another one of Hill's men, a gangster disguised as a high-ranking official named Warren Duke, took it all from her."

Charlie was thinking again. Gordon pressed.

"Neither of these people is any friend of Hill. As a matter of fact, they have their own reasons why they might want to sort some things out tonight. Most important of all, they know your story."

Charlie looked back, behind himself, where a pair of xenon headlights rimmed with orange appeared in the distance like the bloodshot eyes of a rabid robot. At the rate the car was approaching, they'd drive right past them.

"And they believe you," Gordon added. "They're not here to arrest you. They're part of the child-protection unit. They want this finished as bad as anyone. Except maybe you."

Gordon could tell Charlie wasn't convinced. This would change his suicidal plan. He was recalibrating.

"They'll tell your story," Gordon said desperately. "If you blow yourself up tonight, trying to take this goddamn place down, they'll tell everyone why."

Gordon thought he might be getting through to the kid. *The man, now*, he thought, belatedly.

"Please, Charlie," Gordon asked, blatantly begging now.

"Turn on the headlights," Charlie said.

Gordon scrambled to reach in the window and flicked on the coupe's weak headlights again. The Charger's engine slowed abruptly. They'd seen him.

Charlie lowered the gun. He kept his eyes on the approaching car until the headlights illuminated him from the boots up. By the time Gordon had to shade his eyes, Charlie had the gun back in his front pouch, but he was still holding it.

The Charger growled low as Marty shifted it into park, then both doors opened. Gordon was afraid Marty was going to come out shooting, but instead he held his hands out first then followed with his body. Dana did the same until both partners stood in the harsh backlight as if they were the ones being held up.

"Charlie?" Dana asked, hesitant. "We just want to help."

Charlie looked between them then at Gordon. The young man needed to decide his way forward. Gordon had done all he could.

After a moment more, Charlie said, "Then shut those high beams off."

Marty dipped back in and, with a flick, plunged them all into a purply darkness. Nobody moved while their eyes adjusted to the night again.

"Gordon? Are you okay?" Dana asked.

"Yeah, I'm fine," Gordon replied. "I think we're all on the same page here."

"Yeah?" asked Marty, a slab of shadow like an obsidian rock face in the darkness. "And what page is that?"

"We're going in," Gordon said before Charlie could snap off something provocative.

"Well, looks like you got lost, then," Marty said. "Road is thataway."

"If we go in the front door, it's not going to end well," Gordon said. "For any of us."

"So where are we going, exactly?" Dana asked. She was finally resolving in Gordon's eyes and lowering her hands slowly until she had them at her sides. She looked slumped and unsure.

"There might be a break in the fence this way. It's how Charlie got out," Gordon said.

"I can speak for myself," he said. "I'm gonna blow a hole in Pod D. Then when everybody is scrambling, I'm going to find Tasha. If I die in there, I want her to know I did it fighting for her. That I didn't abandon her."

In the dark, without the gun visible, he sounded heart-breakingly young again.

"And ain't nothing any of you can do to stop me," Charlie added when none of them responded. "Not least 'cause I think Hill wants all you dead only a little less than me."

"He ain't wrong," Marty said. "Came damn close with me already. I think they'd like to finish the job."

"So that's it, then?" Dana asked. "That's your big plan? Same as the old plan? Smash shit up and pray?"

"My plan is to find Tasha, to die by her side if that's

what it takes. She's all I got left. That's always been the plan," Charlie said.

"No, it wasn't," Dana continued, stepping forward. Charlie pulled the gun from his pocket again but kept it pointed at the ground.

"Dana—" Gordon began, trying to calm the situation with his hands.

Dana ignored him. "You didn't alert the world to all this by killing Bagshot so you could *die by her side*. You didn't slash Brighton's face to *die by her side*." Her voice was strengthening as she grew a little more confident with each step.

"You didn't strap Karen Jefferson to a chair and carjack Gordon because you wanted to die. You did it to get all of us here. And here we are. So give us better than *die by her side*," she said.

Charlie backed up in the face of her approach. "Maybe so," Charlie said. "Maybe I thought you could help. But that was before I knew where she was. Breaking into New Hope is one thing. This is *Ditchfield*. You know once we go in, there ain't no coming back from this. Especially for me."

Dana exhaled hugely, her breath puffed out into a blue cloud lit by the moon.

"Great. So instead of crashing and burning separately, we get the pleasure of crashing and burning together. Unless we do something about it," said Dana.

"And fast," Marty said, tugging at his vest uncomfortably. "We're sitting ducks out here if anyone cares to look."

Charlie turned toward Gordon. "We're going to the fence. Now." He turned back to Dana and Marty. "You can follow if you want. Whatever."

"Follow?" Marty said, incredulous. "Absolutely not."

"Fine," Charlie snapped.

"No, it's not like that. I'll scratch the shit out of my car," Marty said.

In the silence that followed, everyone looked at Marty.

"I've got ground effects on that baby. It's five inches from the pavement. Plus, I just shined it up."

"Are you serious?" Gordon asked.

"Dead serious," Marty said. "We're squeezing in your Pinto or whatever the hell it is."

"I don't even know what to say to you right now," Dana said, but with a smile in her voice.

"How about 'Get in the Pinto, Marty'?" he replied, already moving toward the car. He tugged down at his vest again and winced.

Dana wrapped her arms around her chest and looked out at the stadium lights of the prison. She seemed like she was trying to capture a thought that was as elusive as the cold mists around her.

"Pop the seats forward. I can jam in the back. If it means saving my car," Marty said.

Charlie said nothing, but he did pop his seat forward and watch as Dana climbed in and squeezed herself into the dinner-plate-sized space next to Marty.

Gordon eased his way in last. His seat wouldn't even lock. He was literally resting on Marty's knees. He closed his door gingerly, like the whole coupe might explode.

"Off we go," he said. He threw the car into drive and started praying to whoever was listening to give them enough horsepower to get where they were going.

CHAPTER TWENTY-ONE

Gordon killed the coupe's headlights a few hundred feet back from where the forest broke. The last incline was proving to be too much for the car. Twice already, the wheels had spun out. Gordon eased the pedal again, and they moved minutely, then the wheels lost traction again, kicking pebbles that clacked loudly against the undercarriage.

"You want me to get out and push?" Marty asked.

Gordon couldn't tell if he was being sarcastic or not, over the raking sound. He threw the car into park and pulled up the emergency brake.

"How about just get out?" Gordon asked. "We've got to be getting close anyway."

"Fine by me," Marty said. "Haven't been able to feel my legs for ten minutes."

Dana nodded but was quiet, watching Charlie carefully. While Gordon had nursed his car's four-cylinder engine and bald tires through the wilderness, she'd laid out the plan.

They'd revised once and had to stop the coupe to go

back for supplies in Marty's car. All the while, Charlie remained aloof, nodding along, but faintly. Gordon knew her plan was extremely risky for all of them, but none more so than Charlie. If the chips didn't fall the way Dana thought they would, their lives were likely forfeit. But for everything to work, they absolutely had to keep Charlie alive.

The problem was, Gordon knew Charlie had come to Ditchfield expecting to die, maybe even hoping for it. Dying for his sister was easy, though. Living beyond Ditchfield would require a different kind of sacrifice from him, one he was having to wrap his head around.

Gordon turned the car off and got out. Marty squeezed his way free from behind. Charlie and Dana did the same until all of them were standing around the car in the dead of night. The wind was flat. Exhaust from the coupe floated lazily up and over them, hazing the moon. The engine ticked as it cooled.

Gordon waved the smoke away, coughing. "Look, before we get ahead of ourselves, let's at least see what we've got working against us up there."

Gordon also wanted to give Charlie time to think, to weigh the options and tally up the balance book in his mind the way he seemed to whenever he made a decision.

As the four of them walked toward the clearing ahead, the fence came into view: a long, straight line that boxed off the western edge of the property and ran away into the distance for at least a few football fields. It looked about twelve feet high and was topped with shimmering loops of razor wire. Charlie had chosen the spot well. It was halfway between the corners on the west side, where the reach of the spotlights was weakest. It was also probably an eighth of a mile away from anything. The closest building was Pod D, and it looked small in the distance. They would be crossing a lot of land exposed, but that wasn't Gordon's immediate concern.

The fence was mended. Gordon couldn't see a break anywhere.

"Shit," Dana said. "There goes everything."

"Maybe we can ram it," Gordon said lowly.

Marty turned to him. "Your car would have trouble knocking over a trash can, much less reinforced chain-link fencing."

"Well, we have to get through somehow," Gordon whispered furiously. "This gets a lot harder without the car. Impossible, even."

"Let me think for a minute," Dana whispered, rubbing her temples.

All the while, Charlie was walking toward the fence. He assayed the distance to the corners along the right and left, counting off ticks in measured time with a pointing finger.

"There," he said, walking quickly to an area of the fence that looked slightly wavy. The other three went quiet as Charlie found where he'd clipped through, shook it a few times, hard, then fingered the edges of the break. He turned around again.

"Zip ties," he whispered.

"That's it?" Marty asked. He fished in one of the tactical pockets of his Kevlar vest and pulled out a small box cutter. "That's no problem at all."

"Ol' Hop always struck me as the lazy type," Charlie said. "Get the quick fix and worry about it later."

As Marty moved toward the fence, snipping out the razor, Gordon said, "Wait."

Marty paused until Charlie had joined them again back in the shadows of the trees.

"So does this mean you're in?" Gordon asked Charlie. "To do it Dana's way?"

Charlie stood still, his breath clouding his hoodie. He nodded. "You all would really do that shit for me?"

"It's the only way," Dana said.

"Unfortunately, I agree," Gordon said. "Unless we make a clean sweep tonight, even if we get out of here, they'll never let us live. Not for long. Not with what we know."

Charlie looked specifically at Marty. "You too?"

Marty's answer was longer coming, but eventually he nodded too. "It's the only way."

"Remember, Charlie. Whatever you do, don't shoot. If you shoot, it's all over."

They'd debated getting rid of the gun entirely, but Charlie had simply shaken his head in silence. His trust went only so far. Ultimately, the final test of whether Charlie was on board or not would be if he kept the gun under wraps.

"All right," Dana said. "Then let's get to it. We got a few things to do and about five minutes to do them."

Marty tugged at his vest again, stretching his neck as if he had a terrible itch somewhere in there. Gordon had never cracked his sternum, but he bet when it wasn't hurting like hell it was itching like hell. Marty never complained. He flicked open the box cutter and got to work. Each zip tie popped like the slow tick of a metronome, counting down.

CHAPTER TWENTY-TWO

The office of the warden had been occupied at Ditchfield for eighty-two years running. Ken Abernethy had been sitting in that hallowed chair for almost twelve of those eighty-two years, longer than any of his predecessors. From fence to fence, Ditchfield was his home. The second someone turned off I-70 at the sign, they entered his dominion.

Over the years, Abernethy had assured many a donor, board member, frightened parent, and furious child that his primary concern was rehabilitation. *Empowering Youth to Live Productive and Law-Abiding Lives.* That was the Ditchfield mission, and by then, he was very good at messaging. Abernethy had an easy Southern bearing that won over Marylanders despite themselves. His confident gentility lulled people. He could spin up a speech so stirring, so impactful, that it might bring his audience to tears. Sometimes, he even came close to convincing himself that it was true.

But in reality, as far as Ken Abernethy was concerned,

he had one aim in life, and that was to hold tightly to his dominion.

He'd had his fair share of trouble over the twelve years he'd sat in the warden's seat. Josiah Hill wasn't the first major donor he'd had to appease to keep the taps flowing. Positioning Ditchfield for a piece of the state-penitentiary pie as a psychiatric hospital was most notable among them. A lot of people had to be greased—and quieted—to get Ditchfield that dual government designation. He'd done worse over the years than turn his back to let Hill move his operation into the northern border property.

He was quite sure that whatever Hill was doing out there was illegal and immoral. He'd seen tarted-up girls ushered quickly and quietly into the old barn at the base of the mountain. He had an idea of what might be going on. Nothing happened in his dominion without his at least being aware of it. He just didn't care. He had bigger problems, namely, keeping the financial support Josiah Hill had earmarked for him. That support would allow him to secure a second one-hundred-year lease on the one-thousand-acre property upon which his throne sat.

Abernethy was in his office, surveying his maps underneath his antique brass magnifying glass and thinking about how Charlie Cunningham was placing all of it in jeopardy. *A boy.* That one boy had been a nonentity in Abernethy's life until recently—safely *stuck and stowed*, as they said.

Until he wasn't anymore.

When Abernethy heard Cunningham had run down Bagshot in cold blood, that was the first blip of good news he'd had all week. After the way that fat-body loser had botched his watch rotation, Abernethy had been afraid if Bagshot showed up at his penitentiary again, he might kill the moron himself.

Even Duke, for all his steely-eyed fury, hadn't been able to corral the boy. And he had half the Baltimore Police in his pocket. He was just another bureaucrat, unable to do what needed to be done. Abernethy would remember that fact when the time came to vote on the mayoral ticket, on which the trust-fund baby was all but guaranteed top billing.

Abernethy stood straight again, arched backward, and rubbed at his aching back. He shut off the desk light and plunged his office into darkness. Usually, when he couldn't sleep, surveying the building plots and plans for Ditchfield's expansion to the north served to calm him—not that night.

Abernethy could've used a bit of good news, but he firmly believed that while good news rained off and on, bad news poured. Thus, he wasn't at all surprised when the comm to his right, quiet all night save for the all-clear calls after the bed checks, suddenly chirped to life. It was Jack Mitchell, who had graciously stepped up to fill in on night watch for the week after Bagshot got waxed.

"Looks like activity along the west fence. Midway in," Mitchell said.

Abernethy snatched up the comm. "Is it Hop?" he asked, knowing full well it wouldn't be Hop, not at one in the morning.

The old groundskeeper had probably been asleep in his little A-frame at the south end of the property for at least five hours by then.

"No, not Hop. A little junker car I don't recognize," said Mitchell. "We doin' repair work on that break tonight, boss?"

"No," Abernethy said.

Outside of himself, Hop, and the ten men in his employ, only one other person knew about that break. Cunningham was back. Maybe it was Stockholm syndrome or some sort of obsessive vendetta on Ditchfield. Either way, Abernethy felt a break in the clouds that had been gathering over his head. The fool boy was serving himself up on a platter.

"Mitchell, you engage with extreme caution, you understand me? Take Horowitz with you. He's closest. But do it now. Report when you have visual," Abernethy said.

"Roger that, boss. Who you think it is?" asked Mitchell.

"I think our flown pigeon has come back to roost," Abernethy said, smiling.

DANA AND GORDON held tightly to the handles fixed above the windows—the oh-shit handles—aptly named for that night as Gordon drove his coupe at a bone-rattling twenty-five miles per hour over the lumpy, uneven earth of Ditchfield's inner grounds. She watched him warily. She'd thought this part of the plan was solid until she saw how much he was jiggling all over the place. When her teeth weren't clacking together, she managed to get out a full sentence.

"There's no way you're rolling out of this car," Dana said.

"What?" he asked. The thumping and rattling was too loud.

"You've got a bum knee, and you're on the far side of forty!" she said more loudly. "There's no way you're rolling out of a moving car!"

Gordon glanced at her, but then the coupe hit a particularly nasty sounding rock, and both looked forward again. *That definitely punctured something*, Dana thought, but that didn't matter. All this bucket of bolts had to do was get them about another hundred yards, hang on while they made some adjustments, then...

Straight on till morning, she thought grimly.

Instead of responding, Gordon nodded hard, in a way that said *We've already discussed this. It's happening.*

Something caught her eye behind Gordon, through the driver's side window. Flashlights were bobbing in the distance. Gordon saw them too. They shared a look that said everything without speech. *No backing out. See it through.*

Dana was surprised they'd gotten that far without being noticed. *Pretty shoddy security for a prison.* Then again, Ditchfield was way more than a prison. For years, they'd done whatever they wanted and never had cause to fret about a damn thing. They'd gotten lazy.

Gordon pressed the gas. Dana winced as the coupe rattled at a higher pitch, but perhaps sensing her swan song had arrived, the old car pressed on. The flashlights receded in the distance. The guards giving chase were on foot. That was good. That would buy them a little time.

"There," Dana said, pointing.

Ahead, the blacktop of the main road stretched out in the distance, illuminated at intervals by the cold blue light of overhead halogen lamps. They'd come around the long way, but they'd bypassed the front gate and guard station.

Once they passed Pod C on their left, the main manor came into view. Only a few lights were on, lending it a jack-o-lantern glow. The intake room looked empty. The whole manor looked empty, which was a good sign.

Gordon hit the sidewall of the road and bounced both of them an inch into the air where they sat. He swung the car hard left and gunned it down the straightaway. Both looked back over their shoulders—no flashlights yet. Then

Dana saw a second pair coming from the other side of the property. She lost them behind Pod B as the car picked up speed, but they would be back soon.

After another hundred feet, Gordon screeched the car to a halt, midway between overhead lights, where the road was darker. The main manor was less than a hundred yards away, yet it looked much farther. Dana didn't think Gordon's hunk of a car could stay on target for that long. When they'd planned this all out, hastily, in the freezing dark of the forest, still safe behind the fence, she'd asked Gordon when he'd last gotten his steering aligned. He'd said sometime in the nineties.

Too late now. See it through.

Gordon threw the car into park, and they both jumped out. Dana picked up the old rag they'd dug from the depths of the trunk earlier. It still reeked of siphoned gasoline. She raced around the back end while Gordon worked furiously at the base of the driver's seat. They worked in silence, a two-person pit crew in the dead of night.

She popped the gas tank open and jammed one end of the rag as far down the hole as she could while leaving a bit exposed.

"Ready," she whispered.

Gordon grunted, lifting something heavy into place. The rock they'd hauled in from the Maryland wilderness beyond the fence was perhaps a tad overkill, but better safe than sorry. He got back in the car and lined up the steering wheel straight.

He took a deep breath. Then he popped the cigarette lighter out and handed it to her. Before she could think, she pressed it against the rag, which started to smolder.

"C'mon, c'mon," she whispered, pressing more tightly.

She thought she heard yelling in the distance. They were running out of time.

"Twenty-five feet," Dana whispered to Gordon. "That's it. Then you roll."

The acceleration on the coupe wasn't good, so she hoped it wouldn't be going faster than twenty miles an hour at that point.

The rag smoked. She turned to Gordon to remind him to guard his head, to tuck and roll. But suddenly the rag burst into flames.

"Go!" she whispered harshly, stepping back.

With the driver's side door still open, Gordon lifted the rock off the floorboard and dropped it onto the gas pedal. He was jolted backward in the driver's seat as the coupe took off down the straightaway.

INSIDE THE CAR, Gordon gritted his teeth and counted down from twenty. He figured that was the easiest way to count out distance, the way least prone to panic blindness. That was a good thing because he was fully panicking, no way around it.

Once the steering wheel was as straight as it was going to get, he snapped his old Club antitheft bar fully across, locking it in place. Ditchfield manor was rapidly approaching. He found himself grinning grimly. *Knock, knock, assholes.*

One last time, he slapped the dash of the coupe he'd driven for twenty-two years. "Bye-bye, ol' gal. Do us proud."

He looked down at the blacktop whizzing by, feet from his shoes.

When his mental countdown hit three, he gave himself

a little push and rolled out into the empty air to the left of his moving car.

He remembered to cover his head, and he remembered to tuck and roll, but when he hit the road, it still felt like a baseball bat to the side, then a second baseball bat to his elbows, and so on and so on, a mob-style pummeling all over his body. But not his head, and not his knee, which was why, when he finally came to rest in the dead grass off the side of the road, he was still conscious.

Dana was there in an instant. He found her eyes and tried to speak, but his wind had left him. He nodded instead. He wasn't dead. Of that much he was sure.

"Anything broken?" she asked.

He eased out his arms and legs. They felt a little numb, but nothing like the deadness punctuated by shooting pain that he'd felt when he broke his leg before. He shook his head and pushed himself up to sitting.

He followed the car as it careened toward the manor. The flaming rag looked like a little streamer in the dark. Dana started to speak, but just then the two flashlights appeared again, rounding the nearest pod. Dana dropped beside him and pushed him back down flat.

Dana whispered something about not moving. Gordon could only watch, mesmerized, as he witnessed the last flight of his coupe. He'd locked the steering as true as he could, but the car was definitely veering right. *She always veered right*, Gordon thought, his cheek pressed on the cold ground, watching through strands of scraggly winter grass.

For a few terrible seconds, he thought they'd done all that only to watch their ratty little rocket miss the entire manor house or maybe run weakly into the hedgerows to either side. As if echoing his fears, the little red streamer seemed to sputter out in the distance.

Gordon turned to look for the two officers they'd seen coming closer on their other side. He expected to get called out at any time and told to stand with their hands up. They were inconspicuous, but they weren't exactly hidden. Then his car blew to pieces.

Luckily, his startled yell was covered up by the echoing clap of his coupe turning into a fireball, like the final thump of thunder that comes after a warning crackle of lightning. He turned back in time to see what was likely the undercarriage sailing through the air at about ten feet.

She would have missed the manor house, Gordon thought in wonder. But the explosion set her right. When the gas tank blew, it cracked the whole car in half. The front end clobbered the front of the manor, just to the right of the old double doors, shattering the old brick and caving in the ancient stone until it lodged like a bizarro impressionist piece of art, smoking and burning four feet up.

When he squinted, Gordon could still see through the back half and out the shattered windshield.

The guards screamed, and all their attention turned toward the main house. They cut quickly to the paved road and took off running toward the wreckage. Dana kept a hand pressed on Gordon until they were well out of range. Gordon tried to speak again, but she pressed a finger firmly to his lips.

The first two guards to give them chase broke from the pods directly behind them. If they'd stood, they probably would have run right into them. Instead, the guards paid them no mind, running at full tilt after the others, boots smacking the blacktop loudly, all their equipment clinking and jostling.

The lead man was screaming into his comm, "All watch to the main house! There's been an explosion!"

They clanked away. Dana pressed on Gordon for another minute, then she stood. She held out a hand, and Gordon carefully rose alongside her, completing a litany of physical health checks as he did so. *Legs bear weight? Check. No nausea or vomiting? Check. No double vision? Check.*

He was scraped up but not bleeding profusely. All in all, he'd come out of that a lot better than he'd thought he would. He was fully expecting Ken Abernethy would be scraping him off the pavement in the morning.

"Ready to move?" Dana asked.

Gordon felt a bit like he was playing on house money. Or perhaps that was just the adrenaline talking. Either way, he had to take advantage of it.

"Let's go," he said.

The two of them stood and looked toward the north, where he hoped the second half of the plan was already in motion. Gordon had taken two steps when he heard a yell from behind.

"Hands in the air! Don't move. I see you move, I kill you."

Gordon put his hands in the air and looked at Dana and found her doing the same, her eyes already seeking his. *I love you*, he mouthed.

I loved you first, she mouthed back.

Gordon and Dana turned around to find a guard shining a high beam directly at them, perched above the barrel of a gun. The guard's aim shifted twitchily back and forth between them.

"We don't want any trouble," Dana said.

"Well you fuckin' got it, sweetheart," said the guard. He switched his comm on quickly then got back to standing them up with the gun and light. "Boss, it's Mitchell. I got two trespassers here. I saw them roll out of the goddamn car that just smashed into the main house."

There was a crackly pause on the radio as all three waited. White smoke wafted through the space between them. Then the comm chirped.

"Bring them to me," said Ken Abernethy, not sounding happy about it.

～

MARTY WATCHED the old coupe take off through the field toward its rendezvous with the main manor and said a little prayer to the big guy upstairs. *Don't let it blow up with them inside it. It can crap out on the grass or blow an axle somewhere between here and there if it means they won't die, but just don't let it blow up with them in it.*

"It'll make it," Charlie said. "The old cars got the most fight."

They stood side by side just inside the fence. They'd helped push the coupe up the hill then given her one final push to get her up to speed and through the fence, and just like that, phase one of the plan was underway.

"All right, we're up," Marty said. "You sure you want to do this? Breaking and entering goes on your permanent record, you know."

Charlie turned to him. "Is that supposed to be some sort of joke?"

"Yep," Marty said, adjusting his vest again and unzipping his backup leather jacket, which Dana had been surprised to see he owned. Marty was surprised she was surprised. If you had a leather jacket, you had a leather backup. That's how it worked. "Just trying to lighten shit up a bit. C'mon, try to keep up."

Marty didn't bother crouching or concealing himself. They were all going to be found sooner or later. The key was what they did in the meantime. So he ran, taking off straight through the inner grounds, heading due north at the spot where Gordon and Dana had peeled off toward the main manor. Charlie had to hold his loose jeans up with one hand, but he seemed like an old pro at it, and he settled in solidly behind Marty soon enough, keeping to his line and matching him stride for stride.

Before Gordon went careening off in his little car, he'd told Marty he was "fairly sure" an abandoned barn marked the north edge of the property. He'd seen a large structure surrounded by several smaller structures in the original plat that had been attached to the 501c3 filing. Gordon also admitted he was "kind of drunk at the time" and "in a bit of a mania."

So that wasn't perfect intel, but it was as good as they were gonna get. Hill's man had mentioned the barn back at New Hope too. Marty was confident that if they could find it, they'd find the girls. And barns, being barns, were usually pretty big—not something one missed if one got near enough.

They passed Pod C in a blur. Marty wasn't sure how long they'd been running, but his lungs were burning. His chest itched like a whole nest of ants were using it as an elevator. He badly wanted to rip the vest off and scratch like a dog.

"Hey," Charlie said, breathless. "Company up ahead. Right."

A flash of light peeked out from around the back side of Pod D. Marty slowed and dropped low, and Charlie followed. A guard came around the far side, flashlight panning the windows high above him. They were still out of earshot, but if the guard looked their way, he would likely spot two lumps that shouldn't have been there. Pod D was the last structure before the north side, the only thing standing between them and the barn somewhere beyond. But if they moved any closer, they'd be spotted instantly.

"Do we take him out?" Charlie whispered.

"No, we don't *take him out*," Marty whispered, still breathing hard. "Jesus, kid. I'm tryin' to like you, but you gotta meet me halfway."

"So we wait?" Charlie asked, sounding unhappy about it.

Marty wasn't pleased either. Every second they wasted would make succeeding harder. The guy might linger and possibly have a smoke. Maybe his job was to watch Pod D all night long. If that was the case, Dana and Gordon would be in a cell of their own before he and Charlie could even find the damn barn.

Charlie crouched like a runner on a starting line, looking like he was about to bolt for it and see if he could make it past. But the angles, the visibility... Marty knew about these things, and it wasn't gonna work.

Then something exploded.

A single pulse of the hungry orange color unique to fire warmed the black sky in a spot just above the buildings to their right. The sound followed half a heartbeat later—a cracking boom that bounced around the box canyon until it escaped into the night, lessening by degrees.

Marty and Charlie looked at each other. *Please don't let them have been in the car,* Marty thought again.

The guard swung his light east toward the source of the sound. He pressed his comm and frantically repeated something a few times that Marty couldn't catch in the reverberations.

"Get out of here," Marty whispered, mentally urging the man onward. "Go check it out."

The guard shook his head and gave the door one last sweep with his light before he took off at an ugly gallop toward the main house. Once he disappeared behind the far side of the pod, Marty nodded at Charlie, and the two of them resumed their pace, racing past the form and function of Ditchfield until they crossed beyond the spotlight banks keeping the darkness of the north side at bay.

The light bled from the landscape as they pressed farther north until they both had to slow to avoid turning an ankle or tripping over the brush.

Charlie stopped Marty again, with a light touch to the shoulder. "You see that?" he asked, pointing ahead and to the right.

Marty squinted. Sure enough, the more he focused on the darkness, the more there seemed to be a strange glow in the distance.

"That's it," Charlie said. "It's gotta be it."

They increased their pace, focusing as hard as they could on the ground while still picking a line through the trees. The forest was weak there, but that almost made it worse. Twice, Marty slammed his hip against little runt trees, and Charlie tumbled once over a knotty patch of bushes that Marty only narrowly avoided himself. Charlie landed hard on his shoulder but rolled out of it, pressing on without a word.

A fence appeared out of nowhere. Marty almost ran full sail into it but stopped himself by sliding, thankful it wasn't electrified. Nor was it as high as the fencing on the front of the property.

Still, it had razor wire that caught the moon like shards of glass, daring them to climb. Marty looked left and right down the fence line, which had to have a break somewhere, an entrance gate for construction, but he couldn't see one, and they were running out of time. They were close enough to see well-defined lighting in the distance—a single spot that cast an eerie redness. The sound of a generator hummed faintly.

Charlie didn't wait for Marty's say. He gripped the fence and started climbing.

Marty grabbed his hoodie at the back. "You'll slash yourself to pieces."

"I don't care," Charlie hissed.

"Razor cuts don't heal, kid. They bleed and bleed. That's the point."

Charlie ignored him and tried to climb again.

"Goddammit, Charlie, wait!" Marty said. He looked around as if seeking a witness for the sacrifice he was about to make. Of course, he found none, only backcountry Maryland hell.

He shrugged out of his backup leather jacket and handed it up to the kid.

"Climb up *carefully* and lay this across. Make a gap. I'll follow."

Charlie looked down at him inscrutably then grabbed the jacket, turned, and climbed. At the top, he picked his spot. He scraped lightly against one big looping set of razors, rattling the whole line softly like a can full of rice. He cussed.

"Told you," Marty whispered.

Charlie ignored him, rebalanced himself at the top, and pressed the jacket until it caught the razor wire. He pushed one sleeve through a loop in the chain link and hastily tied it with the other sleeve on the other side to hold the razor wire at bay. It wasn't much, but it was a gap. Then he flipped over and scrabbled down.

"Good luck, big man," he said from the other side. He sucked at a cut on the back of one hand.

The last time Marty had scaled a chain-link fence was three months into the job, when he was still working the East Baltimore project beat and had to get into a chop-shop impound lot. The last time he'd scaled a fence with razor wire on top was never. But he wasn't about to let Charlie know that. He visualized the gym in his garage, where he'd put a few rock-climbing grips because he wanted to work his way up to three fingered pull-ups, then he started climbing.

His chest hurt abominably every time he reached up for the next link, but he kept reaching and kept the pain off his face, and eventually, he was up top. He threaded through the narrow gap in the razor wire as best he could, but he knew he was too broad to come out unscathed. Instead, he just decided where he'd take the hits: the vest kept his chest and back clean, but his arms and shoulders were fair game.

He pushed through the bright flares of pain and managed to flip around with minimal agony. His sternum grinded once, and he was forced to grip the top crossbar for a few seconds while the spots in his eyes faded, but soon enough, he was on the other side.

He looked at his backup jacket mournfully. By the time he worked it free, it was slashed cleanly apart at the pockets and sleeve, like some wily pickpocket had assaulted it. But he wasn't about to leave it perched like a huge dodo bird atop the fence. He didn't have a backup backup.

By the time Marty hit the ground, Charlie was already running again. Marty hurried to keep up.

They found the barn. It was a weather-worn Quaker structure that seemed to want to fade away into the side of the mountain. Under different circumstances, it might have been hard to spot. As it was, it was hard to miss. The explosion behind them had set off a beehive of activity inside.

Marty pulled back on Charlie while they were still far enough away. Charlie stopped reluctantly.

"What?" he asked, exasperated. "Tasha's in there," he added, desperately.

"Let's just take a minute," Marty whispered harshly. "We don't know what we're running into."

One man was outside, watching the glow to the south. He was talking on a comm, his voice coming to them in unintelligible snippets, but he sounded frantic. Marty looked backward for the first time and saw why. They couldn't see the main manor from where they were, but the sky was reddening in the area over where he knew it stood. The campfire smell of wood smoke was tingeing the air.

"I think Gordon's car put on one hell of a final show," Marty said. *Please let them have gotten away. Please don't let that wood-smoke smell also be little bits of them.*

The barn doors swung open, pushed from inside by two men. Marty saw movement within. Shadowy figures scrambled about in that unsettling red light, some of them cowering, their shadows thrown large against the walls.

"That fire can probably be seen from I-70," Marty said. "This place is about to get a lot of visitors."

A van rumbled their way along the fence, bouncing violently along a barely there path. It cut hard toward the barn well before it reached them then swung a tangent toward the open barn doors before backing up, beeping the whole way. Soon, its rear doors were bathed in the red light as well. Another man jumped down from the driver's side and moved quickly around to open it up.

Two of the four men standing outside, including the one

yelling into the comm, took off into the night, tracing back the way the van had come. At the same time, a line of crouching young women was ushered out of the barn toward the van.

"They're trying to move them again," Charlie said. "Now or never."

Marty doubted he could stop the kid if he tried, but as things stood, he agreed with him. He laid a hand on Charlie's shoulder one last time. "None of this works if you fire that gun you got in your front pocket. Remember that. You kill anyone, it's over for all of us. Tasha too."

Charlie looked like he understood, all right—understood that he was about to meet the architects of his misery. But at that point, Marty had to let go.

"I'll be right beside you," Marty said.

Charlie stood up, adjusted his hoodie, and pulled down on the neckline. Marty straightened his shield and laid it flat on the outside of his vest. He adjusted his jury-rigged camera setup as best he could.

Charlie started walking toward the van, his arms in the front pocket of the hoodie. Marty walked beside him, step for step.

When they were still about a hundred feet away, Marty called out, "Ahoy, there!" while holding up his badge to the smoky moonlight. "I'm with Warren Duke!" Riffing then, he added, "We got a fire at the main house that's getting out of hand."

The two remaining men swung flashlights into blinding focus, right in their eyes.

"Don't move!" one yelled.

Marty recognized the voice. It was the other man from the church, the one Hill had called Brother Dameon. He'd taken off after Alonzo blasted Marty in the chest.

Marty stopped. No shots were fired this time. That was something, at least.

"I have something for you," Marty said. "Some*one*, actually. You've been looking all over for him."

Charlie kept walking forward. He had to get close, had to see the girls. Marty's job was to get him there.

"I said don't move!" said Dameon.

But Charlie kept walking.

"Don't you recognize him?" Marty called. "Charlie Cunningham? The whole city's had an APB out for him for most of the week." Marty tried to shade his eyes, but the glare was too intense.

Charlie was walking in totally blind, but they were past the point of no return. All Marty could do was keep talking. "No? Look, can I talk to your manager or something, then?"

He was answered by the two-click snap of a cocking handgun. He couldn't tell if it was pointed at him or at Charlie. He certainly *felt* like it was pointed at him. He'd always wondered what he'd think of in this circumstance. At New Hope, the trigger was pulled before he had any time to take stock.

What came to mind was a single image, frozen in time: Brooke, pulled into his embrace, her heartbeat like a fluttering butterfly against his raw chest, her tears wet on his neck.

"Wear the vest."

He wondered if she would be disappointed in him.

Then another man spoke. "Now, just hold on there, fella."

Marty recognized that voice, too, from his first visit to this hellhole what felt like a century ago: Ken Abernethy, the sweet-talking warden.

"Take the damn lights out of their eyes, son. You're

gonna blind them," Abernethy told Dameon. As Marty blinked to clear the glare, Abernethy added, "Well, how about that? Charlie Cunningham in the flesh."

Abernethy plucked the gun from Dameon's hands and held it loosely, like a marksman waiting for his shooting target to slide fully out on the line. Marty had a bad feeling about the way Abernethy was holding that gun. He was way too comfortable with it.

"Charlie," Marty said, "hold up a sec."

"No, by all means, Charlie, come on in. Who you lookin' for, boy?" Abernethy asked. "One of Hill's whores?"

Charlie seemed to neither hear nor care—not about the men, not about the gun, not about the fire or the barn. He cared only about the girls huddled back against the barn door, shuddering and cringing but weirdly silent, as if their whimpers and screams were on some other bandwidth, too high to hear.

One, in particular, drew Charlie in. She was tall and thin, like him. Swimming in loose and faded sweatpants and a sweatshirt stretched out at the neck, she crouched against the rough wood of the door and seemed folded over, as if trying to hold herself together and hide her height at the same time.

"Tasha?" he ventured. All bravado, even the false kind, was swept clean from his voice. This was a brother asking for his sister.

Tasha Cunningham looked up at the sound, but Marty could see she wasn't all there. She quested for Charlie's voice like a woman swimming in the depths of a bad dream. Dameon stepped toward him, but Abernethy held him off with an unsettling why-the-hell-not gesture that Marty read as the same type of allowance he might give to a man asking for a smoke on his way to the electric chair.

"Charlie, come on back," Marty said, trying to keep his voice level. "I got it all on camera." He tapped his vest. "Let's just back away."

Tasha caught on to the name and seemed to focus for a span of moments, but no relief showed on her face, only shame. As Charlie reached out, she pushed away and tried to hide.

"Don't look at me," she whispered weakly.

"There, see?" Abernethy said, "You got what you wanted. Was it worth it?"

Charlie reached toward his sister again but checked himself. Stunned, he backed away until Marty was able to pull him gently back out of the red light from the barn and into the glowing night. In the distance, sirens wailed.

"We got a shitstorm on our hands, boys. I don't want to have to explain anything, and I'm damn sure the reverend doesn't want to explain anything, so get gone, and get gone now."

Charlie pulled away from Marty and walked like a shell-shocked soldier to the van. He pulled out his gun, and before any of them could react, Charlie pointed it at Abernethy.

"Charlie, no!" Marty yelled.

The revolver lingered on the warden, but only for a moment. Then Charlie turned to the van. He fired once into the front left tire then once into the front right tire. He unloaded another shot into the engine block before the handgun Abernethy held came alive, and the warden shot Charlie full on in the chest three times.

Charlie left his feet, danced for a moment an inch in the air, then swung around and planted face-first on the ground, unmoving. The girls screamed as one. Tasha's voice cracked highest above the others.

"Goddammit!" Abernethy yelled, turning his gun on Marty. "No cop of Duke's gonna let that boy anywhere near a gun."

Marty barely heard the warden. He ran to Charlie but was cut down at the knees by Dameon, a low body tackle he never saw coming.

"I know this cop," Dameon yelled, leaning hard into Marty's side, pressing him to the ground. "He ain't got nothing to do with Duke. Alonzo shot him at New Hope."

Marty registered all this only peripherally. He was looking for any sign of life from Charlie, even with his own face pressed into the dirt and pine needles poking into his cheek. But he saw nothing.

Dameon said, "I think Alonzo got him right *here*," and he slammed an elbow into Marty's sternum.

His entire chest felt like it caught fire, like his skin was being raked by claws from within. He bellowed in rage. His pain gave him strength, and he jerked out from directly underneath Dameon and into a bit of leverage. He lifted hard at the knees until both men were standing, Dameon with his arms halfway around Marty's chest and throat from behind.

Marty drove himself backward with his heels. Dameon was big, but Marty was more powerful. When he felt the man lose his footing, he threw himself backward with total abandon. Both of them fell back, Dameon under Marty.

Marty loosened his bull neck and made sure that when Dameon hit the ground, he snapped the broad back of his skull right into the man's face. The squelchy pop of Dameon's shattering nose brought a grim grin to Marty's face. He barely felt the pain as the man's front teeth caved in on his skull.

Dameon was unmoving underneath him. Marty scrambled toward Charlie again and almost ran right into another bullet that blew a clod of dirt into his eyes. Abernethy had sighted Marty again. Marty froze, blinking, guarding his head and waiting for the punch that would end him.

"A dead escapee is one thing," the warden said. "A dead cop is another. So we gonna do this a bit differently."

The sirens were loud by then. The glowing sky pulsed faintly red and blue. Marty heard Dameon groan and shuffle into a sitting position. If Abernethy had any sympathy for the wounded goon, he didn't show it.

"Leave the boy. I'll clean him up later. We bring the cop with us."

Marty was staring numbly at Charlie's broken body when Abernethy whip-cracked him neatly at the temple with the butt of the nine millimeter, and he lost consciousness.

CHAPTER TWENTY-THREE

The fire that started when Gordon's car exploded spread quickly up the face of the main manor house. By the time Ken Abernethy was able to deal with the Charlie Cunningham situation on the north side and get back to the main property, three fire trucks had arrived, along with three police cars.

Catastrophic destruction aside, Ken Abernethy thought the sight of the grand old house burning was spectacular, like something out of another era. The flames were so bright and so high that they seemed to suck the light away from everything else until Abernethy felt displaced, as if he was watching an ancient temple in a lost city burn in an unknown time.

A firefighter hailed him, pulling him back to this place and time. He walked over, full gear rattling, and confirmed what anybody within a mile of this place could plainly see.

"It's a total loss, Warden. We're setting up a defensive line to make sure it doesn't spread to the housing units."

Abernethy nodded grimly. The flames were consuming the structure from front to back with the relentless surety of a mass of lava. The car itself, or what was left of it, was pinned like exposed rebar to the glowing stone. The warden's office, seat of his dominion, was a firestorm with a single smoking window for an eye. When the car exploded out front, it had jostled everything in the office. His mirror and art, his coat stand and computer. When the front half slammed into the house, the place fairly shook. Tokens of gratitude, awards and accolades, all of them were jarred off his desk. His magnifying glass had tipped off the map and clattered to the floor.

Abernethy had just enough time to look out that window and down at the burning wreckage before the fire alarms went off and the overhead sprinkler system activated —poorly, it would seem.

After he evacuated, he figured it best to deal with the whole mess up north and shut off the lights before the cavalry came to town. And boy, had they ever.

"Think you can keep it contained? I've got guests in those pods," Abernethy said. "They're the most important thing."

The firefighter squared his oxygen tank and reset his mask. "You got lucky cause there's no wind and it's muggy as shit. Ayup, I think we'll keep it to the one structure. Still, I agree that evacuating the prisoners is the right thing to do."

Abernethy realized the firefighter mistook his words for fatherly concern. He nodded sagely anyway. Abernethy was able to stare clear-eyed into the destruction of the manor house because it wasn't really the heart of Ditchfield. He could rebuild the house and might even be able to spin some charitable campaign out of it. He'd officed in that house, but the true seat of his dominion was on the shoulders of the boys in the four pods arrayed around it.

They were the most important thing because they were

the actual monetary value of Ditchfield. Prisoners. And the unrealized future value of Ditchfield was the space for more prisoners—that and the moonlighting Josiah Hill had to do up north. Palms needed greasing, after all, especially if those palms held sway over a thousand-acre lease at the foot of a national forest.

Looking at the hungry way the fire consumed the ancient wood of the manor house, Abernethy already knew it would eat itself there. The pods would be safe. The three trucks showered the house from above with a triple punch of high-powered water. He could feel it briefly cool his face in between bouts of wafting heat. Still, he would prep to evacuate to the safety zones even though that would be a colossal pain in the ass. He would do it because when the press arrived, it would look bad if a hundred kids were a solid stone's throw away from a five-alarm fire and nobody had given an evacuation order. Thankfully, Duke had sent six city police who were in his pocket. Abernethy would need them to assist his guard unit in keeping the pods in line.

Abernethy called Mitchell over and pulled him close, even though nobody could hear a thing they said even at an arm's length away, given the roar and hiss of the fire surging and being beaten back.

"You take care of the two insurgents that burned down my manor house?" he asked.

Mitchell cleared his throat and covered his comm. "They're put away."

"Good," Abernethy said. At first, he'd thought he would have to spare the detective. He was active duty and distinguished. The woman was a sergeant. She was on the dishonorable discharge track, but still... a sergeant was a sergeant.

Duke had told him otherwise, saying that even if all three went missing, he would find a way to shuffle it off, especially the doctor and the woman.

So at some point in the very near future, Ken Abernethy was going to have to figure out how to bury one current cop, one former cop, one psychiatrist, and four underaged hookers.

The day was shaping up to be perhaps the strangest in his tenure, which was saying an awful lot.

But first, he needed to make sure of one thing.

He pulled Mitchell close again. "You take point. When the press shows up, you keep them focused on that manor house burning to the ground. Nobody looks north, you understand me?"

He pushed Mitchell out but still held him at the shoulders, boring right into his eyes. Mitchell nodded gravely.

"Good," Abernethy said.

Then he turned without another word and went back to his truck, where one of Hill's strongmen sat complacently, watching the raging inferno like it was about as interesting as the daily weather readout. Blood was streaming down his face from a buckled front tooth, but he didn't seem to mind.

As soon as Abernethy was strapped in, Dameon pulled the warden's truck around in a slow circle, and the two of them headed back north.

One of Abernethy's most prized possessions—currently burning in the manor house he stoically watched in the side-view mirror—was a surveyor's packet for Howard County, dated June of 1863. The packet referred specifically to his thousand acres as the "leveled acreage," at that point owned by a wealthy farmer named Thomas Beck, a pro-slavery spitfire who took up cause with the Confederacy at an advanced age and never came back from the war. His derelict sons eventually sold the land to Richard Ditchfield to cover gambling debts. Such was the inglorious birth of Abernethy's dominion, ever striving for better and ever succeeding... allowing for a few bumps along the way, of course. The surveyor's packet was notable to Abernethy for many reasons, not least because it outlined the true legal dimensions of the plot, but also because it documented a cave at the far north of the property.

At the time, Baltimore was a smuggler's cove. Abernethy would argue very little had changed in the ensuing century and a half—mostly just the nature of the contraband. Back then, the rum runners and gun jockeys needed a place to store their goods away from the eye of the port authority. Ditchfield was private and was the perfect distance from Baltimore to avoid eyes and make a lot of pirates a lot of money.

Again, Abernethy had to allow that not much had changed.

Dameon killed the headlights of the truck a quarter mile out and drove the rest of the way to the cave by moonlight. They'd blacked out the barn too. Hill's operation would have to be put on hiatus for a while, until things died down again.

But they would die down eventually. They always did.

Still, Abernethy wondered how he could quietly be rid of seven human beings. Part of him wished they'd just shot the whole lot the second the fire broke out. Nobody had been around for miles. But now, the Howard County Fire Department would be putting out embers all night. In short order, four pods of boys would be spaced in shivering rows in the yard, under the careful watch of ten guards and six cops. That was a lot of ears.

Dameon slowed the truck until he rolled to a stop at the

base of a pocked formation of basement rock. The fist-sized indentations up top got wider and wider as they went down until one could walk right inside at the base—or get thrown inside, as the case may be. Some old bootlegger had fashioned a steel-plate covering God-knew-how-long ago, but it still sealed the front of the cave well enough. Abernethy could hear weeping within.

"I think we've got to smoke 'em," Abernethy said. "No way around it."

"Say what?" Dameon asked, his words lisping through his battered maw.

"Can't shoot 'em. Too much noise. Plus, it's two against seven, and two are cops. So here's what we do: let's take the gas tanks on the truck, dose some logs, light them, and chuck 'em in. The smoke will take care of them eventually. Plus, we can say the cops and the doctor succumbed at the manor fire." The more Abernethy thought the plan through, the better it sounded. He had nothing against any of his new prisoners—nothing personal—but they had to go. He was simply protecting his domain.

"They'll put it out. They got clothes on. They'll take 'em off. Smother it with their bodies if they got to," Dameon said.

"Then we'll put more logs in," Abernethy said.

"What about the body cam?" Dameon asked.

"Body cam?"

"On the big cop. The one Alonzo shot. He wears vests. They got cameras."

"Christ almighty," Abernethy said.

The big man had mentioned something about a vest cam. Abernethy had let it flit from his mind on account of his entire livelihood burning down around him.

"Some of them hook up to the internet now," Dameon

persisted. "Maybe it's got a suicide switch or something. He saw everything. He was right there."

Ken Abernethy muttered and cursed. He kicked out at the dead grass at his feet. It was a five-percent chance, maybe. But a five-percent chance sealed up in a cave was still a five-percent chance. A body cam's battery could take a long time to die and maybe or maybe not send one last gasp to some police server somewhere that would ruin his life. And Reverend Hill certainly didn't like loose ends.

"Goddammit," he hissed. "Fine. Open up the hatch. And get your gun up."

Dameon thunked the lock open—it sounded like some Civil War–era version of the power locks they used on the pods—and swung the hatch open. The smell of wet dirt and body odor seeped out on the wave of the desperate cries of the girls.

"Anybody comes at us, they die," Dameon said with the flat and even tone of a man who means it.

Expecting a bum rush, Abernethy instead heard scrabbling away and then silence and counted that as another small victory on a day full of defeats.

"Detective?" Abernethy asked, peering into the full darkness of the cave. Beyond the moonlit perimeter, he couldn't see a damn thing. "You still alive in there, or you been concussed out of the game?"

Just when he thought he might actually have to go into the damn place, Marty Cicero responded. "I'm here."

"Step forward, please," Abernethy said.

Silence. Stillness. Inaction when Abernethy knew well they couldn't afford it.

"Do it now, or my associate here fires one shot randomly into the dark. Maybe it hits you. Maybe it hits one or two of these girls," Abernethy said.

That got the bleeding-heart bastard moving. He could hear the shuffle.

Marty Cicero appeared, oozing blood from the forehead, his face a smoke-dusted, mud-smeared mess. He had his hands up, which was good. He also had the vest on.

"Take off the Kevlar," Dameon said. "Easy. Then head back in. Nothing funny."

Marty never even looked at Dameon despite the fact that he was the man holding the gun. His eyes shot death at Abernethy, though, which made him want to wrap this up even more quickly.

Marty took his vest off and handed it to Dameon on a single outstretched finger.

Dameon snatched it, backed away, and threw it to Abernethy, keeping his gun trained on the big cop.

The second Abernethy took hold of it, he knew something was wrong. It was lumpy, fractured, mutilated. He felt around to confirm.

"Did you shoot that fella outside of the barn?" he asked Dameon.

Dameon gave him a brief, confused glance.

"I thought not. This vest is worthless. It's been blasted and looks like the camera was stripped already," Abernethy said. So much for that. Case closed.

The detective backed away, fading into the darkness of the cave again. But he had a look on his face that Abernethy didn't like.

While Dameon rolled the steel plate back in place, Abernethy held the vest limply in one hand and thought of loose ends.

Something wasn't right. And over the past week, whenever things had taken another turn for the worse, his thoughts came back to Charlie Cunningham.

"Give me the keys," Abernethy said.

"What? I thought we were gonna—

"You stay here and make sure things stay in line. I'll be right back."

Dameon tossed Abernethy the keys. "I'd just as soon get this done if we're gonna do it," Dameon said.

"Five minutes," Abernethy said, helping himself into the old truck.

Dameon muttered something Abernethy didn't hear as he fired the engine and flicked on the low beams. He drove south.

The barn came into view as a hulking mass of angular lines. It was cold and dark once more, the way it had been since being abandoned in the early nineteen hundreds when the estate moved south. Abernethy wasn't there for the barn, though.

He swung the truck around out front, looking for where he'd shot Cunningham. He thought he found the place but realized he was too far out. He was amazed at how disoriented a man could get in the pure blackness of the place. He thought it strange that he couldn't immediately see the body. He would be the first to admit he was getting old, but he could count on two hands the number of men he'd killed. He knew he was in the right place.

Creeping fears of loose ends had made their way from his gut all the way up his back by then.

Abernethy thought about flicking the high beams on, but at least twenty nonaffiliates were now down at the southern end, and he couldn't risk one of them looking his way and spying a glow, not with what was in that cave.

Abernethy killed the engine and took a small Maglite from the glove compartment, along with the standard Ditchfield service-issue .357. His boots kicked up dust as he stomped down out of the vehicle. He focused the business ends of both tools on the ground and started sweeping.

Three times Abernethy repositioned himself, triangulating his location with the barn doors, the shot-up van, and the trees. He reenacted the entire encounter, top to bottom, from the moment the detective had walked Cunningham onto the scene to the moment he'd killed the boy with three shots to the chest.

He stood over the packed patch of dead land where he was ninety-nine percent sure the boy had died. But the boy wasn't there. His flashlight glinted off flat metal instead of a body. He eased himself to one knee and picked his ill-gotten prize off the ground. The warped-pancake shape gave it away. It was a slug stopped by a Kevlar vest.

He looked briefly for the other two but found no trace and no blood, either. If they'd hit home, blood would've been everywhere.

Dameon had said the vests had body cams, said the detective had seen everything. Well, Cunningham was even closer. Cunningham had run up to his sister among the gaggle of other terrified whores, for Chrissakes. *Talk about seeing everything.*

The other two slugs were likely still embedded in the vest he'd worn, along for the ride to wherever he was going with the footage that would spell the end of Ditchfield.

He always thought if things were crumbling down around him, he would have some grand gesture to make, some final rage into the dying of the light.

Instead, he had the .357 loose in his hand and the glowing embers of his domain laid out before him.

He leaned against the driver's side door, his arm draped across the crook of the mirror. Scenarios spidered out of his brain. If Cunningham made it out with that cam footage, things weren't going to get better for Ditchfield.

If Cunningham had limped, slowly dying, into the dark winter brush, they would find his body somewhere and the cam footage with it. Maybe if Abernethy had a full shift of guards and some peace and quiet instead of half a shift and a five-alarm fire, he could go after the boy. But that wasn't happening.

In the best-case scenario, the boy limped off to die, and nobody ever found him. But if Charlie had come into Ditchfield wearing the vest, that meant he probably had a plan to get out. From what Abernethy had seen, the boy wasn't a quitter.

And an investigation into the fire was sure to follow, along with the rehousing of a hundred boys, many of whom were, to be blunt, not well treated. Things would come to light.

To say nothing of the cave. It was up north a ways, but to think it would never be found was folly. If he had time and help, he could probably gas all of them and carry them down to the fire like they'd been there all along, but time was running out. With Charlie on the lam, Hill's men would stay away. Dameon had probably already bolted. That young man was born and bred on the bad blocks of Baltimore's east side. He'd done time for a botched robbery before Hill "reformed" him. He could read a room.

Abernethy saw no scenario in which he ever sat on his throne again.

The .357 twitched in his hand.

CHAPTER TWENTY-FOUR

Thomas Brighton was gliding. He didn't know what time it was and was only vaguely aware of the day. He'd been working nonstop to help the boy who'd slashed his face open from the moment he'd done so.

Piles of paperwork surrounded Brighton's desk. He held one highlighter in his hand and another in his teeth. Every now and then, he would get to studying one of the photocopied receipts or printed photographs or detailed spreadsheets too long, and a drop of blood would dribble off his chin and splatter on the paper, snapping him briefly back to the present.

Whenever the blood spattered, he knew he had to change his dressing. He was no doctor, but sopping dressings on his face struck him as reckless. He liked the scar, but he didn't want to lose half his face to gangrene for it, so he blasted it with rubbing alcohol and slathered it with Neosporin every few hours, and he barely felt the pain. He was too eager to get back to the case.

Brighton built legal cases—the ones he cared about, anyway—from the ground up. He used a pillared system.

One big truth, the point he was trying to prove, was up top: the New Hope Foundation aided and abetted the sexual trafficking of underaged girls.

That was a big truth. Very big. It was so big, in fact, that it needed several legs to stand on. So Brighton built those legs.

One leg was that Ditchfield was an accessory to said trafficking.

Another was that Warren Duke and select members of the Baltimore City Police Department were complicit in said trafficking

A third was that Thomas Brighton of Brighton and Associates was an unknowing accessory to said trafficking.

Brighton had pictured several scenarios in which his career ended, but he could honestly say that building a case that indicted himself was not one of them. But facts were facts. He was a knowing accessory to legal malpractice—legal abuse, in fact. He was a corrupt attorney.

He'd written it all out on his legal pad before he knew what he was really confessing to, but when it was there in plain black ink on yellow paper, he knew it was the right thing to do.

His case needed legs to stand on. Duke was as slippery as an eel and far more connected, and that leg of the case would likely crumble. The one in which he damned himself would have to bear the weight.

After he'd pieced together his own paper trail such that he was confident it would hold up in court even if Hill threw a curveball at his own confession, Brighton took a break and poured himself an ounce of ice-cold vodka. He sat back in his chair and stared at the whirlwind of self-incriminating paperwork surrounding him. It was strong but not strong enough. If he walked into a courtroom right then, he would certainly succeed in putting himself behind bars. *Josiah Hill? Not so much.*

He needed evidence pinning the girls to New Hope, and he didn't have it.

Brighton was so lost in thought that, at first, he barely registered the throaty rumble of an approaching car engine. Kids dragged up and down the streets outside Bail Bond Row all the time, but even they usually dispersed a little after one. Not at four in the morning. *How did it get to be four in the morning?* Brighton got up to change his dressing again.

When the guttural growl crept right up to his front door, he took notice, especially when headlights illuminated his foyer.

The engine shut off.

Brighton was done with surprise visitors. He dropped the pen and paper from his hands and spat the highlighter from his mouth. Gordon had wedged one of his thrift-store wingbacks against the front door, which seemed to have done the trick so far. Brighton had come in the back way. He hoped the wingback would hold.

Heavy clomping sounded up the old wooden stairs. Brighton peeked around the corner leading to the hall, but the lights washed everything in a disorienting black-and-white relief.

During a pause, a shadow hovered by the door, lit weakly by the chandelier overhead. Brighton reached over to his desk lamp and switched it off. He couldn't afford any more scars.

The person tried the door, pushing it open as far as they could, which was about three inches until the overstuffed chair clogged up the works. *Good thinking, Doc.*

Whoever it was leaned in hard, too, even slamming

against it once. All they succeeded in doing was ripping up the felt on the chair. It was jammed in tighter than an otter's pocket.

During another pause, Brighton thought of his gun, how it might be nice to have right then. Then again, maybe not. The only thing that gun ever did was sit in a drawer until it got stolen right out from under him. Even if he had it, he'd probably end up shooting himself in the ass somehow.

Then he heard something. Either he was hallucinating, or someone was politely knocking on the front door.

Brighton peeked out again. He still couldn't see anything but a shadow, but he was fairly sure the knocker and the would-be breaking-and-entering suspect were one and the same. *Baltimore. Where wonders never cease.*

"Hey," came a harsh whisper. "Brighton, it's Charlie. You let me in now, or you got a lot more blood on your hands."

That got Thomas Brighton up really quickly. First and foremost, he needed to shut off the outdoor lighting that was shedding a halo on the most wanted man in the city as he stood like a Jehovah's Witness on his front porch.

After flicking the switch that dropped them all under a curtain of darkness, Brighton leaned awkwardly over his fat chair. "Are you alone?"

"Yes. Let me in."

"I can't move the chair. Come around back."

"Are you serious?" Charlie whispered.

"Yeah, I'm serious. Am I supposed to leave my office open to the whole inner city? You were the one that crowbarred the lock, remember? Not my fault. Now, come around back, and I'll let you in."

Charlie faded back, and Brighton scrambled through the office to kill the back lights and meet him at the rear door. He heard Charlie trip once and curse, but the kid kept coming.

Brighton opened the door and ushered him in. Then he locked it in two places. The first thing he noticed, upon turning around, was that Charlie seemed to have trouble taking a deep breath.

"What the hell happened?" Brighton asked, still whispering.

Charlie spoke at a normal volume. "I got shot. Three times. Then I had to drive for a little under an hour, feeling like I was gonna choke and puke at the same time. That's what happened."

Brighton looked for the blood. He'd been no stranger to blood recently, and he figured he'd see a lot of it on Charlie, even if the shots grazed him. But no blood was visible. For the first time, he noticed Charlie was carrying something that looked like a ratty harness.

"How are you standing?" Brighton asked. He guided Charlie into his office and flicked on his fake Tiffany lamp to get a better look.

In the boy's hand was a bulletproof vest, well used.

Brighton thumbed at an embedded slug then looked back up at Charlie, who seemed to unconsciously rub at a tender spot on the left side of his ribcage.

"You should see a doctor," said Brighton.

"So should you," Charlie replied, drawing a line down his cheek to mimic the rift in Brighton's face.

Brighton tongued the weak back side of his newly forming scar through the inside of his cheek.

"That's fair," Brighton said. "Sometimes, you've gotta gut it out."

"The vest ain't important no more," Charlie said. "It's the camera that matters. Can you get that footage out?"

Brighton flipped the vest around and found the camera rig. The memory card was a standard flash drive. He wouldn't even need a sniffer. He pushed a little slit on the camera's side, and the chip popped right out. Brighton held it up to Charlie.

"Play it," Charlie said.

"Do I want to see this?"

"You're gonna see this," Charlie said, with the same razor edge to his voice that he'd had when he picked up the pencil last time around. "And then you're gonna go to Ditchfield and find everyone."

"Find everyone?"

"By the time I could get up, they'd moved the girls. And Marty. But they can't have gone far. No idea about the other lady cop or Pope."

Brighton opened his drawer and dug around until he found a flash reader. He plucked it out and plugged it into his laptop. The chip slid in with a simple click.

Brighton downloaded the contents of the folder to his computer then to his external drive, just in case. Then he opened it up.

It had one file, a video twenty-eight minutes long. Brighton clicked Play.

He saw muddy footage of what looked like a football field at night, viewed from the cheap seats. Somebody whose voice he vaguely recognized said, "All right, we're up. You sure you want to do this? Breaking and entering goes on your permanent record, you know."

"Fast forward," Charlie said.

Brighton clicked and dragged right. Suddenly, they were outside a ratty old barn. A single spotlight lit the immediate surroundings and threw everything else into harsh relief. Brighton glanced at Charlie but found the boy's gaze impenetrable.

The same voice again: "Charlie, hold up a sec." But the camera moved forward. Brighton peered into the screen, moving his face up close. That was Ken Abernethy in the lights, holding a gun.

"No, by all means, Charlie, come on in. Who you lookin' for, boy?" Abernethy asked. "One of Hill's whores?"

Brighton's jaw dropped. That certainly helped their cause. One leg of the case just got a steel-beam reinforcement.

Charlie's camera thumped forward, jostling slightly left and right as he walked. Brighton found himself donning his legal armor, analyzing the footage for how it would hold up in court and also removing himself by a degree to make the whole unearthly scene easier to process.

The way the girls appeared reminded him sickeningly of a time last fall when animal control scoped his attic for a bat's nest. They just appeared, huddled against a barn door, drenched in low red light, screeching softly. The camera footage turned their eyes to black pits. He heard Charlie call for his sister and saw the heartbreaking way she pushed him away in shame.

Got 'em, Brighton thought grimly. *Checkmate on Ditchfield. Now, to save Charlie.*

No matter how noble Charlie's cause was, he was a convicted criminal, and he'd murdered Bagshot in cold blood. He would never walk, but Brighton had a best-case scenario of twenty-five years less time served if all the cards fell their way.

He took time-stamped notes of who appeared when and what identifying words they used. He noted the vaguely menacing way Abernethy held his weapon and also noted when Charlie seemed to slip away from reality and point a gun at the warden—Brighton's gun.

I knew nothing good was ever gonna come from that revolver, he thought again as he winced and waited for Charlie to kill Ken Abernethy. The court wouldn't like that. *Sure-fire life sentence right there.*

But at the last moment, Charlie relented and unloaded three shots into the van before Abernethy unloaded on him.

In Brighton's mind, the court swung back in Charlie's favor.

After Charlie had been shot, the rest of the footage was dark.

"Ditchfield is done for," Brighton said, looking over his notes. "Ken Abernethy is too. Hill is always a wild card, but if we can get one of the girls on the stand, he'll go down too. As for you..."

When Brighton looked up, he was alone.

CHAPTER TWENTY-FIVE

Gordon's thoughts wandered toward despair in the pitch black of the cave.

Once Gordon had determined none of them were in immediate mortal danger, they talked through their options. They were limited, to say the least.

It had to be a cave, Gordon thought. *Of all the places in all the world to get forgotten and shrivel up and die, it had to be a cave.*

The four girls, Tasha included, took their confinement in silent misery. Gordon knew they'd been conditioned to be resigned, and they likely still had some sedatives or opiates in their systems, but their quiet defeat still crushed him.

Only the feeling of Dana's shoulder pressed up against his kept him from devolving into a gibbering ball of panic. He didn't even know what the time was. He guessed they'd been in the cave for four or five hours. They'd tried cell phones for a while, but none of them had any shot at service, and the roam and flashlight features were draining battery life.

They didn't know how long they would be in there, so they agreed to turn them off in case they needed the light down the road. What went unspoken was the fact that they would likely die of thirst before they drained the rationed battery juice of three cell phones. But they all knew it.

Marty shuffled where he sat with his back up against the rough rock on the other side of Dana.

"Hey," Dana said to him, "stay awake. No sleeping on a concussion."

"I'm just drained is all," Marty said, his deep voice echoing.

"Then let's talk. What are you thinking about?"

Marty sighed in the darkness. "How I should have bum-rushed Dameon."

"He'd have killed you," Dana said. "He had every advantage, and you had none. So set that out of your mind. What else are you thinking about?"

In a strange twist of fate, Dana seemed to be the only one *actually* keeping it together. She'd rallied them to try to speak with the girls even though they didn't make much progress. She'd explored the cave as far back as she could, but it wasn't deep. Then she'd suggested they all shut off their phones until they really needed the light.

She'd kept them talking when the spaces between words grew too long, and she'd reached out and held Gordon's hand in the dark as if she could somehow sense the revving of his panic. Gordon knew she was holding Marty's hand, too, a human link that kept them both from spinning out.

"Come on," she urged Marty again. "What else?"

"Brooke," Marty said after a moment.

"Good. That's good. Keep thinking about Brooke because that's what's gonna get you through this. Chloe is out there somewhere too. And when we get out of this place, I want Chloe to meet Brooke. I think she'd like her. What about you, Gord, what are you thinking of?"

Gordon was thinking about a lot of things: whether Charlie was alive; how reckless and low-percentage the plan was to begin with; how much his butt hurt sitting on the cold rock; whether anyone could ever get those girls talking again; the steps he would take to try to unpack their pain and anguish; how much air was in the cave.

"To be honest, I didn't think we'd make it this far," Gordon said. *If you can even call this* making it *at all.*

"Neither did I," Dana said, a hint of bewilderment in her voice. "But we did. And we're together. And for the first time in a while, I don't have to share your attention with anyone or anything else. So, whatcha thinking?"

"I'm thinking how I should have asked you to marry me that day I brought pancakes, like I was planning to," Gordon said.

The cave was silent then and so dark that Gordon could halfway convince himself he was alone. Then Dana laid her head against his shoulder.

She said nothing, just listened. Gordon knew that trick, but he still took the bait and kept talking.

"It would have been better than here. Chloe was at the window, you know," Gordon said, and he didn't know when he'd started crying, but he was doing it. Maybe a part of him had started crying the second he and Charlie crossed the Patapsco in his coupe.

"She was in the window. She was so disappointed when I didn't pull the trigger. I can remember her face. I had the ring in my pocket and everything."

"You asked Chloe if you could marry me?"

"Of course," Gordon said. "After I asked your mother, that is. I know how mothers are."

Dana buried her face in his shoulder and let out a few deep sobs. Then she stopped. When she picked her head back up, she wasn't crying, but she was holding his hand more tightly than ever.

"You listen to me, Gordon. We are getting out of this cave, and then you are going to propose to me, and then I'm going to say yes. Do you understand me?"

Gordon tried to find where her eyes would be, were the dark not so saturating.

"I understand," he said.

"Did you just get shot down?" Marty asked.

Gordon heard Dana give him a friendly thwap on the arm.

"Technically, I think I did," Gordon said.

"He did not get shot down. He got postponed," Dana said.

"That's good," Marty said with a tired chuckle. "Because believe it or not, I think you two might actually be good together."

GORDON HAD SLEPT. He knew he'd slept only because he awoke from a dream in which he was buried, and when the darkness behind his eyes and the darkness in front of his eyes were identical, the panic deepened. He jerked to sitting and was trying to stand, but Dana grabbed his shoulder firmly and sat him down again.

"You'll wake the girls," she whispered.

He took deep breaths to gather himself and felt his face to make sure it was there. His hands came away grimy with sweat. He was powerfully thirsty.

"How long was I out?" he asked.

"Not long, maybe thirty minutes."

Those thirty minutes felt like a lifetime and like nothing at all. He was in purgatory, floating and sensory deprived... or rather, deprived of all the good senses. All he felt was grime and dampness. All he heard were wheezing breaths. His nose seemed blasted of everything but the rank, coppery smell of fear sweat. When he stared at one patch of black long enough, his eyes played tricks on him, exploding in muted reds and yellows. Phosphenes, those were called, his own brain trying to make sense of the pure black by putting on a light show to stay sane.

"I'm turning on a phone," he said. He expected resistance from Dana but didn't get any, which struck him as a bad sign.

The phone powering up was so bright that it felt like it physically burrowed into his brain. Even closing his eyes didn't shut out the screen completely. He waited for a span of minutes before looking around the cave. The girls were huddled over one another like puppies, sharing the warmth of Gordon's coat and Marty's shredded leather jacket. They weren't much but had helped ease their tension enough to let them sleep.

Even unconscious, they shied away from the light. Before Gordon turned the phone away, he saw Tasha at the center of the group. The girls had known she was the most damaged. Even if Tasha herself had yet to fully process having seen her brother shot in front of her, the others knew. They kept her at the core like a queen bee. She was deeply asleep.

He shined the light toward the front hatch, which was enough to peripherally light Dana, who looked at him through baggy slits of eyes. Marty had his head back and eyes closed.

"Marty?" Gordon asked.

"What," he replied flatly.

"Just checking."

Red was smeared all over his upper lip, but a little bead of black still seeped from his right nostril. On the one hand, that could have been a nosebleed—on the other, a hemorrhage.

"So how long have we been here?" Dana asked.

"Let's make it a game. Closest guess wins," Gordon said.

"I like Chutes and Ladders more," Marty said.

"Oh, I'm sorry. Do you have something else to do, Marty?" Gordon asked lightly.

Marty rewarded him with a slight smile. "Ten hours."

"I'll go ten hours and one minute," said Dana.

"That's bullshit," said Marty. "You can't *Price Is Right* me."

"And the lady wins it," Gordon said, "with a time-in-cave of twelve hours and nineteen minutes! Which showcase would you like to choose, Dana?"

Dana was smiling. "You've lost your mind."

"One hundred percent," Gordon agreed. "Now, which showcase would you like to choose?"

Dana looked mournfully at the cold, sweating circle of steel plating that covered the entrance. She pointed at it like the Grim Reaper.

"I'll take what's behind door number one," she said.

"Wouldn't we all," Gordon said.

Then the steel plate shook with the reverberation of three hammer blows.

Everyone jumped. The girls started screaming. The entire cave erupted in a deafening cacophony.

Marty turned to Dana in semiconscious wonder. "What did you do?" he asked.

Gordon didn't wait to hear her answer. He ran toward the steel plate, intending to stop and knock back, but he'd forgotten that he'd passed out sitting on a rock floor for thirty minutes, and instead he tipped forward on pins-and-needles legs and slammed shoulder-first into the steel. His yelp of pain was drowned out by the reverberating boom.

Muffled sounds came from outside. He could hear them as clearly as the ear picks up a siren in the dead of night. He started slamming his fist again and screaming as if the entire cave wasn't full up with cries already.

Rusted metal creaked and groaned. Muffled speaking became audible. Gordon pressed his ear to the steel but couldn't catch anything. He went back to pounding with his fist. Something outside went *pop*, like when Marty had snipped the zip ties, but heavier.

Someone yanked from the outside, and the plate groaned again until a sliver of blood-red sunlight slipped through, hurting his eyes. The chorus of cries behind him turned from painful to grateful. Marty was up and at Gordon's side, along with Dana. Together, they all pushed until all three of them emerged into the misty gloaming of a winter sunset in Ditchfield, blinking like newborn animals, a full spin of the clock after they'd been shut in. Two Baltimore City cops had snapped the U-lock. They stared at each other, wide-eyed.

A man slowly emerged from the twilight, and Gordon's eyes adjusted enough to see. The man wore a camel-hair overcoat over a double-breasted suit, held a briefcase in hand, and had what looked like shopping bags over his shoes.

"Hiya, Doc," Thomas Brighton said, pure relief on his

face. Then he turned to Dana and Marty in turn. "Are the girls okay?"

"You found us" was all Gordon could say.

Brighton held up a copy of the surveyor's assessment Gordon recognized from his own boxes of paperwork. "Funny thing. Long time ago, Josiah Hill made me hammer out the property line with the county. I remember this cave. If I recall correctly, I said it could be a liability to him." He stood watching Gordon until Brighton cracked a smile. "Get it? Liability? Come on, I planned that line out like an hour ago on the drive up—"

He might have said more, but Gordon enveloped the man in a fierce and tribal bear hug and drowned out the words.

"Watch the face," Brighton managed, but he did pat Gordon lamely on the back.

The girls came out last, holding each other. For a span of moments, they simply stood in the fading light, looking lost and frightened, as if waiting for the next fresh hell to arrive.

"Officers, your jackets, please," said Gordon.

The two patrolmen looked at each other only briefly before they removed their heavy canvas coats and handed them to Gordon. He carefully approached the two girls without coats and handed them over. Tasha was still wearing Marty's shredded leather coat.

"Does she want my overcoat?" Brighton asked. "It'll be a little long, but I don't care."

Gordon looked at Tasha to see if she understood and saw that she did. Her eyes were clearer. Still, she shook her head and gripped the coat proudly, looking at Marty with pained gratitude. Perhaps she hadn't been as far gone as they had supposed when she saw what he did for Charlie.

He exchanged a glance with the big detective, who only shrugged. Marty was in a thin T-shirt himself, steaming in the still night. His body was likely running hot, still trying to fight off infection from the trauma to his chest, as well as the gun butt to the head. He flashed down a short list of the toughest people he'd ever met in his life—most of them were children—but he had to put Marty Cicero right at the top.

Brighton spoke to the girls. "I know you've been through the unimaginable. But do you think you can walk with us for a bit? Until we can get you somewhere safe?"

The four of them looked at each other—conferring without ever talking, which struck Gordon as a very sensible mode of communication for four young women imprisoned in a place where someone was always listening.

Tasha said the first words Gordon had heard her speak: "We'll walk with you."

Brighton motioned Gordon, Dana, and Marty over as they headed down the slow, rolling slope leading from the north side back to the heart of Ditchfield.

"A few things," he said. "One. We've got a great shot at shutting this place down forever."

Gordon's heart quickened as Brighton looked meaningfully at him, and Gordon recalled when a certain green psychiatrist had walked into the office of a certain crooked lawyer and said, *"I want to take down Ditchfield."*

"Two," Brighton continued, stepping carefully down a small embankment in his grocery-bag shoes and slipping a bit before recovering. "Ken Abernethy is dead. Shot himself sometime in the night by the fence. Which means he can't testify, which means it'll be harder to get Hill."

Gordon hung his head. Marty cursed under his breath.

"I said *harder*, not impossible. Especially if we can get one of the girls to take the stand. So buck up. Three..."

Brighton paused, pressing back on Gordon with the flat end of his arm like a mother might a child who isn't buckled in at a hard stop. "We don't have a case against Duke and won't be pursuing one."

"What?" Dana hissed. "Are you serious? After all he's done? His father is on the fucking board of this unholy organization."

"I know. I know," said Brighton. "But we gotta pick our battles. Especially you, Dana. Because it's time to get ready for the Duke show. He's down at the scene of the fire."

"He's here?" Marty asked. "Now?"

"You better believe it," said Brighton. "Duke knew he was cornered, so he flipped the script. Went full surprise and delight. He would have come to the goddamn cave himself, but he got caught up in a mess of press that just happened to show up because I just happened to tip them off."

Gordon looked down the property and could just make out flashes through the trees. The cameras were probably focused on Duke talking his way into another promotion.

"Pick your battles," Brighton repeated, looking specifically at Gordon.

Dana seethed. He could hear the air pumping in and out of her nostrils. He didn't know what to say to her, what comfort he could give her, but thankfully, Marty stepped up. He threw an arm around her like they were about to take a team photo at the sandlot.

"Think about it this way, Sarge. We got a rap sheet a mile long on the chief. And he knows it. Maybe once we win this case, we take that sheet to his desk and ask for your badge and gun back. Or else."

Dana's anger didn't quite melt away, but it did thaw.

She looked at Marty as if half amazed still to see him standing, much less offering comfort.

"Brighton," she said. "Let's spare the girls as much of this shitshow as possible."

"One step ahead of you," Brighton said.

And he was. As they broke through the brush line and into the lights of the press—just as the cameras started to target the girls—a chardonnay-colored minivan pulled onto the grass between the Duke press conference and where they stood. The door slid open automatically. Natasha was behind the wheel.

"C'mon in, ladies," she said between smacks of gum. "I got donuts and hot tea and cold fancy water and everythin'."

The girls didn't move, although Tasha almost smiled, probably at the severity of Natasha's platinum-bleached updo.

"Look," Natasha said, "it's a lot warmer in here, and you won't get creeps taking your picture."

That got them moving.

One by one, they filed into the minivan, then the door closed, and they were behind enough tinted glass to stymie the flashes of what Gordon judged was probably fifteen photographers—way more than the local press and way more than the state, even.

Good.

He turned toward the ad hoc press conference Warren Duke was holding. The smell of burning wood was campfire strong, and intermittent waves of wet heat shifted on the breeze across the collapsed wreckage of the main building. One fire truck was still dousing the place, aiming to stamp out glowing embers.

"Shall we?" said Brighton. "Smiles, now. Duke isn't our enemy. Not today."

Gordon walked forward as if in a dream. He shielded his eyes against the camera flashes and made sure to keep his eye on the tall man in the navy sports coat and jeans. He was even sporting a ball cap that was no doubt meant to look tactical.

And Warren Duke kept his eyes on Gordon.

"We couldn't be prouder of these three," he heard Duke say. "They are the personification of Baltimore, honest, loyal, and determined. I may be the one standing here today, talking about winning this battle in the war on sex trafficking, but it's only because of Detective Marty Cicero" —a brief pause—"Sergeant Dana Frisco, and—"

That was his longest pause, almost as if his years of finishing school had failed him and he simply couldn't say the words. But then he recovered.

"And Dr. Gordon Pope." He added, "Please, no questions at this time for these three. They've gone through a terrible ordeal themselves, and I'd ask you to respect that."

Warren Duke shook their hands, each in turn. Gordon was last.

He wasn't sure what Marty or Dana had said, if anything. But when he got in close enough to smell the chief's expensive cologne, he leaned in toward his ear. "Tell your sugar daddy we'll see him in court," he whispered.

He didn't wait to see Duke's reaction because he didn't really care. Instead, he walked back toward the minivan, along with Dana and Marty. He wouldn't get any sort of last laugh that day. Nothing about Ditchfield was a laughing matter.

But if Gordon put in the work and the cards fell the right way, he might just get the last word in court.

CHAPTER TWENTY-SIX

Waterstones restaurant continued. Gordon wasn't quite sure why it shouldn't, but he found himself strangely surprised to see the place running like a Swiss watch, the same as always—as if perhaps it might be slightly reeling just like he still was, even two weeks out of the cave. But no, Waterstones was a rock in the river. Its charm came from the fact that it was unchanging in the face of a constantly changing world.

His mother was similarly unchanging. Deborah Pope was seated at her table, wearing a light-gray dress and a faded denim jacket that somehow looked both thrifty and outrageously expensive. She was taking up too much of her favorite waiter's time, as usual, but Caesar was only too happy to catch up with his favorite customer. He was the one that first noticed Gordon's party, which was a good deal larger than their usual standing reservation.

Deborah stood, surprised but looking thrilled nonetheless. Caesar picked up her martini and shifted it to a larger table to their right and started resetting.

"My son! And with an entourage? What a wonderful surprise."

Marty Cicero looked back and forth between Gordon and Deborah with a half-suppressed smile on his lips. "Entourage? No, ma'am. Your son showed up in my life one day, and he ain't left since. All due respect."

Deborah moved to the big detective and patted his forearm. "He tends to do that, dear. You must be Detective Cicero. I've heard all about you. You are twice as handsome and half as beefy as Gordon said. It's wonderful to meet you."

Even though she was less than half his weight, she pulled Marty into a hug he couldn't help but return. Gordon saw it all happening and was powerless to intervene. They were on his mother's stage, now.

"Mrs. Dr. Pope, this is Brooke, my girlfriend," said Marty.

Brooke stepped up with her hands clasped demurely in front of herself. She looked at ease in Waterstones, or at the very least like nothing could faze her. And Gordon couldn't blame her. After having nearly lost Marty twice, she'd been through quite a trial by fire.

"Thanks for having us," she said.

"My, you're gorgeous," said Deborah. "I'd say I used to look like you when I was in my thirties, but I'd be lying. Come sit. Come sit."

"Hi, Deborah—" Dana began until Deborah cut her off with a pre-emptive hug that lasted a long time.

"You saved my son," she said. When Dana started to protest, his mother simply shook her head. "He told me the whole plan was your idea. And also how you kept everyone sane in the cave."

"I was just doing what I could," said Dana.

"That's what they all say," said Deborah. "Now, I know there's someone else here, but she's hiding behind her mom for some reason and not saying hello to me."

Chloe stepped out boldly from behind her mother and stood with her hands in the pockets of her pink jumpsuit. Still, she looked slightly bewildered by the scene until Deborah somehow bent down to her level, all eighty-two years of her.

"How've you been, Chloe?" she asked. "Tell me honestly. Your mom, Gord, Marty, everyone has been running all around Maryland doing all sorts of scary stuff, and I want to know how you feel about it. One word."

She answered, "Sucks."

Deborah nodded with an instant approval that had eluded Gordon himself most of his childhood. "I bet you were scared. I was too. Scared to death. But that's over now. Let's get you a drink."

Deborah stood and found her waiter. "Caesar, would you bring a Shirley Temple for the young lady? That is your drink, right, sweetheart?"

Chloe nodded somberly, and Gordon found he had to hide a smile, especially when Chloe pushed herself up and into the seat right next to his mother.

"As a matter of fact, Caesar, it looks like I finally have an excuse to order a bottle of champagne." She looked around the table, now seated. "Five glasses?" she asked in a way that brooked no argument.

Caesar nodded and departed.

Marty and Chloe seemed to have settled in well enough. Gordon always worried about such things, the mixing of worlds personal and professional, especially given the history. But, as usual, he found his overthinking was far worse than the reality. Everyone looked happy.

That was good. That was step one.

Step two was proposing to Dana.

Chloe hadn't stopped staring at him since she'd sat down. When Caesar brought her the Shirley Temple, she sipped it with one unblinking eye upon him, like some old-time tough in a Western saloon.

She was the only one he'd told about what was happening that night, and she looked like she'd been ready for it to happen for a whole month. Gordon knew the feeling. In fact, if he didn't do the deed immediately, he would never be able to stomach the champagne, much less the Cobb salad. All of it would sit right at tonsil level until he took care of business.

It had to be now. But she was talking, apparently in a genuine conversation with Brooke. Marty looked at him skeptically. He knew something was up too. He glanced at his mother, who was also staring at him with a strange intent. He knew at once that she also knew. *Am I that obvious?*

Gordon cleared his throat. Dana didn't notice. Chloe rolled her eyes. Caesar came over with the chilled bottle of champagne and started working the cork, but Deborah stilled him with a soft touch.

"Dana," Gordon said, which slowed her conversation. "Dana," he interjected again, grasping for her hand and holding on for dear life.

The conversation slowed, and Dana looked at him as if he might be ill. "Gordon, is everything okay?"

He hobbled out of his seat and somehow managed to crank down onto his one good knee. By then, his surroundings had narrowed to a binocular view in which he only saw her.

He had a speech. He'd written it out then turned the

highlights into bullet points to try to remember—something about when he first saw her in the courthouse and then progressing through their first date in the sleep lab and so on. All of it fled him. In its place, he pictured a flash of light: Karen's ring on the side table.

How devastating that had been at the time, and how little it hurt him now. That was all because of her. She was stronger than everything the world had thrown at him, and she made him strong too. He wanted to make her understand all that.

"Dana, until I met you, I was convinced that this world never gives you anything you want until the moment you no longer need it. But the longer I live next to you, the more I realize there is nothing in this world I need more, and nothing that I want more, than you."

He grasped her trembling hands in his, barely registering her swimming eyes.

"Will you marry me?"

Silence. Shock, maybe, although she certainly knew it was coming. He wondered if he'd stuttered. She was wiping at her eyes. He heard Chloe clear her throat heavily. He looked over at her, along with Dana.

Chloe tapped her chest just below the shoulder, as if trying to signal in secret.

The ring!

Gordon let go of Dana's hands and fumbled around in his breast pocket. He couldn't believe he hadn't brought it out first thing. That was supposed to be the order: take a knee, pull out the ring, ask the question.

Smiling, Chloe nodded encouragement. He managed to pull the ring out from where it had been marinating for weeks. He held it out to Dana like some sort of peasant offering wheat for taxes.

"Gordon," Dana said, her eyes looking at the ring and past the ring at the same time. Her voice instantly calmed him. "Do you remember Erica Denbrook?"

Of course he did. She was the young girl that sleep-walked herself right into a construction dumpster. Dana had risked her life climbing a trellis, only to dive down a trash chute in the hopes of finding her.

She took his hands and held them surely between hers. "My heart was yours the minute I saw how far you'd go to save a child you'd never even met. And what's funny is that back then, I thought it was a one-time thing for you. But you sacrifice yourself for these kids every day. How wonderfully wrong I was."

"Is that a yes?" Gordon stammered.

"Yes, Gord. It's a yes."

He held on to her as she helped him shakily to his feet and didn't stop until Caesar popped the champagne. Chloe was clapping like a maniac.

A Cobb salad and two scotches later, Gordon was feeling as fine as he ever had in his entire life. Outside, Baltimore was dark and cold, and the Ditchfield trial was set for ten the following morning, but in Waterstones, at that moment, the pressing darkness was kept at bay. Dana's ring caught the low light easily, in single flashes, each of which was a marvel to Gordon. She wore it like a natural.

Deborah made many toasts. She said that she'd known all along, of course, that his son was going to marry Dana, that she knew the day he'd first mentioned her name. She even pointed out the seat where it had happened.

Marty tried toasting twice. Each time, he was overcome with emotion that only doubled when Brooke came to his aid and rubbed his broad back. His snappy Baltimore accent devolved into a sort of husky bark, but Gordon understood.

Chloe stepped in when Marty had to gather himself. She was eloquent as ever, and at least four Shirley Temples deep.

As for Gordon, he found himself at peace, saying very little after having said so much, content to observe and take in. That was why he saw Josiah Hill stand from his place at the long mahogany bar.

He turned and looked directly at Gordon—no nod, no acknowledgement, no dapper aw-shucks charm—only a dead, flat stare before donning his wool fedora and walking to the doors and outside.

Nobody else at his table saw, which Gordon thought was a good thing. Still, the darkness of the Baltimore night felt closer than ever... until another well-dressed man stood up from the bar.

Brighton turned toward them and gave a single wave, hoisting the remains of his martini glass high in salute. He was wearing his very best, a soft gray suit—double breasted, of course—with forest-green pinstripes. A camel-hair scarf was draped lazily around his shoulders. Anyone that glanced his way could easily think he owned the place until they saw the scar. Then they might start to wonder.

He gathered his things and was making his way to the door when Gordon called to him and waved him over.

He came reluctantly. And when he arrived at the table, he nodded at each of them in turn, as if he'd known them all for years. To Deborah, he said, "You must be Gordon's mother."

His mom cut right to it. "Thomas Brighton. For a long time, I thought you were nothing but an ambulance-chasing fraud. When I heard my son was taking your money, I told him to wash his hands."

"Probably smart," Brighton said, distractedly. He was watching the door as if Hill might spring back in at any moment. "Gordon," he said, as if in a daze, "I don't suppose you've heard anything good from Brookhaven, have you?"

Gordon had not. He'd called the chief attending at Brookhaven Clinic—a workhorse of a psychiatrist he'd leaned on before, named James Cohn—multiple times a day for two straight weeks. According to Cohn's report, they ate and drank in survival mode, huddled close, and said nothing. They'd been weaned of the opiates in their systems through a step-down regimen of methadone and naloxone that he said was a fairly brutal experience, but they'd gotten through it with round-the-clock care.

It was the anti-Ditchfield, in other words. But none of that seemed to matter. The girls still weren't talking.

Cohn kept them together in a calm, minimal-stimulus room with one of three primary care providers on constant rotation. Gordon himself had been there five times. He'd tried everything he knew to get them to open up: group therapy, individual sessions, speaking, silence. Nothing worked. They couldn't seem to find the words.

Gordon felt strongly that Tasha Cunningham could break the cycle of silence. The others seemed to look to her. If she decided to stand up, they might too. But according to Cohn, Tasha had so far done nothing but stare out the window and sleep.

He had an idea who she might be looking for.

Brighton pulled his cuffs straight under his overcoat. "This is probably my last night out for a while. I wanted a martini in a place about as far as possible from Ditchfield," he said. "I should have figured Hill would show up and find a way to ruin it."

"Did he threaten you?" Dana asked.

"Of course," Brighton said easily. "He reminded me what jail is like. As if I don't know. Said he had people inside. Blah blah blah. I don't want to talk about Josiah Hill. I want to say congratulations, Dana, and you too, Doc. That's what I came over here for. I saw Gord drop to one knee. I think the whole restaurant figured he was either having a heart attack or proposing."

Dana stood and grasped Brighton's limp hands. "Thank you, Thomas. God only knows where we'd be right now without you—"

"In a cave," Chloe interjected.

"Thank you, honey," Dana said in stride. "But, Thomas, listen to me. If you think we're gonna get blown out of the water tomorrow in court, maybe we file for a postponement? Maybe we need more time."

Brighton shook his head. "We've sprung the trap. He knows he's caught, but he's probing the walls. It's now or never."

"What happens if we win?" Gordon asked. "To you, I mean."

Brighton buttoned his overcoat and fluffed his hair. "Well, best-case scenario, Ditchfield gets shut down. Hill gets a life sentence under Title Eighteen for child trafficking." He cleared his throat again. "And I'll probably serve five for legal malpractice. Maybe less. But I'll certainly go bankrupt."

The table was silent.

"Now, now, please, hold yourselves together. There's a child here," Brighton said.

"Thomas—" Gordon began.

Brighton shook his head and staunched Gordon's words. "This is my decision. And it's one I want to make."

Dana cleared her throat. "Have you heard from him? Since?"

Brighton buttoned his overcoat. "No. And I suspect I'll never hear from him again. In my mind, he's boosted a '57 Chevy and is taking Route 66 out west. Far away from here."

That was a nice thought. Gordon could picture Charlie with the top down, one arm out, surfing the wind blowing by.

But that wasn't reality. The Charlie he knew would never leave the job unfinished. He wouldn't rest until he knew Tasha was somewhere out of the clutches of the shadow land into which she'd fallen. And judging by the way Marty was hiding behind his beer, he wasn't the only one who felt that way.

"Anyway, congrats on the upcoming wedding, Doc. You clearly outkicked your coverage," Brighton said, nodding at him and then turning to Dana. "Sergeant. Watch out for him. He tends to stumble into messes. Yours truly included."

He spun on the heel of his leather shoe and walked away. Gordon thought about calling after him, but by the time he could think of what to say, Brighton was out the door.

CHAPTER TWENTY-SEVEN

A t nine in the morning and not a moment later, Gordon Pope walked through the doors of the Baltimore City Circuit Courthouse and slowly shuffled through security.

He nodded at Harold, the security guard, who looked exactly the same as he had the day Gordon first set foot in the building all those years before. Either the man didn't age, or he'd been born old. Gordon would've put his money on the latter.

Gordon beeped as he walked through the metal detector. He always had. The wand beeped at his belt, a few notches wider than in the early days. *That'll happen when you're happy*, Gordon thought in a flash.

And he was. The realization struck him like a bolt out of the blue.

He didn't know what was going to happen in the courtroom that day, whether Josiah Hill would sweet-talk his way out or say nothing at all and just cash in on favors—or maybe the long arm of the law would extend all the way out to Ditchfield.

Either way, Gordon was happier walking through BCC security than he'd ever been. Maybe that came with knowing he'd literally burned the house down at Ditchfield, knowing that if Hill somehow walked now, Gordon would dedicate his whole life to waiting until the man slipped up again. And there he'd be, along with his friends.

Or maybe it had to do with Dana.

Probably, it was because of Dana and the ring she was wearing on her finger.

Harold pointed at the pass-through basin. Gordon slid in his ID. Harold looked at it blandly.

"I look a little constipated because I had to sneeze," Gordon said.

Harold raised an eyebrow.

"At the DMV. I had to sneeze. They made me take the picture anyway. They aren't patient people."

Harold huffed like a walrus and handed the license back. Gordon was walking away when he paused and back-tracked.

"Did I just make you laugh, Harold?"

Harold looked up at him blankly.

"I'll take it," said Gordon, and he moved along.

He sat down at his old spot, by the vending machine, and eyed the moon pies, as always. He thought about getting one but decided against it. God knew how long they'd been sitting there. One of them had a bit of yellowing on the package.

Brighton was not late that time. He walked right up and sat next to him, eyeing the moon pies himself.

"I don't suppose you have any last-minute good news about how the girls have become a font of information, do you?" Brighton asked.

"I do not," Gordon said. "They're all silent. But Tasha

wanted to come here today. Dana is going to sit in the stands with her. The only reason I can think is because she's trying to piece together the reality from the nightmares. Maybe she needs to convince herself that Josiah Hill is a real person. It's healthy, believe it or not."

Brighton leaned all the way back on the bench until the back of his head rested upon the hard wood.

"But it doesn't help the case," Gordon added.

Brighton stood and assayed the halls of the Baltimore City Circuit Courthouse as if seeing them anew. "You know, they're building a new dedicated juvenile justice center down the street," he said. "I think things might get better for these kids. Not any time soon. But maybe someday."

Gordon pushed to his feet and eased out his knee. "Lay out the case. Hill will be right there, probably with his stupid hat and a mess of lawyers, but they still have to give you your turn. So tell him. Tell everyone."

Thomas Brighton took a deep breath and let it out very slowly. He gingerly patted at the scar that raked his cheek.

"Does it hurt still?" Gordon asked. "Your face?"

"Not anymore," Brighton said. "It's just that sometimes I'm afraid it'll disappear. Is that weird?"

Gordon came up alongside him as the two of them walked to their courtroom.

"Not at all," Gordon said. "But you earned that one. The ones you earn never go away."

Marty's head was itching. Just when the bruising in his chest calmed down, the split at the side of his dome woke up. *Been a bit of a rough week,* he thought as he waited outside the courthouse, eating almonds slowly because each crunch sent a little flick of pain to his temples. But Marty always got hungry when he got nervous.

The air was freezing even at ten in the morning. No amount of weak winter sun could chase away the bone-deep chill of a cold snap in Baltimore. The trial was underway presently. They liked to keep things timely. The judge probably had a full docket. Marty thought it was crazy that the fate of all they'd worked for was just another line item for somebody else.

Ah well. That was the system they had.

Truthfully, Marty was happy to be outside. He didn't have much faith in the court system and didn't want to be around when Josiah Hill walked, not least because he wasn't sure he'd be able to restrain himself if the man passed by his bench in the cheap seats.

And while Marty had taken a late liking to Charlie Cunningham, the cop in him thought he was probably dead. One could place only so much on a kid, especially one as banged up as Charlie was. That any of them were alive and in the sun at all was a testament to the kid's tenacity. He'd done plenty... and not nearly enough.

Ah well. Such is life.

Yet Marty waited... long past when the almonds were gone. He watched every car and looked at every face that walked up and past, and the more time went by, the more he slumped. He felt strange, like he might cry again. He'd gone twenty years without crying, but there he was with a hat trick. The first time was when he'd seen the kid gunned down outside the barn. The second, when Gordon proposed to Dana. And then this.

He missed the kid, the reckless, murdering juvenile delinquent. It made no sense, but there it was. Marty missed him.

At quarter to eleven, Marty walked back inside. He had no plan to go into that courtroom. He just wanted to sit down where it wasn't so cold.

At the door, he felt a tug on his shoulder. When he turned around, Charlie Cunningham was there. He was wearing a clean pair of jeans and a puffy jacket, both of which had a just-stolen look about them. They stared at each other for several moments, but Marty couldn't hide the relief on his face.

"I knew you'd come," Marty said.

"Yeah? Is that why you were walking away?" Charlie asked, a hint of a smile on his lips.

"I'm freezing my ass off. I've been eyeballing every car for almost an hour."

"You think I'm gonna drive a stolen car onto the lot of the city courthouse?" Charlie asked.

The kid had a point.

"I didn't hear that," Marty said. Then he paused. "I gotta cuff you," he said.

"I know," Charlie said, and he turned around, placing his wrists together behind his back.

Marty found himself in tears for the fourth time. "I wish I... that it didn't have to be..."

"It is what it is. We can still win," Charlie said, looking over his shoulder.

Marty cleared his throat and clicked the cuffs into place. "All right," he said. "Let's go."

～

Brighton had given it his all. The defense came at him exactly as he expected, claiming total innocence when it came to the sex-trafficking charges. They outlined the many organizations in which Hill was involved, charitable and business entities alike—forty-eight, to be exact. He had a passing knowledge of Ditchfield and supported it only because he thought they were a great reform institution for wayward boys. Not all investments hit.

The evidence that they said Brighton "claimed to have found" at the site of New Hope was nothing but a bunch of nonsense spreadsheets and, yes, a few very unfortunate photographs and videos, likely placed there by one of the churchgoers. Hundreds of people came and went in that building every week.

After all, "The house of God is always open," they said. "Reverend Hill seeks to shepherd his flock, but he is not legally responsible for them," they said.

Through it all, Josiah Hill sat complacently, as if waiting at a bus stop, happy to engage in conversation if you sat down next to him but just as happy to sit quietly. And he did have his stupid hat. It sat on the table, right next to his gloves and the meticulously prepared defense of three attorneys whom Brighton knew personally as very capable and a little desperate—in other words, a perfect fit for Hill's pocket.

Hill never even glanced at Tasha Cunningham, who sat in the far back, a small, thin creature who clung to Dana but never looked away from the proceedings. Brighton lost his train of thought several times during the prosecution when his glance happened to fall upon her, staring back at him.

Every time he faltered, Gordon urged him on with a sure nod, but Brighton knew. He knew before he'd set foot in that courtroom. He'd known when he was sipping his martini. He was buying time—that was all—because he was going to lose.

Then the door of the courtroom swung open, and Charlie Cunningham walked in with his hands cuffed behind his back—followed at a fair distance by his escorting detective, Marty Cicero—and everything changed.

Charlie looked around as if he owned the place, as if nothing could hurt him. That, Brighton supposed, was the rare positive you were awarded when you hit rock bottom.

He found Tasha well before Tasha found him. Brighton kept talking, not even knowing what he was saying, only knowing that the tables had turned and he had to see the reversal through. The rest of the courtroom seemed to follow his eyes, though, Gordon especially, who was closer to the front and the first to stand.

Soon, everyone was looking at Charlie.

Brighton watched as Charlie knelt down, his hands behind his back, and placed his head on his sister's shoulder. She flinched terribly, but Charlie kept his light touch until she turned, and in an instant, she knew him. She encircled him around the shoulders and leaned against him to stand, and Brighton finally saw the twin in them as they leaned on each other in an embrace. For a moment, there was no Charlie and no Tasha. There was a family.

Brighton couldn't hear what Charlie said to her when he was close to her ear in that embrace. He doubted anyone in the courtroom could, although he was fairly sure the word *never* was in there somewhere.

"I never abandoned you."

Or maybe *"I'll never leave you again."*

Or maybe Brighton's favorite: *"Take the stand, and you'll never see Hill again."*

Whatever it was, it worked. Brother and sister looked at Brighton. She was ready.

"Your honor," Brighton said, clearing his throat. "The prosecution would like to call Tasha Cunningham to the stand."

Hill's team went mad. They objected on every ground imaginable, but Brighton knew no self-respecting judge who wished to maintain their seat in this city would keep a victim like Tasha Cunningham from the stand if she was willing to take it. He'd banked on that, and he was right.

So then Hill's team went after Charlie, objecting on legal procedure, claiming their client felt unsafe. Brighton pointed out that Charlie Cunningham was in cuffs, escorted by a city policeman—a detective, in fact. And no law prevented suspects—or convicts, for that matter—from attending an open trial when in custody.

Eventually, the judge overruled them all and offered up the stand. Tasha seemed reluctant to leave her brother's side, but he urged her forward then sat in her place next to Dana when she moved to the aisle.

Tasha took the walk.

Brighton thought she might look away as she passed Hill, but instead, she peered at him sideways as if trying to see and understand who this quiet animal was, stretched languorously in the depths of the cage.

She sat on the dais, behind the bench, a little lower than the judge, who watched her curiously.

Brighton came up to the stand and rested there easily. He saw her look at his scar and smiled. "Tasha, a lot of people did a lot of very brave things to get us here, to this moment. But I want to tell you, no matter what happens, that what you just did was the bravest of all."

She nodded weakly. Brighton pulled himself together

by the lapels of his suit. Standing tall, he turned to address the court.

"Your honor, I've laid out in painstaking detail the evil Josiah Hill presided over at New Hope, and the evil he was building in Ditchfield. You've seen the ledgers, the codes, the photographs, and the videos. But pictures and words are one thing. People are another."

He turned to Tasha, feeling his sad smile tug unevenly at his cheek. "Would you please state your name for the court?"

Tasha looked back at Charlie, who nodded encouragement at her.

"Tasha Cunningham," she said.

"And Tasha, is that your brother there?"

"Yes," Tasha said, and the love in her voice was palpable.

"Your honor, meet Charlie Cunningham. He is a wanted man, with good reason. But the crimes he committed should be viewed through the lens of the trap that Josiah Hill set for him years before he ever stole his first car. A trap I sprang myself."

Brighton looked at Hill's table. The man himself met his gaze unflinchingly, but Brighton got the sense that it was in defiant pride despite the iceberg that had just smashed into his ship.

"Josiah Hill has a lot of lawyers. Until very recently, I would have been at that table myself, furiously taking notes, thinking of any way to get my client out of the mess he made for himself, because I was on the take. In exchange for money, I tipped the scales of justice the way Hill wanted: toward Ditchfield. But only for certain young men. Men who were the only support system for vulnerable young women. Men like Charlie Cunningham."

The judge leaned forward, arms flat across the bench. She looked down at him over her glasses. "Mr. Brighton, are you incriminating yourself?"

"I am. Although I submit to the court that I thought I was helping to pad the books of a prison. It's no excuse, but I want it on the record that I had no idea of the depths of this man's true plans."

Having said that, Brighton turned back to Tasha, feeling lighter than he had in years.

"Tasha, do you remember how you met Josiah Hill?"

Tasha looked at Hill in a series of fleeting glances as she spoke, as if she couldn't quite stand to place her eyes fully upon him. "He gave me a sandwich and chocolate milk when Charlie and I were hungry."

"And how old were you at the time?"

"Ten."

"A simple sandwich. A kid's carton of chocolate milk. That's how it started. And maybe that's how it would have stayed if Charlie didn't get sent to Ditchfield."

One of Hill's attorneys objected. "This is hardly relevant to the case," he said, but the objection had no vigor behind it.

"Overruled," the judge said simply. "Although since the young lady took the stand, I'd like to keep this to ask and answer, Mr. Brighton."

Brighton bowed in acknowledgement. "Tasha, when did you move into New Hope Community Church?"

"Not long after Charlie went to jail," she said. "I had no money for the apartment. I was running out of food. Reverend Hill offered to take me in."

"And how long until he asked for payment?" Brighton asked.

"He never asked for money," Tasha said. "But one day,

he asked if I could take some pictures for him. He introduced me to Alonzo."

Brighton turned to the judge. "Alonzo Jackson, your honor. Currently recovering from a gunshot wound sustained after firing upon detective Marty Cicero inside the walls of New Hope."

Hill's lawyers objected again. "Your honor, the shooting at New Hope is not relevant to this case. There is not one shred of evidence supporting Ms. Cunningham's claims."

"Overruled," the judge said.

Brighton jumped right back in. "Pictures like this?" he asked, holding up one of the two Gordon had found in his slapdash raid. Tasha looked at it out of the corner of her eye then looked away.

"That's not me. That's Brianna. But yeah."

"And after pictures weren't enough for payment, what then?" Brighton asked carefully.

"Movies." Tasha's eyes glistened.

"And after movies weren't enough?"

"Men," she said. "They brought in men and asked me to massage them. And... and have sex with them."

"Who did?" Brighton asked.

"Alonzo and Dameon."

Josiah Hill sat back in his chair and repositioned his fedora on the table. He crossed his arms.

"But when I said no, they took me to Reverend Hill."

"And what did Josiah Hill say?" Brighton asked.

"He told me I had nowhere else to go. Said if I wanted to stay warm that winter, I had to do what Alonzo and Dameon asked. And he gave me pills. Said they'd help with the pain."

Brighton let that settle. Not even Hill's lawyers seemed able to surmount the weight of Tasha's words.

"Thank you, Tasha," Brighton said. "You've been very brave."

"Brianna said she'd come to the courthouse too and testify if nothing bad happened to me," Tasha said. "The other girls too."

Brighton drummed his fingers on the wood of the bench. "Let's hope it doesn't come to that. Thank you again, Tasha. No further questions, Your Honor."

Hill's team looked blindsided. When the judge looked at them for cross-examination, they seemed caught unawares. One stood, shuffling papers, looking at the materials in front of him and coming up short. "Your Honor, given this new testimony, we'd like to request a brief recess to confer with our client."

"I think that sounds like a good idea," the judge said in a tone that didn't bode well for Hill or his team.

As Hill's party gathered their things, Josiah Hill approached Brighton.

"You think I'm a pervert," Hill said lowly. "I'm not. But you would not believe how many powerful men are. No matter what happens, you've turned many dangerous eyes your way."

"I don't think you're a pervert," said Brighton. "I think you're a monster. And the best way to deal with monsters is one at a time."

Hill watched him coldly for a moment longer before donning his hat and following his legal team down the aisle. He walked like a weight was slowly settling upon him. For a split second, Brighton had a vision in which Charlie Cunningham threw himself at the man as he passed, never mind that Charlie was cuffed. He pictured Charlie tackling him, somehow, and bashing his head into the man's face until both of them were brainless.

And maybe, in another life, Charlie would have done just that. But in this one, Charlie stood tall, squared to face Hill, and said, "Goodbye, Reverend," in a tone so quiet and final that it gave Brighton goose bumps.

CHAPTER TWENTY-EIGHT

TWO MONTHS LATER

The dining room table in Dana's kitchen was covered in little pink scraps of paper from Chloe's arts-and-crafts closet. Each scrap had a name scribbled on it, and each was arranged around a series of overturned teacups meant to represent tables at the wedding venue.

Dana and Chloe had rearranged the seating three times already as they weighed the pros and cons of putting certain members of the extended family together. After a healthy back-and-forth about separating a pair of cousins and some surprisingly mature observations from Chloe about how they might want to split up a table she felt was "too fun" so that "other tables could be more fun," they decided to rearrange again.

Gordon had politely excused himself after their first rearrangement and set about making his famous blueberry pancakes, the reason being that Dana was already up to a hundred guests at the wedding—with more RSVPs coming in daily—while Gordon's list maxed out at twenty. And even twenty wasn't a true reflection. Half of those were his mother's friends.

"Where should we put Karen?" Dana asked.

"Not by my mother," Gordon said from the kitchen. "Anywhere but by my mother."

He heard Chloe muttering something about how Karen was lucky to get an invite at all, which drew a knowing look from Dana.

"Hey, I did almost get her killed," Gordon said. "Inviting her to an open bar is the least I can do."

"Fine," Chloe said, plunking her name along with *Chaaad*, her husband and plus-one, at a table designated by a cracked coffee cup in the far corner of their little layout.

"So we got Gordon and myself at the head table, of course—"

"And me," said Chloe. "Of course."

"Of course," Dana echoed. "Plus Marty and Brooke. Who else?"

"Brighton and Natasha," Gordon said. "You know he earned it."

"Fine, fine," Dana said. "If he can make it, he has a spot."

Gordon whisked vigorously. "Oh, he'll make it. He might have to walk right from prison to the venue the day he gets out, but he'll be there."

Thomas Brighton had to serve one full year then four more on probation. Gordon had seen him three times already in visitation. At first, he was concerned how an attorney might be treated in jail, even at a minimum-security place like Brockbridge, down south. As it turned out, instead of being known as the man who'd sent kids to Ditchfield, like he'd feared, he was known as the man who'd helped burn Ditchfield to the ground. He said he'd been mostly left alone.

"The scar helps," he'd added.

That reminded Gordon. "Make sure we get good vodka on the spirits list," he said. "Brighton's gonna need it."

In addition to jail time, Thomas Brighton had been disbarred. Brighton & Associates was no more. He could apply for reinstatement to the Maryland State Bar Association after his full sentence was complete. Gordon had thought that would destroy the man, but again, Brighton surprised him.

"I'm thinking about trying something else," he'd said.

What that was, Gordon couldn't fathom. But he knew it would be successful. As for Natasha, she'd gone on to a secretarial position at another attorney a few houses down on Bail Bond Row, but she said she was ready to jump when Brighton was.

"And Mimi, too, at the head table," Chloe said, putting Maria's name next to hers. "And Deb," she added, moving Deborah's marker to the other side of hers.

"Honey, we can't have everyone at the head," Dana said, which led to another back-and-forth and the reshuffling of tabs all over again.

"The batter has to rest for a few minutes. I'm going out to get the mail," Gordon said.

The girls didn't acknowledge him. They were deep in the new redesign.

Spring had finally managed to hang on in Baltimore. The sun felt like more than a set piece, and the lawns and flower gardens seemed past the delicate green phase, ready to grow in earnest. A month back, Gordon had had his mail forwarded to Dana's house and was in the process of turning his loft back into the office it was originally meant to be.

This was his home, and he couldn't have been happier about it.

In the distance, an engine roared, and Gordon followed the sound on instinct. He remembered when Dana had been spooked by a similar sound a lifetime before, when Gordon still had her ring in his pocket and Chloe was hanging her head in the window.

Dana had been right to worry... and wrong. Charlie wasn't the enemy, but he was the fuse. In the end, he'd gotten twenty-five years less time served at Ditchfield. So twenty to go.

"There's always a chance at parole," Brighton had said when the sentence came down. "It's better than we could have hoped for."

Still, it stung, especially considering that Josiah Hill got the same sentence, although with no chance of parole, and given Hill's age, it was effectively a life sentence. The weird equivalency bothered Gordon. He wanted a grand gesture for Hill, like life plus a hundred.

"It gets the job done," Brighton had said.

That was true. Sometimes grand gestures were hard to come by in Baltimore. The longer Gordon lived there, the more he realized it was a city where the small things got the job done. The things nobody else wanted to do.

Gordon had gone to see Charlie as soon as he was able. He was serving his time at Jessup, a federal penitentiary that was well regarded, as far as those things go. It was not the supermax Charlie had feared, and it certainly was nothing like Ditchfield, still in the depths of a federal audit that, according to the word on the street, it was never going to climb out of.

On Gordon's first visit, Charlie came out dressed in an orange jumpsuit, clear-eyed and unmarked and also a fair bit thicker. He nodded to Gordon like an old friend before he picked up the pass-through phone.

During their chat, Gordon had told Charlie about Hill's sentence but was surprised to find he already knew. Word traveled fast in lockup. Charlie also said that he doubted the good reverend would have the luxury of dying of old age wherever he ended up.

"He committed two sins," Charlie said. "Bad ones. One, he hurt kids. Two, he hurt kids on his block. There's a lot of people don't take kindly to that shit in here. Or out there. Just ask Dameon."

Gordon couldn't ask Dameon, of course. Nobody could. After he'd disappeared from Ditchfield, he was at large for a week before showing up dead in an impound lot on the east side of the city, not far from the Lexington Heights projects, a bullet blown clean through the back of his head. Alonzo probably would've been dead, too, if he hadn't gone straight from Hopkins to solitary confinement at the Chesapeake supermax.

So debts had been paid, in a manner of speaking. But none of it really felt like justice to Gordon, not when it got stacked against all those lost children. *How much is a childhood worth?* he wondered. *One where you're kept and cared for. Told you matter. Told you're loved.*

He was bringing himself down. *Enough of that.* He walked back toward the warmth of the house, back toward the world where plans were unfolding and futures were being written.

On the way back, he pulled the mail from the box and sifted through each piece. Three more little envelopes were there—incoming RSVPs that would no doubt throw Chloe into a fit of giggles and wreck their most recent seating plan.

One of them gave him pause. It looked like it had been inspected and carefully taped up again, and the return address was Jessup Correctional Institution.

Could it be? On a lark, Gordon had mailed Charlie a wedding invitation. He'd been thinking about the kid, as he often did, and was in the depths of the invitation grind. He'd doubted Charlie would ever see it but thought it was worth a shot.

He popped open the return envelope and pulled out their standard response card. The name field read, "From: Mr. Charlie Cunningham."

And in the response section, he'd ticked Regretfully Declines, to which he'd appended "On account of prison."

In the comment section, he'd written:

I'll make it up to you when I get out.
Thank you.
—C

ABOUT THE AUTHOR

B. B. Griffith writes best-selling fantasy and thriller books. He lives in Denver, CO, where he is often seen sitting on his porch staring off into the distance or wandering to and from local watering holes with his family.

See more at his digital HQ: https://bbgriffith.com

If you like his books, you can sign up for his mailing list here: http://eepurl.com/SObZj. It is an entirely spam-free experience.

ALSO BY B. B. GRIFFITH

Gordon Pope Thrillers

The Sleepwalkers (Gordon Pope, #1)

Mind Games (Gordon Pope, #2)

Shadow Land (Gordon Pope, #3)

The Vanished Series

Follow the Crow (Vanished, #1)

Beyond the Veil (Vanished, #2)

The Coyote Way (Vanished, #3)

The Tournament Series

Blue Fall (The Tournament, #1)

Grey Winter (The Tournament, #2)

Black Spring (The Tournament, #3)

Summer Crush (The Tournament, #4)

Luck Magic Series

Las Vegas Luck Magic (Luck Magic, #1)

Standalone

Witch of the Water: A Novella

Made in the USA
Columbia, SC
27 February 2021

33660017R00195